Beguiled

Books by
Deeanne Gist

A Bride Most Begrudging

The Measure of a Lady

Courting Trouble

Deep in the Heart of Trouble

A Bride in the Bargain

Beguiled

Beguiled

DEEANNE GIST
J. MARK BERTRAND

BETHANYHOUSE
Minneapolis, Minnesota

Published by Bethany House Publishers
11400 Hampshire Avenue South
Bloomington, Minnesota 55438

Bethany House Publishers is a division of
Baker Publishing Group, Grand Rapids, Michigan.

Printed in the United States of America

ISBN-13: 978-1-61664-099-6

Acknowledgments

It was Mark's idea to set this book in the historic district of Charleston. Deeanne had never been there, but its rich history appealed to her very much. When she made a trip to check Charleston out for herself, she fell in love with it.

We'd like to thank those who welcomed us with open arms and who gave up their valuable time by answering our many, many questions. In particular, we'd like to acknowledge Willie Morris of InterCoast Properties, Jane Barrett Dowd of Disher, Hamrick & Myers, and Kimberly Farfone of Bishop Gadsden. These three people selflessly gave up a great deal of time, educating us on Charleston's culture and landmarks.

Charles and Sallie Duell, Abigail Martin and the folks from the Inn at Middleton Place were fabulous. (If you go to Charleston, make sure you visit their B&B historic home!) Deeanne imposed on Tom Hatley and Lynn Shaddrix of James Island Charter High School and Gayle Evers without any prior warning or appointments. They were all extremely gracious and giving of their time.

Authors always owe their editors a debt of thanks, even if it typically goes without saying. In this case, we simply must acknowledge the support of David Long, who championed the project from the beginning, served as a sounding board for ideas, and gave suggestions that made the book far better than it otherwise would have been.

DEEANNE GIST has a background in education and journalism. Her credits include *People, Parents, Parenting, Family Fun* and the *Houston Chronicle*. She has a line of parenting products called I Did It ® Productions and a degree from Texas A&M. She and her husband have four grown children. They live in Houston, Texas, and Deeanne loves to hear from her readers at her website, *www.IWantHerBook.com.*

J. MARK BERTRAND is the author of *Rethinking Worldview: Learning to Think, Live, and Speak in This World* and has an MFA in Creative Writing from the University of Houston. His crime novel *Back on Murder,* the first in a series featuring Houston homicide detective Roland March, will be published in summer 2010 by Bethany House. He grew up in Louisiana, spent fifteen years in Houston, and now lives with his wife in Sioux Falls, South Dakota. Find out more at *www.backonmurder.com.*

Chapter One

Something wasn't right. Rylee Monroe unclipped the leash from Romeo's collar, then stood still in the quiet kitchen, all senses alert.

The toy schnauzer clicked across the wooden floor and lapped up water from his bowl, sloshing it over the sides in his enthusiasm. Not a speck of dust touched the slick black granite countertops. An assortment of spoons, ladles, and spatulas hung above the chrome-plated gas stove. Above that, a row of dinner, salad, and dessert plates rested between vertical dowels.

From the kitchen, she could see the sunken sitting room and the archway opening into the dining room. White sheers hung in front of two bay windows, foiling the sun's effort to fade the richly upholstered furniture. No cushion had been disturbed. Nothing was out of place.

She slowly closed the back door, turning the knob to reduce any noise she might make. Romeo looked up from his bowl, water dripping off his wet cheeks. Squatting down, she quietly patted her thigh.

He trotted over, tail wagging a mile a minute.

"Listen," she whispered, wiping his chin and picking him up. "You hear anything?"

Outside, a tour bus struggled to accelerate. Distant sounds of electric saws, chisels, and hammers kept up a continual din. All normal sounds for the historic district of Charleston.

The floorboards above her squeaked under the weight of a footstep.

She stiffened. Had Karl come back to get something? She checked her watch. Ten o'clock. Too late to return for a forgotten item. Too early to quit for the day.

Romeo began to squirm. She tiptoed to the laundry room and set him behind the doggie gate. He immediately began to whine.

"Shhhh." She gently held his mouth closed. "I'll be right back."

She glanced at the set of kitchen knives resting in a wooden block. The temptation to grab one was strong, but what if it was Karl? What would he think if he caught his new dogwalker creeping up the stairs with a butcher knife in her hand?

She kept to the edge of each step, where the wood had less give. Sweat beaded her hands, playing havoc with her grip on the railing. At the halfway landing, she paused, her own breathing loud in her ears.

The hum from outside no longer reached her.

A creak from behind.

She spun around. A bust of Henry Timrod, the Poet Laureate of the Confederacy, stared back at her. She glanced down the stairs.

The massive front door with beveled-glass sidelights remained bolted and chained.

Taking a deep breath, she continued up, finally stepping onto the oriental rug gracing the second-story landing. The door to her right stood open. The foot of the four-poster bed and carved hope chest were visible and undisturbed.

The door to her left was closed. She frowned, wondering if it was always closed. She'd never had reason to go upstairs. In spite of how long she'd known the family, the Sebastians were new clients, and it was too soon for her to know what was normal and what wasn't.

A shadow passed below the door.

Her heart tripped.

Then she forced herself to calm. She was going to feel awfully silly when that door opened and it was Karl.

The floor creaked again.

"Hello?" she said.

The shadow stilled, stopping in the center of the doorway.

"Karl?"

A scrambling from inside.

She touched her throat. What if he had a woman in there? Karl was unmarried. In his early thirties. And GQ-gorgeous.

Heat crept up her neck. "Karl? It's me, Rylee. I don't mean to be a bother. I just thought I heard something and wanted to be sure everything's okay. *Is* everything okay in there?"

A whoosh. A clatter. A grunt.

Her pulse picked up again. He should have answered by now.

"Karl? I'm coming in." She placed her hand on the knob, the brass cool to her sweaty palm. Slowly, slowly she turned the handle and peeked inside.

The bedroom stood immaculate. Another four-poster bed. A kentia palm tree. A mahogany chest of drawers. A tall urn.

She pushed the door the rest of the way open. Nothing.

With a crash, one end of the window's curtain rod swung down.

She whirled around, her heart slamming in her chest. A man's leg, tangled in gold brocade curtain, protruded from the window. He yanked the limb free, pulling the rod the rest of the way down.

Screaming, she bolted, banging the doorframe on her way out.

The noise set Romeo off. His loud, incessant yipping echoed through the kitchen like a homing beacon.

She scrambled down the stairs, swung around the landing, and rushed to the kitchen phone. Jumping over the dog fence and into the laundry room with Romeo, she slammed the door shut, then punched 9-1-1.

"Please! There's a burglar! He's outside on the second-story balcony. Hurry!"

The operator verified her location and kept Rylee on the line and talking.

Romeo stood with ears and tail up, barking so loudly she couldn't hear a thing.

The shakes took hold. Her legs quaked. Her arms trembled. The phone slipped from her hands twice.

She slid down the door and onto the floor. "Yes, yes. I'm fine. Just hurry."

The questions and reassurances continued for a few minutes until a deep male voice rang out from the kitchen. "Miss Monroe?"

"Yes! In here." She cracked the door open.

The uniformed man looked to be in his fifties but plenty robust. "You say you saw a prowler, ma'am?"

She nodded. "Upstairs. First door to the left. He was crawling out the window."

He pushed a button on the walkie-talkie strapped to his shoulder, dropped his voice an octave, and mumbled something indecipherable into it.

He looked at her. "Close that door and don't come out until I return for you."

Swallowing, she did as instructed. The shakes were worse now. Had the robber managed to get untangled and off the balcony? What if he was still there? What if he was younger and stronger than the officer? What if he had a gun and got the first shot off?

She'd be a sitting duck.

Romeo crawled into her lap, sensing her distress. She cuddled him close, drawing comfort from him. Most schnauzers had bobbed tails and ears and shaved bodies. Not Romeo. For whatever reason, he'd never been clipped. His ears and tail, along with the rest of his coat, were long, shaggy, and adorable. She'd fallen in love with him on sight.

She gave his head a kiss. Maybe that's why they named him Romeo.

Picking up the phone she'd had earlier, she speed dialed Karl at the law offices of Sebastian, Lynch & Orton. "Rylee Monroe calling. Would you tell Karl it's an emergency, please?"

Innocuous elevator music filled her ear before Karl picked up.

"Rylee? What's happened?"

"There's been an intruder."

"At the house?" he exclaimed. "Are you all right?"

"I'm fine. The police are here now."

Someone knocked on the laundry room door. "Officer Quince here. You can come out now."

She scrambled to her feet. "I'll call you back, Karl."

"No need," he said. "I'm on my way."

Cracking the door, she peered around it. "Did you catch him?"

"He's long gone, ma'am."

Unhitching the doggie gate, she and Romeo joined him in the kitchen.

The officer listened to her story, making occasional notes as she spoke. "So you didn't get a good look at him?"

"No, sir."

"White, black, Hispanic?"

"I couldn't really tell. All I saw was that leg and boot trying to kick free of the curtain."

"Is anything missing?"

"I don't know. This isn't my house."

He looked up. "Not your house?"

"No. I'm the dogwalker. The house belongs to Grant and Amelia Sebastian."

"Have you called them?"

"They're on their honeymoon. I'm walking the dog while they're gone. But Mr. Sebastian's son lives here, too. He's on his way now."

She gave the officer the last of her personal information just as Karl pushed open the back door, a lock of sun-kissed blond hair falling over eyebrows pale to the point of translucence.

He ran his gaze up and down her. "Are you all right? Did he hurt you?"

She shook her head. "I'm fine."

"You sounded pretty shaken on the phone." A well-tailored tan jacket nipped around his graceful frame, his white linen shirt lay open at the collar. His jeans gave the look a relaxed charm. Not exactly the attire she'd expect of a law-firm associate—she'd never seen his father in anything but suits and ties—but Karl knew how to wear his clothes.

"I interrupted him while he was in one of the bedrooms upstairs."

He sucked in his breath. "Which bedroom?"

"Second floor, the one on the left."

A pained look crossed his face. "That's *my* bedroom."

With the officer leading the way, the three of them headed upstairs. Now that there wasn't a burglar to distract her, Rylee got a good look at the room. Not what she would have expected from a single man in his thirties. In spite of herself, she was impressed.

The crystal chandelier would have been better suited for a formal dining room. His bed was neatly made. Instead of clothing strewn all over the floor, a single linen jacket hung on an antique wooden valet with a pair of polished shoes underneath. A flat-screen

TV atop the chest of drawers angled toward his four-poster. A dog-eared issue of the *Robb Report* and a DVD lay next to an urn.

She squinted, then smiled. Season Two of *Heroes*. She loved that show.

On the bedside table rested an iPod, a James Patterson paper-back, and three remote controls, all neatly arranged.

Karl scanned the room, went into the bathroom, came back out, and then disappeared inside his closet. "My jewelry casket!"

"Jewelry casket?" The officer joined Karl. Following behind, Rylee noted the empty spot on the low shelf above his slacks.

Karl clamped a hand over his mouth, shaking his head. "It's nothing."

"You sure about that?"

"Karl," Rylee said. "What is it?"

"If he took something, sir, we really need to know about it."

Karl looked at them both, then surrendered with a shrug. "Yeah, it's missing. A kind of shrine-looking jewelry box." He gestured with his hands. "It has all these hand-painted panels and finials that look like Roman statues. Dates to the mid-1800s. Been in our family for years."

"Was the jewelry inside it worth much?"

His eyes wide with distress, he strode out of the closet. "No."

The officer nodded. "Then it was the actual, um, casket that was valuable?"

He tunneled a hand through his hair. "To me, it was. But it's not near as valuable as that amphora." He indicated the urn Rylee had seen earlier. "Why couldn't he have taken that?"

"How much is this urn worth?" Quince asked.

Karl paced. "Twenty-five thousand? Thirty? I'd have to check to be certain."

Rylee swung her attention back to the urn. It was about a foot-and-a-half tall, had a narrow neck and two handles. Engraved silhouettes of male and female figures decorated its bowl. She'd seen something just like it at Hobby Lobby last week.

"And the jewelry box?" the officer asked. "What's your best guess there?"

Karl rubbed his forehead. "I really couldn't say for sure. Not much, though. Somewhere in the one to two thousand dollar range?"

Rylee frowned. Two thousand dollars? And he'd have preferred for the robber to have taken the thirty thousand dollar urn?

She wondered if the jewelry box had a sentimental value. Inwardly cringing, she fingered the pearl drop hanging around her neck. It was the only memento she had of her mother's. And no price could be put on that.

"Well, that fits the *modus operandi* of our Robin Hood burglar," the officer said.

Karl shook his head. "It's not him."

"I'd be willing to bet, sir. This will make the third time he's hit a house south of Broad and left with only one piece—and a piece that wasn't close to being as valuable as some of the other items in the house. We'll know for sure when—if—the piece gets donated to some nonprofit somewhere." He scribbled on his pad. "You sure nothing else is missing?"

Karl blinked, as if he didn't understand the question, his self-assurance suddenly gone.

Rylee moved next to him, touching his sleeve. "Did the box have sentimental value?"

His tanned skin had lost all its color. "Yes," he said softly. "Very much so."

She squeezed his arm. "I'm so sorry."

The officer cleared his throat. "Is anything else missing, Mr. Sebastian?"

Karl opened a few drawers, went back into his closet, and then came out again. "Not that I can see." He stopped at the window.

The curtain rod lay at his feet, rich brocade pooling around it like liquid gold. "The guy came in through here?"

"We're not sure. He definitely left through there, though."

Karl nodded.

"Would you mind taking a look at the rest of the house to see if anything looks out of the ordinary?"

"Of course not."

A search of all four stories offered up no further clues.

In the kitchen, the officer shook Karl's hand. "We'll be in touch. In the meanwhile, see if you can locate a picture of that jewelry casket."

"Will do, Officer. Thanks." He closed the door, then turned back to Rylee.

"I'm so sorry, Karl."

"Yeah." He shook himself. "But it's only stuff. You know? It could have been worse. Something could have happened to you. Are you sure you're all right?"

"I'm fine."

"I saw you rubbing your shoulder."

She touched her right shoulder. "I ran into the doorframe trying to get out of the bedroom."

He frowned and stepped toward her. "Let me see."

"It's nothing. Really."

He lifted a brow, his eyes more turquoise than blue.

Flustered, she dipped down the side of her summer cardigan.

He brushed her shoulder with his fingers. "Looks like you're going to have a nasty bruise."

He was close. Very close.

She shrugged the sweater into place. "It'll be fine. I hardly even feel it."

A small smile tugged at the corners of his mouth, deepening his laugh lines. "Liar."

She softened. "It's good to see you smile."

She'd had a crush on him for three years. Ever since his father, a longtime friend of her family, had helped sell her house on Folly Beach. Anytime Karl made the society news, she always took note. But she'd never expected him to notice her.

She swallowed. "Well, unless you need anything else, I probably ought to get going."

"You'll be back tonight?"

She glanced at her watch. "Yes. I'll make sure Romeo gets in a good walk and some dinner."

"Tonight, then."

She skirted around him, then darted toward the door.

"Rylee?"

She turned.

"This yours?" He held up a pink and yellow Vera Bradley messenger bag.

"Yes." She took it and slipped it over her head, careful not to wince when the strap hit her sore shoulder. "Thanks."

"You're welcome."

She backed up. "Right. Well. See ya, Karl. See ya, Romeo."

With a quick wave, she stumbled out the door.

Chapter Two

Rylee wasn't afraid of the dark. If anything, she preferred it. The tourists flooding Charleston all day cleared out of the Battery after sundown, so she had the wide streets and cobbled alleyways all to herself.

But now that she'd come face-to-face with the Robin Hood burglar—or face to foot, anyway—the possibility of running into him again put her on edge. He'd hit the Sebastian house in broad daylight, but most of his break-ins had occurred in the dead of night.

Therefore, she'd decided to now start her evenings with the smallest and friendliest canines in her charge, saving her biggest dog, Toro, for the late-night walks.

"Nobody's gonna mess with us." Sitting on the Davidsons' piazza, she gave Toro a vigorous scratch, then strapped on her rollerblades. "And if they do, you be sure to take a bite out of them. Okay, boy?"

The Argentino mastiff panted in response.

She slipped her bag across her shoulders, then stood and pushed off. The two of them headed up Meeting, then hooked a right on Tradd. Toro paused to do his business in front of the old tavern—the carved crescent moons on its green shutters signaled its purpose in the olden days. Across the street—and quite convenient—was what used to be a brothel. Its cream shutters sported hearts.

Rylee looked up and down the street wondering, not for the first time, what it would have been like to live at a time when the most recognizable icons weren't golden arches, but hearts and moons.

A flash of movement down the alley caught her eye. Stiffening, she scrutinized the area. The darkness ebbed and flowed, making as many varied shapes as the clouds in the sky.

She tugged on Toro's collar. "Come on, boy. Let's get moving."

They turned on East Battery and passed Romeo's house. Toro began to slow, eventually stopping beside an old carriage post.

She shifted her weight, trying not to hurry him but anxious to keep moving. This particular spot evidently had some enticing smells, though, because she had a hard time drawing the mastiff away.

Glancing behind her, she gave the leash a determined yank. "Come *on*, Toro."

They cut across Atlantic Street to Meeting, then to South Battery. Less than an hour earlier, the antebellum homes opposite White Point Gardens had been ablaze with life. Now they sat dark and foreboding.

Swiveling on her rollerblades, she skated backward. No sign of anyone following. Nothing but a couple of streetlamps and a lot of black to hide in.

Toro trotted along, totally oblivious to the possibility of any-one lurking. Straining to listen, she heard nothing but the clack of her rollerblades and the treetops stirred by the balmy evening breeze.

She faced forward and looked at her watch. Eleven o'clock already. Just one more block to the waterfront, then they'd turn around.

Toro edged ahead on the straightaway, snapping the leather leash taut. His body strained with energy, pulling her forward, dispelling her worries with exhilarating speed. Her lips curved into a smile. She crouched lower on the rollerblades, letting Toro do the work.

This was what she loved about her job, the physical bond between walker and dog, the feeling she was invulnerable, at one with the world around her.

Toro halted abruptly, ears back, tail stiff. Rylee jerked to a stop, glancing back toward the alley. "What is it, boy?"

But it wasn't the path behind them that held him riveted. He growled into the darkly wooded park up ahead. Following his gaze, she peered into the darkness.

A shape moved behind the hedges. The outline of a man—no, two men—materialized.

Her heart jumped. The figures crouched low to the ground; then one of them straightened and moved forward, coming straight for her.

She tried to speak, but no sound came out.

Toro leapt forward.

"No, Toro! Down! Down!" Grinding her blades against the concrete, she jerked back on his lead with both hands. But it was no use. She couldn't stop him.

The leash threatened to slip through her palms, but she held tight. The last thing she wanted was to be separated from the mastiff.

Toro dragged her into the park, making a beeline for the men. The silhouettes froze for an instant, then bolted.

The first one cut sideways in the direction of a gazebo. As he passed through a gap in the trees, lamplight from overhead faintly illuminated him. A tall black man with something clenched in his pumping hand.

21

Her breath caught. *A gun?*

Toro ignored him, locking in on the other man, who fled toward the edge of the park. The man emerged from the trees onto a circular courtyard surrounding the Confederate Soldier Memorial. In the light, she saw he wore a baseball uniform.

Baseball uniform?

Before she could process that thought, Toro closed the gap, dragging her behind him like an anchor.

The man had nowhere to go. The only thing beyond the park was miles of bay. The moment he stopped for breath, they'd be on top of him.

But he didn't stop. He headed straight for the monument, never glancing back. He traversed the broad steps leading up to the pedestal, then took a running leap. His body sailed through the air, arms extended.

Rylee held her breath. No way was he going to reach the top of the pedestal. It was far too high. But his fingers hooked the edge of the stone, and after dangling a moment, he hoisted himself up.

Any other time, she'd have been impressed with his jump. Instead, she focused on the low brick wall surrounding the monument. She barely cleared it, her rollerblades slamming down on the opposite side.

As the memorial's steps rushed up to meet her, she yanked again on Toro's leash. Hard. There was no way she could navigate the steps at this speed.

But the mastiff wasn't stopping. At the last moment, she let go of the leash, swerving to a breathless stop.

Toro launched himself against the pedestal, then threw his body again and again into the air, snapping at the man but unable to reach him.

He stared down at the dog wide-eyed. His face flushed, his chest heaving.

She wasn't sure what to do. She glanced back into the park. Apart from pools of light here and there, the grounds were dark. A shadow flicked from one tree to another. A chill ran up her spine.

Was the other guy circling back? Would Toro be able to protect her from both men?

She dug through her bag—a jumble of leashes, poop bags, keys, a flashlight, and a water bottle—until she seized on the plastic body of her cell phone and dialed 9-1-1. Twice in one day.

"Yes. There are a couple of guys after me. Please hurry. I'm in White Point Gardens by the Confederate Memorial. I have one of the men cornered."

"What are you doing?" the man shouted in disbelief.

She glanced at him again. His muscles were taut, his face twisted in outrage.

After answering the dispatcher's questions, Rylee hung up, only to realize she'd cut off her lifeline. Hesitating, she slid the phone into her cardigan pocket, then peered into the surrounding darkness. Nothing moved.

Behind her, Toro placed his paws on the base of the statue and gave out a deep, booming bark.

The man shimmied farther up the statue's leg. "Call that albino off!"

She continued to scan the area, resenting the man's tone. "He's not an albino. He's an Argentino mastiff."

"Whatever he is, just call him off!"

She whirled around. "You call off your friend!"

His laugh caught her off guard. "He's long gone. Now will you please get control of your dog? I can't stay up here all night."

His exasperation seemed real enough, but she wasn't about to put her back to the park. Gliding to the front of the statue, she positioned herself where she could see both the shadowed grounds and the guy in the baseball getup.

His blue T-shirt, which had *Mets* plastered across it in big red cursive letters, stretched tightly across his muscled chest. Rust-colored dirt had been ground into his silver pants. He lifted his blue cap, wiped his brow against his sleeve, and gave her a hopeful grin.

She bit her lip. Maybe she'd acted too fast calling the police. Looking at him now, he seemed harmless enough. But why had he been hiding in the dark? Why had he run? Maybe he and his cohort had been canvassing the houses opposite the park.

She unsnapped her blades just in case the other guy showed up. She didn't want Toro dragging her right to him.

The man glanced at the dog nervously. "Why'd you call the cops? You think I'm some kind of pervert or something?"

"Or something."

"Dressed like this?" He plucked at his T-shirt, prompting Toro to let out a low growl. "Listen, we were just taking a few photos."

"In the dark? From behind the bushes?"

"We're on an assignment."

"An assignment?"

"That's right." He sighed. "My name is Logan Woods. I'm a reporter for the *Post & Courier*. I've been covering the Robin Hood burglaries. Maybe you've read one of my stories?" Reaching into his back pocket, he gingerly removed a thick brown billfold.

Toro leapt to attention and started to salivate.

"Here's my business card." The card flicked toward her, spiraling to the ground.

Holding the card to the light, she recognized the newspaper's logo. There was his name in black ink. Anyone could print up fake business cards these days, but this one looked legit.

She glanced at him again. *This is the guy who wrote the articles on the robberies?* A sinking feeling came over her.

Her idea of a reporter was a pale, paunchy, middle-aged man, and Logan Woods was anything but. He looked as if he spent more time at the gym pumping weight—lots of weight—than sitting behind some desk.

His muscles had mouth-watering definition. Thighs that bulged, a stomach as flat as a wall, a chest that swelled, and serious biceps.

Flashing lights lit up East Battery. Seconds later, a squad car pulled up to the curb. A young officer climbed out of the driver's seat, slipped a nightstick into the loop on his belt, and headed in their direction.

"Rylee Monroe?" The officer took in her stocking feet, Toro, and the man hugging the statue. "I'm Officer Kirk. You all right?"

"Yes, but there's another man out there somewhere."

As Kirk scanned the trees with his flashlight, an old Mustang rattled up behind the squad car. The engine cut off and another baseball player in a Mets jersey jumped out.

Kirk saw the man and straightened. "Detective. I didn't expect to see you here."

"Just passing through after the game to make sure everything was quiet. Saw your lights and figured I'd lend a hand. What's up?"

"Not sure yet, sir. I was dispatched here on a prowler call."

The detective inspected the man on the statue. His jutting face caught the gold light, dominated by a prow-like pointer of a nose. He ran a hand over his bristling crew cut, then burst into a grin.

Rylee frowned. "Who are you?"

He flipped his badge open. "Detective Campbell, ma'am. Looks like you caught a live one there."

"Very funny," Logan said.

She glanced from one man to the other. "You *know* him?"

The detective hitched up his baseball pants. " 'Fraid so."

"So he's not a burglar?"

"Why don't you tell us what happened."

"This man and another one were prowling—"

Logan laughed. "We weren't prowling."

"—were creeping in the shadows along South Battery when my dog here spotted them and they took off running."

"I didn't run until that thing charged me."

Campbell shook his head. "What's the matter, Logan? This little critter scare you?"

"You'd be up here too if that snarling albino was coming at you with his teeth bared."

"Is he friendly?" Campbell asked, pointing to Toro.

"Yes, sir." She patted the dog between the ears. "Very loving and gentle. His name's Toro."

Officer Kirk's walkie-talkie let out a blast of static. He turned down the volume, then looked at Rylee. "You live around here, ma'am?"

"Actually, I'm pet sitting for someone who lives in the neighborhood." She rummaged through her bag for her address book, producing a creased business card from inside the cover. Kirk looked at the card, then passed it to Campbell.

All she wanted was to get out of there. If the man on the statue really was a reporter—and by now, it was obvious he'd been telling the truth—she owed him an apology.

Her cheeks burned with embarrassment, and she had a hard time meeting his gaze. She waited for the officers to declare it all a misunderstanding, so she could apologize and get going.

Perched on the statue, every muscle in his body burning, Logan finally ran out of patience. The whole thing was absurd, and he couldn't believe it was still dragging on. The woman should have realized right away she'd made a mistake. She should have gotten her animal under control and let him come down. Instead, she'd dragged the police out, and Nate Campbell showed no sign of resolving the situation speedily.

He was probably having fun. It wasn't every night Nate had a pretty, long-legged girl in his power, and he wasn't going to rush things any.

Pretty was an understatement. Once she'd come into the light and he'd had a chance to take a closer look, Logan had seen right away that the dogwalker was stunning. Tall and slim, moving with graceful poise in spite of her apparent fear, her cheekbones framed by the jagged tips of her stylish pixie haircut.

And Nate was just eating it up.

"Aren't you guys forgetting something here?" he called down. "I'm the one who was attacked. What if I want to press charges for assault with a deadly weapon?"

"Toro did not assault you." She put a hand on her hip. "And he's *not* a deadly weapon. He wouldn't have done anything at all if you hadn't run."

"I'd be in the hospital if I hadn't run." He gave Nate a pointed look. "Are you gonna help me out?"

Now that he'd had his fun, Nate put on his serious-cop face. "Actually, miss, this man does have the right to walk in the park without fear of molestation by your dog."

"Walk in the park?" Her jaw dropped. "He wasn't walking, he was lurking." She jabbed her finger toward the trees. "And he had somebody else with him—"

"Your dog charged this man and drove him up onto that statue." He paused and looked at Logan. "How did you get up there, anyway?"

Logan peered down at the cobbled circle bounding the memorial, shaking his head at the height. "If I knew I'd tell you. I'm sure it was impressive."

Nate snorted.

The dogwalker's eyes flared with outrage. "This isn't funny. Maybe I was wrong, but I really thought this man was a threat to me."

Logan had looked forward to this woman's comeuppance, but if she'd really been afraid, if she'd thought someone was after her . . .

"Hey, Nate. It's all right. I can see why she was startled."

But going easy wasn't in Nate Campbell's nature. He had a bit of the bully in him. She might have brought it on herself, but it was, after all, just a misunderstanding.

He tried again. "Look, I just want to get down from here, all right?"

The dog seemed to understand, gazing up at him with wolf-like eyes. A long, low rumble rolled in his throat.

Even with all the distance between them, even with the police there and the leash firmly coiled around the dogwalker's fist, Logan's mouth dried up. He knew better, but he couldn't shake the image of that animal leaping up at him, fangs sinking into him, its head snapping back and forth to pull a chunk of flesh loose. His throat seized up and he began to cough.

"What's the matter with you?" Nate said. "You can come down anytime. Nobody's stopping you."

The dogwalker looped another circle of leash around her hand. "He won't bite, Mr. Woods. I promise."

He closed his eyes, forcing himself to take deep, slow breaths through his nose. The growling stopped, cut off by a jerk of the leash, but it was too late.

"Give me a second," he said.

On the ground, they kept talking, but Logan checked out of the conversation. His hand gripped the statue, but he felt powerless now that the trembling had taken hold. The others wouldn't be able to see it. If he just toughed it out, maybe they'd never pick up on his fear.

He took deep breaths and tried to imagine climbing down to join them. He wasn't ready, though. Not yet. He didn't trust his arms to hold out.

When he opened his eyes, he wasn't sure how much time had passed. But Nate was in the dogwalker's face, hissing in a quiet, menacing way. And the woman, in spite of the bravado she'd shown a few moments before, looked ready to cry. Meanwhile, Officer Kirk watched with a poker face, giving no hint what he thought of the situation. Logan made a point of not looking at Toro at all.

He closed his eyes again and tried to think happy thoughts. His mom standing on the porch, calling him in to dinner. Dad closing the newspaper after finishing one of his articles, a smile across his lips. The crack of his bat against a baseball, the white speck disappearing into the stratosphere. Slowly his heart rate returned to normal.

Nate's voice thundered below. "Don't take that tone with me."

There was no response. Logan opened his eyes again.

He'd expected to find the dogwalker cowed and submissive, but instead she looked ready to throw a punch.

Before things could get out of hand again, Logan lowered himself down, kicking awkwardly in the air until his foot found a purchase. Getting up had been easy in comparison, and by the time he let go and dropped the final yard, the conversation had stopped so all three of them could watch. Four, counting the dog, but Logan was trying to pretend it didn't exist.

"And he sticks the landing," Nate said, clapping his shoulder. "So what do you say, Logan? Feel like pressing charges?"

"Of course I'm not pressing charges." He cast an apologetic glance toward the pretty dogwalker, hoping to distance himself a little from Nate's brusque behavior, but she wasn't having it.

He sighed. The detective had some rough edges. Deep down, though, the guy was all right. Logan counted him as a friend—and over the past couple of years, he'd proven to be quite an asset for a crime reporter to have, considering how talkative he could be. But that didn't excuse him for bullying the girl.

He glanced at the dog. Now that he was back on the ground, its proximity couldn't be ignored. It took a tentative step toward him, a gourmet diner edging closer to the table.

Logan's limbs felt rubbery from the climb. If it turned into another sprint, he didn't fancy his chances. But it was too late for fear. He stood up straight and did his best to look nonchalant.

"In that case," Nate said, "why don't you get going, ma'am? In the future, don't call us, we'll call you."

"And what about the other man? Suppose he's still out there?"

Nate arched an eyebrow at Logan.

"She means Wash Tillman, my photographer."

"Ah." Nate turned to her. "If you run into him, be sure to smile for the birdie."

She shot Nate a look of loathing, then snatched up her skates and headed back the way she'd come. At the edge of the memorial, she turned again, her eyes boring a hole through Logan.

Hey, wait a second, he thought. He didn't want her lumping him together with his friend. He had half a mind to go after her and explain.

Nate must have read his mind, because the detective burst out laughing.

"You're a piece of work, you know that?" he said. "Woman chases you up the flagpole, and you wanna run after her to apologize. When I reflect on the fact your batting average is so much better than mine, it really pains me, Logan."

But Logan wasn't listening. He strained his eyes watching her, not turning until she finally disappeared into the night.

Chapter Three

The morning sun sparkled on the harbor, and a warm breeze blew the state flag anchored proudly above the Sebastians' house. Sweeping her gaze over their breathtaking four-story Regency, Rylee studied the windows off the second-floor balcony.

No sign of an intruder. Releasing a pent-up breath, she slipped through the gate and fished an oversized key ring from her bag. It held a dazzling array of color-coded keys. She found the right one with practiced ease and opened the back door.

Karl stood pouring a cup of coffee, a half-eaten slice of toast in his free hand.

"Karl! I'm so sorry. I should have knocked."

He grinned in reply, raising a finger as he finished chewing his toast. "Don't be silly. You don't need to knock. We're practically family."

She smiled, though that wasn't exactly true. Back in the day, Sebastian, Lynch & Orton had been Sebastian, Lynch & Monroe. Until Rylee's father simply walked out, abandoning his wife, daughter, and law partners. Shortly after, the Monroe was replaced by Orton. Karl would have been eighteen at the time, Rylee only five.

Karl's father, Grant, had helped with the financial wreck her dad had left behind. Since then, he'd swooped back into their lives during emergencies and been present for the various milestones in Rylee's life.

In spite of the shared history, though, she and Karl had lived most of their lives in two different worlds.

"Want some coffee?" he asked.

"I better not. I have two more dogs after Romeo, and they'll be awfully uncomfortable if I keep them waiting too long."

His eyes held a glint of amusement. "Well, we can't have that."

Her heart took an inadvertent jump. It always did when he used that conspiratorial tone, like the two of them shared a secret.

Realizing she'd been staring, she scrambled for something to say. "So, your dad told me you're moving out when they get back from their honeymoon. Have you decided on a place yet?"

He brushed crumbs from his fingers. "Actually, he asked me to hold off awhile on that."

"Oh. Well." *I'm an idiot.* "That's nice of you to accommodate him."

"I missed you last night." He leaned a hip against the counter and took a sip from his mug. "You didn't come for Romeo at your usual time. He's not proving to be too much trouble, is he? Because if he is—"

"It's nothing like that." She flicked her thumbnail against the strap of her bag. "I made Romeo my first walk of the night, since he's one of my smaller dogs. With the burglaries and all, I decided to save my biggest dogs for last."

"Nothing else has happened, has it?" He lowered his mug. "If you were in trouble, I'd want you to tell me."

Her first instinct was to pretend everything was normal. But after the burglary here, her fear from the night before, and the condescending way the police detective had treated her, Karl's concern was like a balm.

"Actually," she said, "there was an incident last night. I had this feeling someone was following me, and then there were these two men creeping around the Confederate Memorial. I actually called 9-1-1."

He straightened. "Again? Are you all right?"

"I'm fine." She plucked a leash off a peg by the door. "Just a case of mistaken identity."

Before he could ask more questions, Romeo zoomed around the corner, ears perked, wriggling all over at the sight of her.

Smiling, she put her bag on the table and squatted down. "Morning, Romeo. How's my sweetie pie?" She tried to clip the leash to his collar. "Hold still, you silly."

She finger-combed his salt-and-pepper hair aside, trying to locate the loop on his collar. He moved his nose closer and closer to hers. His eyes grew dreamy, and right before she clipped on the leash, his bright pink tongue shot out and swiped her across the lips.

Laughing, she nuzzled his neck and scrubbed behind his ears.

"Lucky dog," Karl said, eyes shining. "You've stolen his heart, you know. All he does is mope until you show up."

She smiled. "I admit, I'm a bit smitten with him, too." She eased Romeo down. "I was wondering if it would be all right if I took him to a retirement home later this week. Your stepmother said it would be all right, but I wanted to check with you just in case."

Karl rinsed out his mug and set it in the drainer. "No, no. That's fine. Take him as often as you like. I'm sure he gets bored cooped up all the time."

"Oh, thanks so much. That would be great." She slipped her bag onto her shoulder and headed for the door.

"Speaking of being bored," he said. "There was something I wanted to ask."

She stopped, her hand on the knob.

"You wouldn't happen to be free this Friday, would you? For dinner?"

Her breath caught. "Dinner? Friday?"

Slipping his hands into his jeans, he gave her a sheepish look. "It gets pretty quiet in this big ol' house sometimes. I thought a little break in the monotony would be nice."

"Monotony? You're always at the best parties, the ones I only read about in the papers."

He shrugged. "They get old after a while."

Maybe they did, but she couldn't imagine someone with his looks and background being without a long list of women willing to go to dinner with him. Women who moved in his world. Women who weren't working for his family.

Still, she couldn't help but be tempted.

Digging deep, she made herself resist. "Much as I'd like to take you up on that, Karl, I'm afraid I can't. It's against my policy to date clients."

He lifted a corner of his mouth. "But I'm not your client. My stepmother is."

She released the knob and turned to face him. "You know what I mean."

He closed the distance between them, a hint of his woodsy aftershave teasing her senses. "Do you really consider me a client? I mean, we've known each other forever."

"Not really, Karl. Let's be honest. We hadn't seen each other since your dad sold my house. And even then, it was for a very brief time."

"What about when you were a kid?"

"I don't remember much about that time."

"I remember. I remember you in your white-and-navy sailor dress one Easter. And the time you sprained your wrist falling out of that tree right there." He indicated a big oak in the garden behind them. "You'd think you'd broken every bone in your body the way you carried on."

Her eyes widened. He was talking about the time before her parents died. Things she longed to know, but the memories were always just out of reach.

"You came flying through this door screaming loud enough to bring the house down."

"I was *here* when I fell?" she whispered. "At your house? Nonie told me that happened at my house. But she gets so mixed up sometimes."

He shook his head. "It was here. I'm positive. How is your grandmother, anyway?"

Rylee looked to the side. "Sometimes she's fine, and sometimes she . . . she doesn't remember the simplest of things."

He ran his finger lightly, lightly down her arm. "I'm sorry. That's gotta be tough."

She swallowed. "Yes. Well, listen. I better go. I'll see you later. Okay?"

"I'll be counting on it."

She felt his eyes lingering on her as she went out. She hustled Romeo past the three-tiered fountain and around the pool, not looking back until she was on the other side of their green gate.

She'd left her rollerblades in the car, reserving them for bigger dogs and nighttime walks, when the streets were less busy. With Romeo panting merrily at her feet, she replayed the scene in the kitchen. The dinner invitation had come out of nowhere. She wasn't sure what to think.

She was attracted to him. No question. But dating clients was bad for business. If the relationship didn't work out, her reputation could suffer. And in her line of work, reputation was everything.

In her bag, she carried keys to dozens of multi-million-dollar homes. Of all her qualifications, trustworthiness was at the top of the list. Compromise that—even a little—and her livelihood would collapse. Charleston was a tight community south of Broad. People talked.

A group of tourists on the opposite sidewalk paused to admire Romeo. They snapped photos of the little schnauzer as if he and his walker were one of the city's sights. Rylee smiled and waved.

Surrounded by the exquisite, sometimes crumbling, architecture, the Caribbean color palette, and the scent of flowers as she trekked past hidden gardens, she felt she *was* part of the city. One of the sights. Rooted in the heart of her self-proclaimed neighborhood.

Approaching Tradd Street, they crossed to the opposite sidewalk so she could pass by First Scots Presbyterian, her church home for the past five years. Just a glimpse of the fine old building, pillars and spires, was enough to induce reverence.

As they approached, however, her sense of awe evaporated. A police car sat at the curb, lights flashing. No one at the wheel.

Through the gaps in the wrought iron, she caught sight of her pastor, Dr. Welch, engaged in an animated conversation with a police officer. This one was older than the previous ones she had recently encountered and much wider around the middle.

She coaxed Romeo forward with a light tug of the leash. "Let's make a quick stop here and make sure everything's all right."

They entered the gate and bounced up the wide steps into the shade of the church's breathtakingly tall portico.

"Dr. Welch?" she called.

The two men turned, and Dr. Welch smiled in recognition. "Mornin', Rylee."

His brick-colored polo and tan twill pants were tidy and neat, though his shock of gray hair had frizzed up in the August humidity. Next to him, the portly policeman studied her, clipboard in hand. The chrome name tag over his breast pocket read R. MUNN.

"Is everything all right?" she asked.

Dr. Welch bent over to give Romeo a rub. "Fine, fine. But we seem to have a bit of a mystery on our hands. Look what was left on our doorstep last night."

At the top of the stairs, tucked just behind a fluted column, she discovered a two-foot-tall bronze figure. A horse jockey standing with one leg bent at the knee, his hand resting elegantly on the hip. A riding crop dangled by his side.

She crouched before him, trembling with recognition. The expression on the bronze jockey's green-gray face was cryptic as the Mona Lisa's, strangely enticing. An old-fashioned paper tag hung from his neck by elastic, inscribed in black ink: *Sell and give proceeds to the poor.*

"It's a fine sentiment," Dr. Welch said, coming up alongside. "But under the circumstances, I thought I'd better call the police."

She looked up at him. "I recognize this."

Officer Munn snapped to attention. "You do?"

"This is the statue that was stolen from the Bosticks. They'll be so happy to get it back."

Dr. Welch let out a sigh. "So it *is* the Robin Hood burglar? I thought so. Imagine. Of all the places he could have donated the loot, he chose our church. Why do you suppose he'd do that?"

"Search me. But I'll be glad to return it to the owners." She encircled the statue at its base.

"Don't touch that!"

She jerked her hands back and stepped away from the statue, smiling apologetically. "Sorry, I don't know what I was thinking."

Dr. Welch tried to smooth over the awkwardness with a chuckle, but the policeman gave Rylee a hard look, staring her down.

Fine, she thought. After last night, she wasn't exactly a fan of the department.

"Now," Officer Munn said finally, "how do you know the Bosticks?"

"They're clients of mine," she said. "I walk their dog, Cocoa, and pet sit while they're out of town. As a matter of fact, they're on Long Island and won't be back until next Tuesday."

Officer Munn frowned. "The Bosticks were out of town when the burglary took place, weren't they? And now they're gone again?" He didn't try to hide the disapproval in his voice. A lot of locals were none too pleased by the influx of wealthy newcomers who treated the city's historic homes as occasional getaways.

"They're not like that," she said, reading between the lines. "They've lived here all their lives. They just like to travel, that's all."

"And what's your name, ma'am?"

"Rylee Monroe. That's R-y-l-e-e."

He scratched out what he'd written and rewrote it. "Would you mind waiting here while I radio this in? I'm sure the detective will want to speak with you."

She hesitated. "Detective Campbell?"

He looked up. "You know him?"

"I ran into him last night."

Munn made another note, then headed for his cruiser. "Just sit tight and I'll let you know what the detective wants to do."

She didn't want to see Detective Campbell again. Not ever again.

"Dr. Welch?" A woman in her forties stuck her head out the massive front door. "Your appointment's here."

He turned to Rylee. "Will you be okay? You want me to stay with you?"

"No, you go on. I'll be fine. They just want to ask me a few questions."

"Well, if you're sure. If you need anything at all, you come round and get me. You hear?"

"I will. Thanks."

A few minutes later, the detective drove up in his Mustang. The baseball uniform had been replaced with a boxy, bad-fitting suit and a tie with a mottled, synthetic sheen. He and the officer spoke quietly at the curb before Campbell headed toward her.

"Trouble seems to follow you around, Miss Monroe," he said.

She tightened her lips.

"I did some checking this morning when I got to the office. I understand you were involved in a robbery on East Battery?"

"I wasn't *involved*. I walked in on the burglar."

"So you say."

She opened her mouth to object.

"And you work for the owners of this statue right here?"

"That's right."

"And in the presence of Officer Munn you plastered your fingerprints all over it?"

She stiffened. "I didn't *plaster* them all over it, I grabbed the bottom. I was going to return it to the Bosticks."

"Convenient."

"I didn't do it on purpose, Mr. Campbell. I saw something that belonged to my client. I was simply going to return it to them."

"It's *Detective* Campbell, and I'm just making sure I have all the facts."

"Well, now you do. Is there anything else?"

"Matter of fact there is." He rocked back on his heels. "Do you happen to work for Nathaniel Shelby over on Orange Street?"

"No."

"Have you ever worked for him in the past, in any capacity?"

"*No*. What's this about?"

"It's about the fact that two of the three homes that have been burgled by Robin Hood are clients of yours."

She gasped. "Has Karl Sebastian's jewelry casket been donated too?"

"Not yet." He gave her a penetrating stare. "All the same, I'd like a comprehensive list of your clients. Names. Addresses. How long you've been working for them."

"Absolutely not. Don't you need a warrant for that?"

"You got something to hide?"

"I have nothing to hide. But I do have clients whose privacy I'm expected to guard." She wound Romeo's leash around her hand. "Now if you'll excuse me, this whole thing has made a mess of my schedule."

After a slight hesitation, Campbell stepped back and extended his hand in an after-you gesture. "Let's keep in touch, Miss Monroe."

⌒

This is the day, Logan thought.

On his drive in to work, he'd checked his phone for messages twice, and again first thing when he reached his cubicle. Nothing so far. Now he sat in front of his glowing monitor, staring at a blinking cursor on a blank page. His agent would call in his own sweet time, so there was no use anticipating.

He felt a hand on his shoulder and turned, expecting Wash. But it was Lacey Lamar, immaculate in a sleek pencil skirt and signature pearls. She wore perfume, a subtle bouquet, the only person with guts enough in their scent-free workplace.

He started to rise.

"Don't get up." She sized him up with those clear blue eyes of hers, drawing out the pause. "We need to talk about the Robin Hood pieces."

He leaned back in his chair. "Is something wrong with them?"

"The story's good, Logan. It's front-page good. And as of now you're not working on anything *but* the break-ins. We want regular coverage—unorthodox coverage. If the television news isn't taking its cues from us on this, I'm going to be very disappointed."

"Then what's the problem?"

"Like I said, I don't want you working on *anything* but this story."

He nodded. "Okay."

"There's a rumor that you've taken on an extracurricular project—and I'm not talking about the baseball team. Is it true you're working on a book?"

He gave her a look of baffled innocence. "We're on the same page here. The Robin Hood burglar is all I'm working on. Twenty-four seven. Scout's honor, Lacey."

"All right," she said with a skeptical nod. "But if I hear otherwise . . ."

"You won't."

He could say this with all sincerity. Even though it was true he was writing a book after hours, it was also true that the Robin Hood burglaries were the only thing he was working on.

For months, his agent, Seth, had been trying to sell Logan's manuscript in New York, but without much success. His collection of true tales from the Low Country underworld, packed with a cast of likeable, larger-than-life bad guys, was missing something.

Editors seemed to like the writing, but the story needed some kind of hook, a narrative thread to tie all the anecdotes together.

That's what the Robin Hood burglaries offered. At first, he was uncertain, but when the culprit struck the second time, he was convinced—along with the rest of Charleston—that this was no anomaly. Robin Hood was planning to stick around. The thief had some kind of message to impart, which meant there would be more break-ins—a series of future incidents to serve as a backbone to his history of the city's crime.

His agent liked the new approach and found an editor who was interested. Today, Logan was supposed to hear one way or the other. But until his book was sold, he really needed his day job. And that meant placating Lacey. He dragged his attention back to her.

"You're a good kid," Lacey said. "You'll turn into a good reporter some day, too—assuming there are still newspapers when you get to be my age. In the meantime, don't go getting any ideas. And don't do anything stupid."

"Who, me?"

She gave him a pointed look. "Be careful, Logan. I want you on the story, but not if you're harboring any illusions. You may think this Robin Hood character is some kind of wacky eccentric from a Southern Gothic fairy tale, but trust me, guys like this are dangerous."

"Stealing from the rich and giving to the poor? What's the danger in that?"

"Whatever his motives are, they aren't altruistic. Crime is crime. The moment you forget that, you're in trouble."

Turning, she walked down the aisle, her slim skirt and gray stiletto pumps drawing the eye of every man on the floor. Watching her go, Logan thought about the warning. Was it the Robin Hood burglar she wanted him to be wary of, or was it moonlighting?

With a vibrate-mode ring, his phone crawled an inch across the desk. He grabbed it and headed into the storeroom for privacy.

"You sitting down?" Seth asked.

The electricity was unmistakable. They'd been roommates in college long before Seth left for New York, so he could read the agent pretty well.

"Just tell me. Is it a go?"

"Almost. We're at ninety-five percent."

Logan's throat tightened. "What do you mean, ninety-five? What happened to one hundred?"

"The good news is, Dora loves it. She took it to the committee, and it sounds like they were pretty impressed, too."

"So what's the snag? Are they going to offer a contract or not?"

"There's no snag," Seth said. "But there is a wrinkle. You're a first-time author, and you're trying to sell a story that isn't finished yet."

"Of course it isn't. They haven't caught the guy. As long as he's robbing houses, the story keeps going."

"Which is great for the book. But not so great for the deal. They're going to need a finished manuscript before they'll make an offer. They want to be sure the end is as good as the beginning."

By now, Logan was used to almost-but-not-quite successes. Most of the illusions he'd entertained about publishing were long since gone. But he still held onto a dream he could never admit to Seth. He wanted editors to be moved by his writing, to love it without qualification. No snags. No wrinkles. He'd thought this time it would happen.

"Logan, are you still there?"

"I'm here."

"Look, this is excellent news. Finish the book, and if it's as good as what you've written so far, they *will* make an offer. I promise. You've been after this too long to give up now."

He sighed. "I know. It's just, this story could drag on for-ever—"

"Just write it, man. Don't worry about the rest. And think about this. You have an opportunity a lot of writers don't. You are part of the story. You're the one who dubbed the guy the Robin Hood burglar. You're covering it. Hey, you might even be the one who reveals his identity."

"Yeah, right—"

"Actually, *that* would be great for the book. But the point is, you should be living, eating, and sleeping this story from now until the end. Make it yours, okay? Do that and let me take care of the rest."

They hung up and Logan tucked his phone away. Lacey and Seth might be on opposite sides in this situation, but for once they were both telling him the same thing. This Robin Hood story was his future. It was everything.

Which meant he had to do more than sneak Wash Tillman out for some dramatic nighttime photos. He had to get in front of the Robin Hood burglaries and stay there.

Chapter Four

Logan slipped into Wash's office, converted out of the old dark-room from the pre-digital days. To enter, you still had to squeeze into the pitch-black cylinder and slide the opening around, only now the glowing red submarine lights were gone, replaced by bald fluorescents.

Wash sat with his back to the door, browsing Facebook.

"You don't leave a buddy in the lurch," Logan snapped.

He glanced around in surprise. "Bro, that's not how it went down—"

"Don't bro me."

"You think I abandoned you? I had your back, man . . . from the shadows." He cocked his head toward his computer. "Take a look."

Wash tethered one of his cameras to the computer with a length of gray cable. Soon his photos began to load onscreen.

Logan saw a blurry image of himself running, his name inde-cipherable on the back of his uniform shirt, then another one from a wider angle that showed the dog snapping at his heels. In a third, he was leaping for the memorial statue.

The photographer smiled. "I can't believe how fast you were moving."

"So you just stood there and snapped pictures?"

"I figured you had things under control."

The back of the girl's head was just visible in the next shot. Then in the next one she had turned, and Logan saw her from the front. Dark hair. Slender build. Legs that went on forever.

She bent out of the next frame to remove the rollerblades.

"Do you have any—" The following image cut him off. She was looking right at the camera, though she didn't realize it, and the focus was dead on. He stared into her bottomless brown eyes, half-hidden by a reckless fringe of bangs. Maybe he imagined the slight curve at the edge of her lips, the hint of dimples on her sun-glazed cheeks.

"She's . . ."

"Hot," Wash said.

"Unhinged."

"But kind of hot, too, don't you think?"

"She walks dogs for a living. On rollerblades. In the middle of the night. During all these break-ins. Textbook example of crazy."

"Yeah," Wash said, drawing the word out. "A man like you, with big ambitions, he needs to stay focused and keep his eyes on the prize. You don't want to get mixed up with this kind of girl. And I know you don't want me to print this one out or anything."

"Print it out? No way." Logan turned to go, pausing at the revolving door. "You can go ahead and delete them. All of them."

꧅

Wash ignored his instructions and by the time Logan reached his desk, the girl's picture was waiting in his e-mail.

He'd been staring at it trying to think of her name. It was something funny. A boy's name.

The lens had caught her unaware, between expressions. Her face wasn't at all how he remembered. Viewing the picture was like seeing her for the first time.

Then it came to him. Reilly.

Or maybe it was spelled Riley, like the NBA coach Pat Riley. Maybe her parents had been Showtime-era Lakers fans and named her after him.

He tried to work out her age, looking at the photo. Younger than he was, for sure. Early twenties, maybe.

Riley. Honestly, what kind of name was that for a girl? Did she hold it against them?

He clicked on the corner of the picture and it disappeared. He had work to do. He needed a lead. Some new info. Something.

Pulling up his notes, he summarized the first break-in. The thief entered through a window and stole a two-foot-tall bronze of a horse jockey. His story on the crime barely received three inches. If it hadn't been for the historic angle—a picturesque treasure in a creaky historic house—the theft would have gone unreported.

The second incident was more interesting. The thief, striking at night when no one was home, entered through a back door and made off with a nineteenth-century ormolu clock. Once again, there had been more valuable pieces in the house, and the thief left them untouched.

After his story on the stolen clock ran, things really got crazy. A nonprofit in North Charleston called the police to report that the clock turned up at their back door, still ticking away. Nate Campbell had tipped him off, but it was Logan who christened the thief.

"You're saying this guy breaks into a mansion downtown, takes a clock off the mantel, and donates it to charity?"

"Yep," the detective said.

"You're saying he robs the rich and gives to the poor?"

"I guess so."

And the Robin Hood burglar was born. His story was followed up with one about the clock itself, another about the nonprofit, and yet another about the history of the house it had been taken from.

Yesterday Robin had made off with an antique jewelry casket. Logan had tried to interview the victim of the theft, an attorney at one of the high-priced downtown firms, but so far Karl Sebastian hadn't returned any of his calls.

Reshuffling his notes, Logan tried to connect the burglaries. He'd been to all three sites the night before and had Wash photograph them, then they'd walked a path from one to the next. The distance was just a couple of blocks.

All that was left was to call Nate Campbell. He dreaded the conversation. Nate wasn't the sort of buddy to let you forget he'd just rescued you from a barking dog.

The detective picked up on the second ring.

"It's Logan. I never did get a police report for the Sebastian break-in."

"Hey, I was just thinking about you."

"Spare me the details."

"Remember your little friend from last night?"

"The dog?"

"Not the dog," Nate said. "The girl. Miss Monroe."

Riley *Monroe*—that was her name. "What about her?"

"You're gonna want to talk to her, assuming you can work up the nerve. The missing jockey, from the first break-in? It just turned up on the steps of her church. When the priest or minister or whatever he's called discovered the statue, she turned up and identified it. It belongs to one of her clients."

"Maybe they should have left their dog at home to guard the place."

"Anyway, looks like your Robin Hood angle is right on target. This one had a note: 'Sell and give proceeds to the poor.' Thought you'd want to know."

He felt a surge of energy. This burglar, whoever he was, clearly intended to redistribute the wealth. "Can you give me her contact info?"

"The girl? Sure."

Nate rattled off the number. "And the name is spelled funny," he added, listing the letters one at a time.

"Rylee?" Logan smirked. "Seriously, she's got to hate her parents."

"She's certainly a piece a work. Got a real mouth on her."

"Oh, I don't know. As scared as she was, I thought she handled herself pretty well."

"You got to be kidding. We can't have every person who sees a couple of guys in the park at night calling 9-1-1. We'd be out there 24/7. I tried to tell her that, and she got right in my face."

Logan frowned. "She may have overreacted, Nate, but she was afraid."

He scoffed. "You should have seen her this morning with that statue. Defensive as all get out. Something doesn't smell right."

Logan hung up the phone but didn't dial Rylee Monroe's number right away.

If he put himself in her shoes—or rollerblades, in this case—it was hard not to sympathize. She'd been frightened enough to call the police. Even if she read the situation wrong, the fear was real. And instead of reassurance when Nate showed up, she'd gotten the brush-off.

Now he was acting like she might be a suspect. Logan didn't have a sister, but if he did, and the cops had treated her that way, he'd have a problem with the officer in charge.

Fact of the matter was, the girl deserved an apology. And it was pretty safe to say she wouldn't be getting one from Nate. But that didn't mean Logan couldn't offer one on his behalf.

Picking up the phone, he punched in her number.

"Hello?" Her voice was tentative.

"Miss Monroe, hi. It's Logan Woods. From last night?"

A pause.

Wash sauntered into his cubicle and tossed an 8x10 glossy of Rylee on his desk.

Logan picked it up. "Are you there, ma'am?"

"What's this about?"

"I was wondering if I could talk to you about what happened this morning at your church. My paper is covering the story, and since you were an eyewitness to the discovery—"

"I don't think so. I—"

"Hold on." He gripped the phone more tightly. "Before you say no, let me assure you, this won't take up a lot of your time, and you'd be doing a public service by sharing your perspective."

Public service? Wash mouthed. He sat on the edge of Logan's desk, making no effort to mask his interest.

Logan cleared his throat. "Listen, about last night. Detective Campbell was a little out of line."

"You think?" A bite in her voice.

"Could I make it up to you? Maybe over a cup of coffee?"

Wash lifted his brows.

"I'd rather not."

Logan swiveled his chair so his back was to Wash, but he still held the photo pinched between his fingers. "Just a quote, a sound bite, would be all I'd need."

"I thought you wanted to make it up to me."

"I do."

"But you also want a sound bite."

"If you don't mind."

On her end of the phone, a trolley car bell drowned out her next few words. " . . . just answer your questions over the phone?"

He ran his thumb up and down the edge of the photo. "We could do a sound bite over the phone, but I've always thought apologies should be done in person."

A hum of silence.

He sensed her wavering. "There's a Starbucks on—"

"What about City Lights?" she said, her voice resigned. "You know that one?"

"City Lights?" He glanced at Wash, raising an eyebrow in question.

"It's on Market between Meeting and King," she said.

"Right." Logan checked his watch. "What time?"

"Can you do it right now? Otherwise, it'll have to be tomorrow afternoon."

"Now is fine. I'm on my way."

―

"Looks like she's gonna make you grovel." Wash snapped a picture, then indicated the tables outside City Lights.

Rylee pulled out a chair and sat at one of them, glancing through the big bay window.

"Oldest female trick in the book—make 'em come to you." Wash focused his zoom. " 'Course with a girl like that, groveling would be a pleasure."

Logan quickly scanned the menu chalked on the blackboard. "Let me have two coffees of the day, please." He placed some bills on the counter. "You stay here, Wash."

"What? Is me being out there gonna cramp your style?"

"I was thinking about her."

Wash grinned. "You sure you don't need a witness? In case she calls the police on you again?"

Logan narrowed his eyes.

"All right. All right."

Logan dropped his change in the tip jar, picked up the mugs and a couple of creamers, and then pushed out the door.

She waited at the table, her eyes hidden behind sunglasses. A dark-wash denim mini-skirt sheathed her thighs, and her frilly top left her shoulders and arms bare.

He started to smile, then stalled midway. At her feet, a tiny white and gold dog stared up at him, the leash hanging limp in Rylee's slender hand.

"I can't bring him inside. Don't worry. He doesn't bite." She leaned over to scrub the thing's head with her nails. "Do you, boy? Do you?"

"I didn't realize you were working."

She straightened. "I'm always working. Will Tippy bother you? You're not allergic, are you?"

He shook his head, trying to ignore the tightness in his chest. "I got you a cup of basic black and some creamers. If you'd rather have something else . . . ?"

"No. I love black." She ventured a sip, then nodded. "Thanks."

He settled into the wrought-iron chair next to hers but opposite the dog, then leaned onto the table, close enough to inhale her scent, close enough almost for their arms to touch. "Listen, I'm sorry about the way things went down last night. I usually see Nate either in his office or on the baseball field. If I'd known how . . . excited he was going to get, I never would have enlisted his help."

She crossed her legs, swinging her foot back and forth. Her flats were fire-engine red. "What made you think you needed help? I told you I had Toro. I told you I wouldn't let him get you."

He could have launched into an account of his sad history with canines and even shown her some traumatic childhood scars, but he bit his tongue instead. Apologies were best unqualified. "It was wrong of me. I'm sorry. And I'm sorry for the way Nate acted."

Her foot stopped. He wished he could see her eyes.

"He's a real jerk, your friend."

"We all have our moments."

"Are you making excuses for him?"

"No. He was totally out of line, and I'm both sorry and embarrassed."

She pushed her sunglasses up onto her head. The sunlight shrank her pupils, leaving brown irises the color of toffee. The camera hadn't done them justice.

Her voice was so soft, he almost didn't catch her words over the sound of traffic. "I really was scared. This Robin Hood thing is freaking me out. Stuff like that isn't supposed to happen south of Broad." She searched his eyes. "You have no idea how frightening it was to have you and your photographer pop out at me like that."

He curled his hand around his mug. "I know. And I'm sorry for that, too. We were going for a kind of dramatic angle for our photos. That's why you didn't see us right away."

As apologies went, it definitely ranked up there. And he seemed sincere. But his motive was still suspect. Was he genuinely sorry, or had he apologized simply because he wanted his sound bite? Or worse, what if his detective buddy put him up to it in order to fish for information?

Tippy wandered toward a communal canine water bowl under the front window, the leash lengthening as it went. The dog lapped up the liquid, then made his way toward Logan.

He looked different without his baseball cap. A thick mop of brown hair streaked by the sun lay in artful disarray, the ends curling slightly in the humidity. His chocolate-colored eyes were surrounded by eyelashes longer than hers, yet there was nothing feminine about him.

His eyebrows looked as if an artist had made a quick slash with his brush to frame each eye. A defined nose and jaw drew her eyes to his mouth. Subtle grooves on each side hinted at a lifetime of smiles.

He eyed Tippy as the dog scratched its ear, paw thumping Logan's shoe after each scratch.

She snapped her fingers. "Come 'ere, Tippy."

Logan's shoulders relaxed the tiniest bit. He flipped his notebook open, setting it on the table in front of him. "So." He cleared his throat. "Are we good?"

"Depends."

"On what?"

"On whether or not the detective sent you here to question me."

"Nate?" He reared back. "Why would he do that? Nate conducts his own interviews. I have nothing to do with his work and he has nothing to do with mine."

She bit her lip, still unsure.

He held out his hand. "Let's start over, okay? I'm Logan."

The appeal in his eyes was impossible to resist. After a slight hesitation, she reached out. His hand was warm to the touch. "I'm Rylee."

"You had quite a morning, I hear."

She took another sip, then placed her mug down gently. "Yes, I did."

"You know the Bosticks, then. The people whose jockey got stolen?"

She nodded. "It was kinda surreal, seeing it there at the church. I was, like, *Wait a minute—I recognize that thing*. Then, like an idiot, I offered to take it back to them. There could be fingerprints, and I put my hands on it."

He pulled a digital recorder from his pocket and set it on the table. "Do you mind?"

"No, I guess not."

He pressed the record button. "This statue, it was the first of the thefts. Did you talk to the Bosticks about it?"

She gazed up at the striped umbrella they sat beneath, tapping into her memory. "I remember Mr. Bostick saying they were going to change the door locks, which was funny because the guy had jimmied the window overlooking the garden. When I asked him what was wrong, he showed me the mention in the paper." She turned to him. "I guess you wrote that?"

"I did."

"You know how you said which night the break-in occurred?"

He nodded.

"Well, that was actually the night they discovered the statue was missing."

"It wasn't stolen on—" he flipped through his notebook "—August ninth?"

She shook her head. "They don't know exactly when it went missing."

"How could that be?"

"You could only tell from the outside that there was damage to the window. When the thief shut it again, it was unnoticeable from inside."

"And the perp came in from the garden?"

She blew on the warm liquid in her mug, sending waves across its black surface. "The Bosticks travel a lot. They have a beautiful garden, but I think the gardener and I are pretty much the only ones who ever go out there."

"You'd think they would notice the statue was gone, though. It's two feet tall, right?"

"Yes, but I can see why they didn't miss it right away. Their place is like a museum. A lot of those historic houses are, but that one in particular." She flicked the hair from her eyes and smiled. "You know how they realized it had been stolen?"

"I don't, actually. I based my article on the police report and a couple of phone conversations with Doug Bostick, who made it sound like the crime was reported as soon as it happened." His eyes had widened slightly, calling attention to caramel accents radiating from their centers.

"I can see how you thought that, but the day they called the police, Mrs. Bostick was telling her husband she wanted to hire a new maid service. In the middle of this discussion, she goes over to the table where the statue was, and starts pointing out the dust on everything. And she sees this square section, perfectly dust-free. 'What was standing right here?' she asks, and he can't remember. They went all through the house and finally it came to her, the bronze jockey. Isn't that something?"

"It is." He made a note, his arms and shoulders crowding the circular tabletop.

Tippy circled the gap between their chairs. Rylee moved her Vera Bradley bag, grazing Logan's arm by accident.

She jerked back, but he didn't seem to notice.

"There's a lot of stuff in that house more valuable than a bronze statue," she said, resting her hand over the spot where they'd touched. "Same with the box that was stolen from the Sebastians."

"You know the Sebastians?"

"Yes. They're a new client of mine."

He made another note. "And the jewelry casket? You'd seen it before the theft?"

She shook her head. "I'd never been upstairs before that day. But Karl said it had been in his family for years."

"I've been trying to get ahold of him."

"You know what really bothers me?" A spark of irritation flashed through her. "How the thief donates his spoils to charity, and suddenly this . . . crime starts looking quaint. Stealing from the rich, giving to the poor. People think it's funny."

"It is pretty unique, you have to admit."

"Well, you didn't see the expression on Karl's face when he discovered the box was missing. Whoever did this took more than a jewelry box from that family."

He copied down a few of her phrases. She watched his hands form the letters in a surprisingly neat script.

Whoever did this took more than a jewelry box from that family.

"Look at this." She dug through her shoulder bag and produced her key ring. It reminded her of the kind a jailer in an old movie would have swinging from his hip. She moved her fingers deftly through the stacks of color-coded keys, isolating a series set apart by pink adhesive dots. "Before the break-in, I had just the one key for the Bosticks, and now there's three. Three locks on every door."

Logan stared at the key ring. "So wait a second. You have keys to the Sebastian and Bostick places? You go in and out?"

"Of course I do. People don't just meet me at the door and hand their dogs over. Some of them are out of town, some work during the day, some of my elderly clients have difficulty with the stairs. And some just don't want to be bothered."

"And all those keys." He indicated the thick stack radiating around the ring. "Those are to other people's places around town?"

She straightened, well aware of what he implied. "I offer a specialized service."

"To Charleston's elite."

"I work south of Broad, if that's what you mean."

"Exactly. The old money."

"And the new. A lot of my clients are out-of-towners who just come to Charleston as a getaway."

"Pretty expensive weekend house."

"Like I said, valuable is a relative term." Uncomfortable with the direction of the conversation, she checked her watch. "Listen, I need to get going. Do you have what you need?"

"Sure. I appreciate you meeting me." He hit the stop button on his recorder and stood.

He had to be around six foot one. She hadn't noticed it when he was up on that statue. But standing next to him, she realized he topped her by several inches and she was five eight in her bare feet.

Tippy jumped up, tail wagging.

Rylee hesitated. "I did want to say that I'm sorry Toro chased you up that statue."

He smiled. A boyish good-natured grin. "No problem."

She moistened her lips, unsure if she should shake his hand or exactly what. In the end, she gave an awkward wave and led Tippy down the sidewalk in the direction of Market Hall.

Chapter Five

Toro nosed the gate, anxious to begin their nighttime run.

"Rylee?"

She turned.

Mrs. Davidson stood at the threshold of the front door in a flowing silk caftan and matching house slippers. "Maybe you shouldn't go out there alone, not with these robberies going on. A young woman, all by herself—" She shivered. "I hate to think about what could happen."

Rylee answered with a broad smile, ruffling the fur at Toro's neck. "I'll be all right. Toro here will watch out for me."

Waving, Rylee skated into the night, not giving Mrs. Davidson a chance to reply. Her concern was touching, but even at night, Rylee knew the city, knew its twists and turns, its hidden gardens, its alleyways and shortcuts.

Ducking under a low-hanging branch, she cut down a cobbled path, Toro surging forward. Now that she knew it had only been Logan and his photographer lurking in the shadows last night, her fears had mostly disappeared.

Then Toro stopped, bringing her up short.

A silhouette of a man at the other end of the alley ducked into the shadows. A streetlamp flickered, the swaying tree canopy baffling its light.

"Stay, boy," she whispered, tightening her grip on the leash. Goose bumps raised along her forearm.

She reached under the flap of her messenger bag, digging around until her hand gripped her flashlight. No way was she calling 9-1-1 again.

She thumbed on the flashlight. A cone of light illuminated the wooden slats of a partition fence.

She swept the beam left and right.

Nothing.

But she could feel his presence.

Toro growled, crouching on his haunches, though he seemed reluctant to charge into the unknown.

"It's okay, boy." She smoothed his head. "Come on. Let's turn around."

They circled with caution, retracing their steps.

A rustle of branches. She whirled, shining the light again.

Nothing to see.

Her heart raced. Part of her wanted to turn and run. But she had Toro by her side. And she wouldn't let her fears drive her off the streets she loved.

She switched the light off but kept it firmly in hand, then set a brisk pace, shaking the leash to get Toro moving. They made for the golden streetlamps of Meeting Street, away from the fragrant, secluded gardens tucked into the side alley.

More shuffling over her shoulder. A dash from tree to tree. A footstep sliding over the cobbles.

She imagined the shadow gaining on her, ghostly hands reaching out.

The hair on the back of her neck tingled, but she kept moving. Ready to shine her light on any noise too pronounced to write off as just the wind or a stray cat.

I'm being followed.

The thought seemed crazy. But this wasn't her imagination. She'd seen the silhouette. She'd heard the movement, in spite of his effort to go unnoticed.

They reached Meeting Street and headed toward Broad, where even at this hour they were bound to encounter a stray tourist, some late-night partygoers, or even a couple out walking the dog.

She glanced behind, and there he was.

Just the crescent of a head eclipsing the light of a streetlamp. Lurking at the alley entrance. She was too far to away to make out any features. It could be anyone.

Then he was gone.

She felt a shiver run through her. All her strength ebbed away. Toro brushed her hip, panting softly, and she nearly fell.

They continued to Prices Alley, where the Davidsons lived, encountering no one. At the alley entrance, she stopped, gazing through the darkness for a glimpse of King Street.

He could have doubled back, cut through to King, and then made his way to the opposite end of Prices Alley.

She flicked the flashlight back on, throwing the beam ahead of her.

She saw nothing amiss, but these streets interconnected. They were full of nooks to hide in. He could stalk her like game and never reveal himself.

Taking a deep breath, she glided forward. Toro loped along, undisturbed by doubts, his bulk reassuring her.

She reached the gate, hustled the mastiff inside, and breathed a sigh of relief.

The ordeal was over. In the warm light of the Davidsons' kitchen, she removed her rollerblades. Surrounded by familiar objects, she could almost convince herself it was all a mistake. Just a man out walking whose path had crossed hers.

"Are you all right?"

She looked up.

Mrs. Davidson stood in the archway, her silk tunic billowing about her ankles, her reading glasses perched at the end of her nose. In her veined hand, she held a closed paperback, her finger marking the page.

The last thing Rylee wanted was to appear as if she couldn't do her job. If she couldn't walk her dogs at night, the Davidsons and all her other clients would hire someone who could.

"I'm fine," she said. "See? Nothing to worry about."

A few minutes later, she headed for her car, Daisy. The old yellow Honda Civic was parked out on Meeting Street, which meant threading her way through the dark alley to get there. She flicked the flashlight up and down the lane, then set off. Her footsteps echoed on the uneven cobbles. Halfway to the street, she glanced behind her and froze.

There he was again. Just outside the Davidsons' gate. Another snapshot of a man's silhouette dashing from light to dark.

Her breath caught.

And then she ran, breaking through to Meeting Street, her heart pounding in her chest. She reached Daisy, jabbing the lock with her key. Finally she wrenched the door open and jumped inside. The car came to life with a sputter, then threatened to die. Her headlights flared and dimmed.

Don't die on me, Daisy.

She crammed the car in gear and gunned it, mentally daring the man to step out of Prices Alley and show his face.

He didn't.

She passed the entrance without so much as a glimpse of him.

Breathing hard, with a white-knuckled grip on the wheel, she drove home, wondering what to do. Calling the police was out of the question.

Perhaps she should call Logan, but what would she tell him? She couldn't identify the guy. No facial features. No distinguishing marks. Not even an ethnicity.

She could call Karl, but again, she didn't want her clients thinking she couldn't do her job.

She sighed. There was nothing she could do. No one she could call. No one she could lean on. She was in this all alone.

＝

While his mom banged pots together in the kitchen, Logan stood on the deck with his dad. The backyard of his childhood, a damp and muddy patch of ground that sloped down to a vast marsh, had been fenced in with wrought iron. The swing set was gone, the ground now carpeted with stone pavers and exotic plants.

"The next thing is gonna be lights all around the perimeter." Dad drew a line in the air with his index finger. "I had them already picked out, but your mom said they looked too modern."

They stood over a water feature. A slender stream gushed out through a rock wall, tumbling into a pool with glowing bulbs underneath.

Dad slid his hands into his pockets. "It's been a while since we've seen you at church."

Logan glanced at him. "I do make an effort. It's just with the job, I work some crazy hours, and when I'm not on the clock there's the book to work on."

They gazed down onto the water's rippling surface, their heads tiny and their legs huge.

"I know how it is, son. You get so busy, you think you can do it all, then suddenly you don't have time for anything else in life. I've been there. The thing is, you can't do it all, not alone."

"I know that, Dad."

"Now your mom, she'd be happy as a clam if you'd just attend church. But I didn't raise my boy to be one of those one-day-a-week Christians. I'm talking about starting every morning in a sit-down with your Bible and the good Lord above."

Logan tilted his head back and looked into the huge branches of an oak he'd spent many an hour climbing. From anyone else the words might've sounded like a sermon, but he knew how important it was to his father. Knew how the old man actually lived what he believed. And besides, it was true he hadn't spent any time reading his Bible lately or driven down to James Island these past few Sundays—maybe more than that, come to think of it.

But the omission wasn't intentional. His hands were full at the moment, that's all. Still, his dad was right. He needed to get his priorities in order.

"Okay, Dad. I'll do better."

"That's great, son." He gave an approving nod. "So tell me what's going on with this Robin Hood stuff. Everybody at the office is talking about it. I should be pumping you for inside information."

"I'm working on a new draft of my manuscript," Logan said. "With the Robin Hood story right at the center."

"That's a great idea."

"Yeah? I thought so, too, at first, but now I'm having doubts. I'd be tying my future to a story that hasn't ended yet, one that might not ever have a proper end if the police don't figure out who's behind the burglaries. Not only that, I'm beginning to think the crime angle sort of cheapens the rest, if you know what I mean."

"In what way?"

He shrugged. "I started off with this idea about the city, all the history, the eccentric people. The ones in my book just happen to be criminals. But they're *Charleston* criminals. To me, the Robin Hood story doesn't fit. It's not a Charleston crime."

"What's a Charleston crime, then?"

Logan rubbed the back of his neck. "I don't know. A crime of passion, I guess."

"Just because nobody's been killed doesn't mean there's no passion behind it, son. Think about what has to go into crimes like these. Somebody knows these houses or has a way of researching them. He chooses these specific items to steal. Like they have meaning, only it isn't monetary. Whatever's behind this, I bet it's fascinating. I bet it is a Charleston crime."

"So you think I should do it?" Logan asked, his voice tinged with skepticism.

"You want to know my opinion?" Dad clapped him on the shoulder. "Nothing you choose is gonna cheapen your book, so long as it's you doing it." They turned to go back inside, Dad's hand still gripping his shoulder. "You know what would really sell some books, don't you?"

He couldn't help but smile. "What would sell some books, Dad?"

"If you somehow managed to solve the crime yourself. Ahead of the police."

Logan eyed him curiously. "Seth told me the same thing. I'm not too sure I could manage it."

"Sure you could. You're an investigative reporter."

"Technically, I'm not."

Dad smiled, putting his hand on Logan's chest. "In here you are."

⌐

Driving home, Logan could still feel the pressure of his father's fingers against his sternum. His heart quickened at the memory. For all his spreadsheets and interest schedules, Dad was sentimental to the core, much more so than Mom, despite appearances.

Where she had perfectly reasonable dreams—wanting the same thing any mother would—his dad still thought his son could turn out to be a baseball star, snag a beauty, and solve a crime. When it came to their vicarious thrills, Mom's were pretty ordinary, whereas Dad's had a touch of the daredevil.

Still, reporters had been scooping policemen since the daily paper came out in cuneiform on clay tablets. And one thing his dad had said kept coming back to him.

You can't do it alone.

Of course, Dad meant something like, you can't it do without Jesus. But the principle rang true. A big break would require more than waiting on a fresh tip from Nate Campbell.

Rylee's face rose unbidden to his mind's eye.

He needed to know if she was holding something back. He needed to know if she had some sort of connection to the Robin Hood burglar. He needed to know . . . *her.*

Chapter Six

Rylee pulled into a visitor's spot at the Bishop Gadsden retirement community, the brakes of her Civic squeaking. On the porch, Mr. Lusky, in a short-sleeved, plaid button-down, perused his newspaper.

She sighed, knowing she'd get yet another lecture from him on the importance of regular car maintenance. She'd have to bear it, though. She could hardly tell him that keeping her grandmother at Bishop Gadsden took some creative manipulation of her finances.

She turned off the key, the engine coughing like a lifelong smoker.

Mr. Lusky dipped the corner of his paper. "That car needs some attention, Rylee-girl," he called. "If one of your dogs made a sound like that, you'd take him to the vet, wouldn't you? It's downright cruel to make your car suffer."

She strode up the walkway, then stopped beside him. "Looks like it's going to be another scorcher today."

He wrestled with the paper, folding it back.

Her breath caught. A picture of Logan took up a small corner at the bottom of the page. He was sliding into home, his face in a grimace, the catcher clearly tagging him out.

He had on his Mets uniform. The same one he'd worn the night Toro had chased him. In the stillness of the shot, the muscles in his arms and legs bulged. She leaned down to read over Mr. Lusky's shoulder.

Logan Woods of the Charleston MABL Mets was tagged out at home by Oriole Harold Hearn in Sunday's game. The Orioles went on to knock the Mets out of the playoffs with a 4-3 win.

Mr. Lusky sniffed. "You follow the Men's Adult Baseball League, Rylee?"

She straightened. "What? Oh, no."

He lifted his chin, peering through the lower half of his bifocals. "That's Logan Woods. He's the center fielder. Good player. Power hitter. Played for the Trojans over at the high school."

Rylee blinked. "James Island High School?"

"Why, sure. They almost won State his senior year."

"When was that?"

"Ninety-nine, I think? Good team that year. One of their players went on to play for the Rockies."

She looked again at the picture. She'd attended James Island High School, too. Doing the math, she realized he'd have been a senior her freshman year.

With JIHS being the only high school on the island, its enrollment was always on the high side. So it was no surprise she hadn't known him. Still, she'd have to look him up in her old yearbook.

"He writes for the paper now." Mr. Lusky narrowed his eyes shrewdly. "Matter of fact, he had an article about one of those breakins down where you walk your dogs. Saw you were quoted in it."

She'd read the article over coffee this morning. A photo of the bronze jockey dominated the page, the text wrapped on either side.

She was quoted twice—once at the opening, talking about how she'd recognized the statue at the church, and a second time in the body of the story: " 'Whoever did this took more than a jewelry box from that family.' "

She hoped Karl didn't read it. Seeing the comment in black-and-white, she felt as if she'd exploited his pain somehow.

"Rylee!"

She turned at the sound of her name. One of the nursing staff jogged toward her. "I thought I saw you pull up. Come quickly, dear. It's your grandmother."

＝

Rylee hurried toward Room C5 of the Cloister. This wing of the facility was reserved for residents who needed round-the-clock care. It resembled a hospital, with an octagonal nurses' station at the hub and halls radiating out like spokes. The rooms had hospital beds, many of their doors open.

But that's where the similarities ended. The Cloister didn't smell like a hospital. The halls were carpeted. There was no intercom system blaring. No dinging elevator.

She checked the numbers posted beside each door, catching brief impressions of the rooms inside—a television playing reruns of *I Love Lucy*, a walnut chest of drawers belonging to a long-term patient, a pair of lonely feet wrapped in pink slippers propped on the footrest of a recliner, and then Room C5.

The door was closed. She gently tapped, then pushed it open. Monitors beeped.

Dr. Craig Morris looked up from the clipboard in his hand.

Nodding to him and Nurse Melanie, Rylee went straight to her grandmother's bedside. Nonie's eyes were closed.

"Is she all right?"

69

Dr. Craig nodded. "She'll be fine. She was making some cookies and forgot to use a hot pad before she removed them from the oven."

She glanced at her grandmother's hands. The right one was wrapped in gauze.

"How bad is it?"

In his late forties, the doctor was young enough to be approachable, yet old enough to instill confidence. "It's a second-degree burn. She has some blisters that'll be red and painful for a while. But it doesn't appear she suffered any nerve damage."

"Thank goodness." Rylee released a long breath. "How could she have forgotten the hot pads?"

He exchanged a look with the nurse.

Rylee looked up sharply. "She hasn't been wandering again, has she?"

"Not wandering, no," Nurse Melanie said. "But she's been losing track of time and events. I'm afraid her bad spells are getting to be more frequent. Not as many lucid moments as before. We make sure she doesn't miss mealtimes. . . ."

Rylee brushed a tendril of hair from Nonie's face. She'd been at Bishop Gadsden for almost three years now. The decision to move her here had not been an easy one. But she couldn't support her grandmother and take care of her at the same time.

The sale of their Folly Beach home had financed Nonie's entrance into Bishop Gadsden and subsequent stay.

For now. But when Rylee had originally done the math, she hadn't taken any future medical problems into account—and there had been plenty. Now the funds were dwindling, and the new healthcare bills would deplete their resources even more.

"Can she hear us?" she asked.

The doctor shook his head. "I gave her something for the pain. She'll sleep comfortably for a while if you need to return to work."

"No, no. I don't have to be back until two. So if it's all right with you, I'll stay with Nonie. Thanks so much."

The doctor slipped out, followed by Nurse Melanie, who promised to check in after a bit, leaving Rylee to contemplate Nonie's fragile form under the covers, the hum of the overhead lights punctuated by the beep and hiss of the machinery at her back. She reached to take her grandmother's hand, then remembered the bandage. Even here, Nonie could manage a minor catastrophe.

She sat and listened to her grandmother's breathing, the irregular in and out, worrying at every overlong pause that this would be the last. Nothing would erase that dreadful possibility from her mind. Rylee struggled as a sense of loneliness and abandonment swept over her again.

Please, Lord. She's all I have.

Chapter Seven

Rylee let herself in the Petries' front door, cocking an ear, trying to determine where the mewling was coming from. She slipped her key ring back into her messenger bag, listening.

Tin Man—a gray tabby with a ringed tail—ran to the door, doing continuous figure eights through her legs. She picked him up, then looked for the other three cats Mrs. Petrie had named after characters from her favorite movie, *The Wizard of Oz*.

She found Dorothy in the parlor curled on the seat of an upholstered armchair, too supercilious to be bothered.

The mewling continued. Probably Lion. He'd been mauled by a Rottweiler as a kitten, so Latisha Petrie had coaxed the Persian into eating by petting him the whole time. Now he wouldn't touch his food without being stroked through the entire meal.

Passing through the dining room, she released Tin Man and dropped her bag on a sideboard. "Li-on?" she singsonged. "Here, kitty-kitty-kitty."

Stepping into the kitchen, Rylee noticed a suitcase by the back door.

She glanced toward the sunroom. "Lion?"

The cat came through the doorway, apparently fine. But the mewling kept up. It was coming from the other side of the half-open door. Rylee edged forward, then gasped.

Latisha sat curled in a fetal position on a padded wicker armchair. Her slacks were rumpled, her hair in disarray, her black suede pumps lay haphazardly at her feet.

"What's wrong?" Rylee rushed to her side. She knelt on the seagrass mat that served as an area rug. "Are you all right?"

"That robber . . ." Latisha looked up, tears flowing down her ebony cheeks.

Rylee sucked in her breath. "He came here?"

Latisha nodded, her long black ringlets bobbing.

Rylee glanced around. "When? Were you here?"

Scarecrow leaped from Latisha's lap, leaving a layer of red hair on her white cashmere pullover.

"I flew back early from London because of a work emergency," she began.

Rylee pictured the suitcase in the kitchen.

"When I got to my room, it was, was . . ." She covered her face, her shoulders shaking.

The hairs on the back of Rylee's neck prickled. "Was he still here when you arrived?"

"No."

"Have you called the police?"

"They've been and gone. But they did nothing. *Nothing*." She slammed her hands on the arms of the chair. "They just took down enough to file their reports, then left."

That was exactly what they'd done at Karl's house, too. It hadn't occurred to Rylee until now that they probably should have done more.

"They told me to call if he comes again," Latisha said. "Can you believe that? They aren't going to dust for fingerprints or take pictures or post a guard or anything."

"I wonder why."

"They said what he took wasn't valuable enough for all that."

Rylee's lips parted. "That shouldn't make any difference. A crime's a crime no matter what was taken. Breaking and entering and all that."

"That's what I thought, too. But all they said was that they'd let the local nonprofits know to keep an eye out for it. Evidently, the stolen item has to be worth a lot more than my mourning brooch for them to do anything. It simply boggles the mind."

"Mourning brooch?"

"Yes. It's an old Victorian one Paul's mother gave me. I always wear it with that red cape. You know the one I mean?"

Rylee nodded as comprehension dawned. "Of course. The onyx one. Did he take anything else?"

"Nothing."

"And you're sure you didn't misplace the pin?"

"Positive."

Rylee deflated, remembering Officer Quince's description of Robin Hood's M.O. He took only one thing, and not the most valuable. He'd definitely struck again. "How did he get in?"

"Right through these doors." She indicated the French doors overlooking the garden. The pane next to the bolt was nothing but jagged edges.

"It wasn't like that when I left last night. I'm positive." Tin Man brushed against Rylee's arm. She ran her hand over his head, back, and tail. "Well, I can't see Paul standing still for all this. He'll make sure the whole thing is investigated properly. Have you called him?"

Sighing, Latisha fell back, resting her head against the chair. "He's still in London and not answering his cell phone."

Rylee glanced at her watch. "What time is it there?"

"Past midnight." She drew in a shaky breath. "Our bedroom's a mess." Her eyes filled again. "I don't want to sleep in there. I don't want to sleep in the house at all. Especially not by myself."

Rylee stood. "Well, don't you worry about a thing. I'll stay with you until Paul returns."

A wobbly smile touched Latisha's lips. "No need for that. My sister's driving in from Asheville, and I've left a message for my girlfriend Cheryl. I expect to hear back from her any minute."

"Good. For now, though, I'll make you some tea, then start straightening your room."

Latisha reached out and grasped Rylee's hand. "You're so good to us. Thank you." She straightened. "Oh, I almost forgot. The detective wants you to call him." She picked up a business card off the side table and handed it to Rylee.

Nathan Campbell. Detective Division. Charleston Police Department.

Rylee fingered the card. "Did he say what he wanted?"

"Just routine things, I imagine. He had lots of questions about who all has access to the house and their comings and goings. Probably wants to confirm that the doors were secured when you left last night." She looked at the broken glass on the floor. "I guess they're following up a little, anyway."

"Does he want to speak with Carmel? And George?"

Latisha crinkled her brow. "Actually, he didn't leave cards for them—though I did tell him we had a housekeeper and a gardener. Should I have them call, too?"

Swallowing, Rylee shook her head. "No. I'm sure he'll let you know if he needs to speak with them."

Tucking the card into her pocket, she moved into the kitchen to brew some tea.

Rylee stood at the threshold of the master bedroom, eyes wide, hands covering her mouth. Family photos had been knocked off the bureau, shattered glass studding the carpet. Drawers ripped free of the mahogany dressers, their contents dumped everywhere. Designer clothes flung from the closets and trampled in a frenzy of destruction.

She felt as if she were falling into a great abyss. Four houses had now been hit. Three were her clients. Detective Campbell would want to know why.

But he'd have to do the calling. Just because he wanted a convenient suspect didn't mean she had to volunteer.

The chaos in the room was so great she didn't know where to start. Finally, she moved to the bed and righted a jewelry box. She picked up a strand of pearls and placed them in a compartment. So smooth. So cool to the touch.

Whoever did this didn't care about money. A person could pay a lot of bills with what they could get from hocking the baubles strewn across the white coverlet.

She fingered a tasseled key hanging from the keyhole of the jewelry box. The thought of a stranger being in the house, in this very room, filled her with the same vulnerability she'd experienced at the Sebastians'.

The doorbell rang, jolting her out of her thoughts.

"I'll get it," she hollered, hurrying down the stairs. "It's probably Cheryl."

She looked through the peephole, pulled back, then looked again. He sure didn't waste any time.

She watched Logan lean to the right, trying to see inside the window of the dining room, before he punched the bell once more.

She'd looked him up in her yearbook. His photo showed the awkwardness typical of school pictures, but his features were attractive even then. He'd matured in the intervening years, though, making the leap from boy to man with flying colors.

She opened the door. He wore his work clothes—an oxford shirt, striped tie, blue jeans and Jack Purcells. Same thing he'd worn to the coffee shop.

His eyes widened, then a slow smile began to form. The grooves around his mouth came into full play, transforming his face. His dark hair begged for a comb's attention, the unruly locks going every which way.

"What are you doing here?" he asked.

She raised a brow. "I was wondering the same thing about you."

"You don't live here, I'm assuming."

"No. The Petries are clients of mine."

"You're kidding." He glanced nervously into the house. "What kind of dog do they have?"

Suppressing a smile, she leaned against the doorframe, blocking the view. "Don't worry, Wonderboy. No ferocious dogs here. Just cats."

"I didn't think cats needed walking."

She let out a huff of air. "I feed their cats. Now, what can I do for you?"

Tucking his hands in his back pockets, he leaned his head to the side. "That kind of makes you three-for-four, doesn't it?"

"I'm sorry?"

"Three of the houses hit by the Robin Hood burglar are clients of yours."

She stiffened, all humor snuffed completely out. "What do you want, Logan?"

"No offense. I was just making an observation."

"Well, I have things to do, so if you would excuse me—"

He stopped the door with his hand. "I really didn't mean to imply anything, Rylee."

She gave him a tight-lipped nod.

"Are the Petries home?"

"They're not available right now."

He pulled a card from his shirt pocket. "Would you just let them know I'm here? It'll only take a minute."

She didn't take the card. She still had the one he'd tossed her last week while quivering atop the Confederate Memorial.

He extended the card into her space. "I'll even stay on the porch, if they'd prefer. I just have a couple of questions."

"Maybe I can answer them for you."

He hesitated. "Were you here when the robbery took place?"

"No."

"Then I'd prefer to speak to them. I got my facts wrong last time, remember?"

"They weren't here during the robbery, either."

"I'd still like to talk to them."

She hesitated.

His blue eyes exuded appeal. He definitely had the all-American-boy-next-door look down to an art. And try as she might, she wasn't immune to it.

Snatching the card, she took a step back. "Wait here."

She'd barely closed the door when Latisha reached the entry-way. "Is it Cheryl?"

"No, a reporter from the paper." She handed the card over.

"He wants to talk about the robbery?"

"I was just fixing to chase him off."

Latisha bit her lip. "Hold on a second. I should talk to him. Maybe it would wake the neighborhood up, so the police start taking these robberies seriously."

Rylee wasn't so sure. Talking to the press was a very slippery slope. Just like talking to the police. "How about I have him call your office and make an appointment?"

Latisha shooed Rylee's suggestion away with a fanning of her hand. "Nonsense. You show him on in to the parlor."

"You sure you don't want to wait until Paul gets back?"

"The sooner we get the news out, the better."

Rylee watched her until she disappeared from sight. Then she took a deep breath and reopened the front door.

Chapter Eight

Logan found Latisha Petrie installed in a floral print club chair, one of a pair upholstered in the same fabric as the open drapes. For a woman whose house had just been burgled, she seemed quite composed. But as she rose to greet him, her outstretched hand trembled, giving the lie to her impression of calm.

He cleared his throat. "I'm sorry to have to meet under these circumstances, Mrs. Petrie."

"I'm glad you're here," she said, a waver in her voice. "Please have a seat."

He crouched on the edge of the sofa, his knees nearly touching the coffee table, while she resumed her place by the window. Rylee stationed herself behind Mrs. Petrie's chair, like a lioness waiting to pounce.

"Mrs. Petrie—"

"You can call me Latisha."

"Thank you." He placed his recorder on top of an oversized picture book on the table—*Paris Interiors.* "Do you mind?"

"Go right ahead.

In response to his questions, Latisha described coming home this morning from the airport, then discovering the broken door.

Without thinking, she'd rushed through the house, finally ending up in the bedroom. Only then did she realize the danger she was in.

"For all I knew, he could've still been in the house." She studied her cupped hands. "But he wasn't. I called the police."

"When did you realize what had been taken?"

Her face slackened. "It took a while. The burglar didn't just dig through my drawers—he ripped them out. When I walked in, I didn't even recognize the room."

"And all he took was a brooch?"

"All? My husband's mother gave that brooch to me." She swallowed. "She's not with us anymore. We lost her last year."

"I'm sorry."

She dabbed at her eyes. "It was a Victorian mourning brooch. There's a cape I wear it with, and I just leave it pinned to the side. The burglar dumped out all my jewelry, but had to tear through the closets before he found the brooch."

"Victorian." Logan jotted that down. "I guess it was worth quite a bit."

She shook her head. "Not compared to a lot of my things. It'll take a lot more money to repair the damage he did than it will to replace that brooch. The value's not what matters, though. He broke into our *home*. He took something that had special meaning to us."

Rylee put a comforting hand on her shoulder.

After he finished with his questions, he asked to see the scene. They started in the sunroom, where the French doors had been forced. Getting inside had been as simple as breaking a pane and reaching through to work the lock. He bent down for a closer inspection, bits of glass cracking under his feet.

"They could've dusted that for fingerprints," Latisha said, pointing one of her glossy fingernails at the oiled-bronze door handle. "But you don't need fingerprints to file an insurance claim."

"The police didn't make much of an effort?" he asked, glancing Rylee's way. "Was Nate Campbell here?"

Rylee nodded. "They were gone when I got here, but he left his card."

He followed the women upstairs, noting how their feet left slight impressions on the carpet runner. Maybe the burglar had left footprints behind, too. The frustration in Latisha's voice as she described how little the police had done elicited his sympathy, but it left him feeling strangely excited, too. He'd made the decision to beat the cops at their own game, and now it looked as if they weren't going to put up much competition.

The women parted on either side of the bedroom door, letting him pass through on his own. He recalled Rylee's story about the Bosticks not even noticing they'd had a theft until they noticed the telltale dust ring.

This time around, there was no chance of that.

The Petries' bedroom looked as if a wild animal had been locked inside, overturning everything in a struggle to break out. He felt guilty just witnessing the aftermath, a voyeur peering in on a private tragedy.

"I can't look," Latisha said. "I'm going back down."

She retreated along the hallway, leaving silence in her wake. Rylee seemed torn, not wanting to leave him unattended. She waited impatiently as he moved through the room.

The burglar had come for a specific item, something of no value in comparison to what was left behind. But in the process he'd battered the room to a pulp.

Great violence could radically alter the place where it happened. Rendering a farmyard battlefield holy. Making a marital bedroom profane. But he'd never imagined the Robin Hood crimes were of this order of magnitude. Now, seeing the fury taken out on this place, the damage done to things the burglar hadn't even come for, Logan had no doubt of the malevolence behind the thefts.

"It's evil, pure and simple."

Rylee made no reply. She shifted her weight, clearly ready for him to finish up. It couldn't be a coincidence that three of the four houses hit were her clients. And whoever was doing these jobs took only things that had a sentimental value attached to them.

Who better to know which items qualified than an employee? Rylee's familiarity with her clients went above and beyond the call of duty.

He gave her a speculative look. He had a hard time picturing her wreaking havoc on a room like this, but that didn't mean she wasn't involved. It would certainly explain the fierce protectiveness she was exhibiting. And she had keys to something like twenty houses in that bag of hers. If a person wanted to rob the wealthiest families in Charleston, they could do worse than snatching her purse.

He wondered if she realized the police suspected her.

"I better go check on Latisha," she said, turning to go. "Have you seen enough?"

"Before I leave, there's something I want to ask you."

She stopped.

"I want you to know, the police might not be taking this seriously, but I am. It's not enough for me just to report what happens. I want to find the guy who's doing this."

"On your own?" She looked at him the way a mother indulges a child who's declared his intention to become an astronaut or the president.

He looked her right in the eye. "You don't think I can?"

"Logan."

Just that. She spoke his name. But she filled it with meaning he couldn't hope to unpack.

"I can't do it alone," he said. "I know that. But maybe if I had some help. From, like . . . you?" *Where did that come from?*

"Me?"

"This guy has hit four houses now, and three of them are people you know. What if that isn't a coincidence? What if it keeps happening? In cases like these, sometimes the police take the road of least resistance." He gave her a pointed look. "And if it's a scapegoat they want, you'd be the perfect candidate."

She crossed her arms, holding them close. "I'd thought of that, actually. And honestly, I don't know what I'd do. In my line of work, if there's even a suggestion of improper conduct, my business would be ruined." A liquid sheen coated her eyes. "I'm my grandmother's sole provider. If I lose my clients, what'll happen to her?"

Her words took him completely off guard. If she was lying, she was the best actress in the world.

Her gaze darted about the room. Picking a pair of reading glasses up off the floor, she fumbled with the earpieces, then placed them on the bedside table. "I do admit to being frustrated with the police. And you know what's strange?"

He waited.

"Your friend Nate Campbell made such a big deal about me putting my fingerprints on that bronze statue, but he didn't even try to lift fingerprints from all this."

He raised his eyebrows. "Good point."

She scrubbed the back of her head, making her short hair stick out at a funny angle. "I don't know how I could help you, though."

He smiled. "I don't either, actually. I just figured, you know, you have access to this world. The people who are being targeted. If there really is a connection, maybe the two of us could work it out."

"You really think I might be of some use?"

He paused, a little uncertain of what he'd just done. His dad had told him he needed help, but enlisting the aid of the prime suspect was probably not what the old man had had in mind.

Yet, looking into her brown eyes, brimming with sincerity, it was impossible to take Nate's suspicions seriously. She had to be innocent, a victim of coincidence.

But was there really such a thing as coincidence?

"Possibly," he said. "Let me think on it, and I'll give you a call later. Okay?"

She gave him her full-on smile, a confluence of straight white teeth, lips tight and glossy, eyes bright as flood lamps in a fog.

"Okay." She clasped her hands together. "And thanks, Logan. Thanks for caring about more than just writing an article."

He flushed, knowing his motivations, whatever they were, could hardly be described as altruistic.

She led him back to the front door. Part of him wanted to retract the offer. He'd blurted it out without thinking. It would be better not to blur the lines.

At the same time, he had made a commitment to the story, and if Rylee Monroe was behind the burglaries—or an accomplice of some kind—what better way to find out? She couldn't keep up the act forever.

Seth was right. He was part of the story. And so was she. What he had to figure out, though, was what part she was really playing.

≈

Outside the Petrie house, Logan checked his voice messages, hoping Nate would have a copy of the police report for this break-in and the Sebastian one. Instead, he heard the voice of Seth, his agent. "Dude, if you're still breathing on this earth, it is imperative that I get some fresh pages from you. I had another chat with Dora, and she is hot to get moving on this thing. H-O-T. She's been selling the concept internally, but she needs something to show. So call me, you hear?"

He had already filled a FedEx envelope with clippings from the *Post & Courier*, but apparently that wasn't enough. He thrummed his steering wheel, trying to decide what to do. Maybe it was time to call in some favors.

He left a voice mail with an informant at the top of his speed dial. Marcel Gibbon, nicknamed the Cherub. But when the Cherub called back, he was anything but angelic. "What's this about?"

"I have a favor to ask."

"What do you think this is, Logan, the help line?"

"When can we meet?"

Gibbon took a long while before answering. "My schedule's full."

"What about tonight? Washington Park?"

"No can do."

"I'll be there around midnight. Maybe I'll run into you on the street."

No response.

With the Cherub, there was no such thing as a simple meeting. In spite of the bald head and chubby cheeks, and the belly swelling behind his buttoned jackets, Gibbon had a cloak-and-dagger streak.

He dressed impeccably, moved with an improbable feline grace, and had an aversion to talking on the phone, which is why he arranged every rendezvous as if an FBI surveillance team might be listening in. Logan hoped a midnight appointment would appeal to him.

Lacey Lamar had made the introduction, warning Logan to be careful.

"Half of everything he says is a lie, and the other half is all too true," she'd said, fingering the signature string of pearls at her throat. "But he knows where the bodies are buried in this town. He put some of them there himself."

"Literally?" he asked.

"You mean, am I positive he actually killed anybody?" She shook her head. "His official list of crimes includes plenty of B&E, larceny, and an infamous swindle or two. One of his best friends is a prominent defense attorney, otherwise Marcel wouldn't be walking the streets. But I've never asked him to his face whether he killed anybody—and I don't recommend that you do, either."

"I won't."

She nodded. "Get him on your side, Logan, and you'll be surprised the things he will talk about."

~

After thirty minutes on the sidewalk outside city hall, Logan glanced down Broad Street and finally saw Marcel Gibbon strolling toward him, a cigar jutting from the side of his puckered mouth. The man looked as if he'd reached the end of a long night. His jacket hung open, his loosened tie pulled to one side, hands plunged into his pants pockets. No one who happened to observe him would conclude this was a man on his way to a clandestine rendezvous, and that was the whole point.

He crossed Broad, glancing both ways, then ambled through the park entrance like he was taking a short cut to Chalmers Street on the opposite side. Logan followed without any pretense to stealth, skirting the obelisk at the center of the park and joining Gibbon on the bench near the Beauregard plaque.

The trees overhead rustled slightly in the night breeze, the scene only half illuminated by cast-off light from city hall and the

Fireproof Building, where the state flag hung from a pole, its white palmetto mostly concealed in the fabric's folds.

"I know what this is about," Gibbon said.

Even in the shadows, Logan could make out the habitual De Niro squint and the wide grin that in daylight would reveal incongruous dimples beneath the perpetual layer of stubble along his jawline.

"You sure about that?"

"I read the paper. Not that there's much worth reading in there."

"So you've been following my stories. That's good."

The tip of the Cherub's cigar flared with a hot orange glow, and then he cocked his head sideways to expel the smoke. "If you have a question to ask, get on with it—"

Logan's hand went to his pocket.

"—but if you reach for that little recorder, I swear I'm gonna put out my cigar on your hand."

"Fine." Logan pulled back. "Here's the thing. My career is riding on this story. I need to find the Robin Hood burglar, and I need to find him before the cops do."

A pause. Gibbon leaned forward so he could study Logan's face. His breath was charred. "You think you're going to jump ahead of the police on this? You're gunning to solve it?" He gave a bark of laughter. "You're gonna splash this guy's face on the front page—the Robin Hood Burglar of Charleston, courtesy of Logan Woods, ace reporter."

He should have let Gibbon laugh. He wanted to. But Logan felt his mouth opening anyway. "It's not for the paper."

The Cherub's grin flattened. "No? Then what's it for? If I'm helping, I have a right to know."

"It's for a book. A book about the city—all of its eccentrics and stories. There's a publisher interested, but to close the deal, I need to see this Robin Hood thing through."

But Gibbon wasn't listening. "A book? You're writing a *book*?"

"Yeah," Logan said. "Why is that so—"

The Cherub moved closer, squeezing Logan between himself and the bench's arm. "Am *I* in this book of yours?"

Logan sprang up, eluding the other man's outstretched hand, then moved into the light around the obelisk.

Gibbon stood, keeping to the shadows, eyes narrowed at Logan. He wasn't grinning anymore. "Am I in this book?"

Logan shrugged. "Kind of."

The Cherub's grin returned with no hint of mirth behind it. "Well, I better be. I hate this town the way a man hates the dog that turns around and bites him. There are more names on my revenge list than you've got girls in your little black book. But you wouldn't be telling the truth about this place without me at the center."

"So it's okay?" It didn't look okay, not with the cold light burning in those slit-eyes.

Gibbon drew on the cigar thoughtfully and then flicked the butt out into the darkness, where it smoldered in the nearby grass. Logan was tempted to walk over and stomp on it, but he didn't move.

"It looks like a prank, doesn't it?" Gibbon said. "You break into one of these multi-million-dollar homes, you pass up all kinds of treasure. You take something pretty much worthless compared to everything you leave behind—and then, to top it all off, you donate your ill-gotten gain to charity. At the end of the day, the injured party's goods are restored. No harm done."

"More or less." Logan pictured the Petries' ransacked bedroom.

"From a technical point of view, nothing I've seen suggests you're dealing with a pro. We've had a few in our fair city—don't get me wrong. But they don't work like this. One thing they've never done is made a statement, and that's what your guy is all about."

"You think it's a man, then?" Logan asked, regretting the question immediately. But he wanted Gibbon to assure him this had to be the work of a man, that it was inconceivable a woman—one woman in particular—could be responsible.

The Cherub eyed him curiously, but misunderstood. "I'm not ruling out the possibility of a juvenile offender, but a teenager wouldn't be satisfied with just boosting a statue. He'd want to trash the place, too, just for kicks. It's about the thrill."

"Then the latest one fits the bill." Logan told Gibbon about the Petrie break-in, the way the violence still clung to the room like a bad smell. Describing the scene, he felt his muscles tensing up. "Ripping a place apart like that. You couldn't do it without some fury inside you."

"Maybe not," Gibbon conceded. "That's what I was getting at before when I said he was making a statement. The stuff this guy steals, it's worthless. But that doesn't make it meaningless."

"Then what does it mean?"

Gibbon shrugged. "How should I know? But I guarantee it means something to him. Find the connection between the objects . . . and maybe you'll find your man."

Turning, he walked along the perimeter, keeping out of the light, edging toward the Chalmers Street exit. His steps had a deliberate quality, like he was squashing dark thoughts into the pavers as he walked. All of Lacey's warnings about Gibbon started chiming in Logan's head. He had to learn to keep his mouth shut about the book.

"Gibbon?"

The Cherub paused at the exit, silhouetted by the streetlights farther out.

"Do you know anything about Rylee Monroe?"

He lifted his brows. "The dogwalker? The girl's a fixture south of Broad."

"But what can you tell me about her?"

"Don't ask me," Gibbon said. "You're the detective now."

Chapter Nine

"Hey there, George."

The Davidsons' gardener crouched near the bushes with a pair of shears. He didn't stir at the sound of Rylee's voice. She passed through the gate, hitching it behind her, then unhooked Toro and let him run free.

"It's shaping up to be a hot one, isn't it?" She made her way toward the gardener, determined to draw him out.

In his late fifties, George Pendergrass was a little old-fashioned. He did his gardening in a button-up short-sleeved shirt, always tucked in. His mahogany skin was toughened by the sun and perhaps hard living.

Every five minutes or so, he consulted his gold Seiko, like he was expected somewhere else. And he probably was. He did gardening for many homes in the neighborhood.

Out on the street, a Charleston police cruiser rolled by slowly. George followed it with his gaze.

"They're keeping a close eye on things, aren't they?" she said.

He grunted. "With the po-lice, there's always a lotta looking, but not a lotta seeing."

His mumbled words were so quiet, she'd barely caught them. But at least she'd elicited a response.

Reaching for the yard bag beside him, she held it open while he dropped his trimmings into it. "Do you like what you do, George?"

No answer.

"I love what I do." She waved her arm to encompass the neatly-trimmed garden, the verdant lawn, and the mastiff circling a tree. "When you find the kind of work that satisfies you, and you do it the rest of your life, well, that's a gift from God."

He retrieved his shears and garbage bag, then set off for his truck, mumbling under his breath. This time, she wasn't able to catch the words.

Taking Toro inside, she fed him, rolled around on the floor with him and played tug-of-war as she waited for Logan to come by. He'd called earlier, asking if they could brainstorm, compare notes.

Her phone beeped. *I'm here. Where R U?*

She quickly texted, *Coming.*

As she locked the back door, George was dragging a grass-stained trimmer through the gate.

"You gonna be at the Sebastians' later on today?"

He shook his head. "Monday."

"I'll see you then." She waved, but he'd already turned away.

Logan met her at the gate. This time his oxford shirt was yellow. *My favorite color.*

Unbuttoning his cuffs, he rolled up his sleeves, revealing tanned arms sprinkled with brown hair. "Who's that?"

"George Pendergrass." She pointed to his white truck with its silhouette of a wheelbarrow, a shovel, and a potted plant on its door. PENDERGRASS GARDENING arched over it like a rainbow. "I'm sure he's a sweet man deep down, but he keeps pretty much to himself. I'm working on him, though."

Logan opened the door of a black BMW.

"This is yours?" she asked.

"A graduation gift from my parents." He patted the hood. "Still runs like a dream, even with a hundred thousand miles on the clock."

He closed the passenger door behind her and hopped behind the wheel.

"What's her name?" Rylee asked.

"Whose name?"

"Your car's. What's your car's name?"

"It's a BMW 3-Series coupe."

"No. Her *name*. You know. Like my Civic. I call her Daisy."

He shot her an amused glance. "You don't."

"I do."

Glancing over his shoulder, he pulled onto the street. "I don't name my cars, Rylee."

She ran her gaze over the well-kept leather seats, the GPS unit and high-end stereo, with an mp3 player screen, and the gleaming dashboard. He may not name his car, but he certainly took good care of it.

Logan drove Rylee past each of Robin Hood's crime scenes, asking questions as they went. Did she know whether Karl's jewelry casket had ever been appraised? Had she ever noticed anyone who didn't belong in the neighborhood checking out the Petrie place? Were any of her clients friends with Mr. Shelby—the widower whose ormolu clock had been stolen? Besides her, who else did work for the Bosticks?

"George does."

"That gardener we just saw?"

"Yes."

"How many other clients of yours does he work for?"

"Three others. The Sebastians, the Petries, and the Davidsons."

"Anybody else work for your clients? You know, housekeepers, pool guys, something like that?"

She shrugged. "Maybe. I don't know them all."

He'd fished his digital recorder out and balanced it as best he could on the console between them. With the road noise, he wasn't sure how good of a recording he'd get, but it was better than trying to take notes as he drove.

"Have the cops told you anything?" she asked.

Helping or fishing for information?

"Nate's been pretty tight-lipped lately. Gave me next to nothing on the Sebastian and Petrie break-ins."

She smoothed down the hem of her top. A plain silver band encircled her thumb. "Probably because he doesn't have any information to pass along."

He checked his rearview mirror. "Possibly."

"You know what I find myself wondering?" she asked. "The Robin Hood burglar, when he enters somebody's house, does he already know what he's going to steal? If these things mean something to him—these particular things—then he has to know in advance, doesn't he?"

The same thing Marcel Gibbon had suggested—*find the connection between the objects, and you'll find your man.*

He downshifted as they approached a light. "The statue, clock, and jewelry casket were things you might notice during a visit, right? And someone might have seen Latisha Petrie's brooch while she was wearing it. Makes me wonder if our guy is one of their inner circle."

"The jewelry casket wasn't on display."

He glanced at her sharply. "What do you mean?"

"It was in Karl's closet."

"How do you know that?"

"I was at his house when the police came by."

"You're kidding. I had no idea."

"Yeah. I interrupted him."

"Karl?"

"Robin Hood."

He stared at her, stunned. Clearly Nate was holding back.

"Light's green."

Putting it in first, he eased forward. He'd interviewed hundreds of people in his years on the crime beat. Spotting a liar had become almost second nature to him. Wandering eyes. Fidgeting. Rapid speech. An exaggerated version of the sincere, furrowed-brow look.

Yet Rylee exhibited none of these. She sat relaxed against the seat cushions, her long legs crossed at the ankles.

"Tell me exactly what happened. Start at the beginning."

She talked him through the robbery, gesturing with her hands in an effort to assist him in seeing what she'd seen.

He braked, allowing a horse and carriage to pull in front of them.

The sun coming through the window gave her hair the same red-bathed tint as a glass of iced tea. So short in back it barely reached her raised collar, affording a clear view of her graceful jaw and long neck, but she had to keep flicking the longish strands in front away from her toffee eyes. Her blue checked top had very short sleeves, revealing the burnished tan line of her bare arms.

She turned suddenly and caught him looking.

He glanced away, tried to think of something to say. "What if it wasn't Robin Hood?"

"What?" She tilted her head, calling his attention to the creamy length of neck she'd exposed.

He took a right on Market. "What if we have two cat burglars on our hands instead of one?"

"How do you figure that?"

"It's just a theory," he said. "And maybe I'm crazy. But the robberies aren't quite the same, are they? Sometimes there's a lot of violence and sometimes there isn't. Sometimes he hits at night and sometimes he doesn't. Sometimes he donates what he steals, and sometimes he doesn't."

"Maybe he donates everything, but the people don't all report it."

"Maybe," he said. "The jewelry casket was the third robbery, right?"

"I can't keep track anymore."

"It was third. The statue was first. Then the clock. Then the jewelry casket. Then the brooch."

She turned in her seat, the checked shirt twisting tight across her chest. "So what?"

"The Petrie break-in is different because of the violence. The Bosticks couldn't even tell there'd been a break-in, and he didn't trash the Sebastians' home either. Something happened between the Sebastian break-in and the Petrie one, something to make him angry. Either that, or it was a different burglar."

"I don't know," she said slowly. "They all have so much in common. He always takes something of sentimental value. The brooch meant a lot to Latisha, and Karl . . . he seemed just devastated."

Devastated? Since the lawyer still hadn't returned any of his calls, Logan had done a little digging—mainly in the society pages. Why would one of the most eligible bachelors in Charleston be devastated over a jewelry box? What kind of man kept a jewelry box in his closet, anyway?

"What's so special about this jewelry casket?" he asked.

"He said it had been in his family for years."

"What was inside?"

"It was empty."

"Then why did he keep it hidden in the closet?"

She scrunched up her nose. "It wasn't really *hidden*. It was on a shelf."

"And you didn't know it was there?"

"Of course not. How would I know something like that?"

She fell silent, letting him drive aimlessly from street to street. The congenial, charming girl of a few moments before had grown somber during the conversation.

He pulled up in front of the Davidson house. "Well, thanks for answering my questions. It fleshes out the Sebastian break-in for me, anyway."

She pulled her bag off the floor, then opened her door. "You're not going to quote me in your paper or anything, are you?"

"I might summarize some of the stuff you said, but no, I can leave you out of it if you'd prefer."

"Yes, please." She unfolded herself from the car, then bent down. "See ya around, Logan."

He lifted his hand good-bye and watched her head toward a yellow Honda Civic. *Daisy*. Ridiculous. What kind of person names a car?

He accelerated toward Meeting Street, joining a line of traffic. He'd never name his. Or if he did, it would be something like . . . Thor, strong and Germanic.

"Thor."

But *no*. He was not going to name his car.

Chapter Ten

"Who in his right mind, when he's got a 1793 Storioni staring him in the face—1793, for crying out loud!—moves it over so he can get to a Ladislav Prokop? From the *thirties*."

Logan did his best with the spellings, writing as fast as he could. Despite the digital recorder, he often took notes by hand, just in case. A sudden pause made him look up. Jamison Ormsby, by all accounts a virtuoso on the violin, stared red-faced at the Storioni, as if he was angry it hadn't been stolen, too.

The music room was filled with instruments, most of them glossy as antique furniture, which he supposed was what they were. One fiddle looked like another to him, but Ormsby, the latest victim of Charleston's Robin Hood burglar, clearly knew what was valuable and what wasn't.

"So a, um, Prokop . . . That's not worth much?"

"A couple thousand bucks, maybe. I mean, it's a nice violin, a very bright, warm tone. But that's a Storioni right there. A Storioni!"

Logan tried to look shocked. Meanwhile, Wash moved the drapes back and forth, trying to focus a shaft of sunlight across the empty stand where the missing Prokop had stood. Now that he was shooting extra frames for possible use in Logan's book, he was getting outrageous with the creative lighting effects.

"When I first walked through the door," Ormsby said, "everything was quiet. Too quiet. I couldn't figure out what was wrong. Then I heard footsteps thundering on the floorboards upstairs. I rushed up the front stairs without thinking. I mean, he could have had a gun, right? But that didn't occur to me until later. I just about had a heart attack. But at the time, instinct took over." He pressed his long fingers to his forehead. "As I went upstairs, though, he must have been tearing down the kitchen stairs. He was gone before I could catch up."

"You didn't get a look at him?" Logan asked, thinking of the leg Rylee had described seeing at the Sebastian house.

Ormsby shook his head.

"And what about the police?" Logan asked. "Did they seem to take it seriously?"

In the background, Wash shot him a look.

"Off the record?" Ormsby peered down at Logan's notebook. "They acted like it was just a nuisance. I knew immediately it was the Robin Hood burglar, but the detective kept saying, 'Maybe so,' like it could all be just a coincidence. They said they'd give me a copy of the report for the insurance company, but it's not the money that matters so much. That Prokop has sentimental value."

"Was it a gift?"

Ormsby hesitated. "It was . . . from an estate sale. I collect them, as you can see."

Before he'd left his office, Logan had pulled up all the information on Ormsby he could find, mostly articles dating back to the late seventies when he'd made Charleston his home. There were concert reviews, which Logan skipped over, and a few gossipy notices about his trading in his wife of three decades for a red-headed accompanist, aged twenty-three.

"Mr. Ormsby, you don't have any pets, do you?" Logan asked.

"Animals? No. They play havoc with my allergies."

Logan nodded. Good. That meant the man wasn't a client of Rylee's.

"No." Ormsby shook his head. "I can't stand having animals in the house. That's something I don't miss about my ex-wife. When she left, she took that infernal dog with her."

"Dog?" Logan's pen stilled once more.

"A German Shepherd. Tiffany." He pronounced the name with exaggerated loathing. "After thirty years, I can breathe in my own home again."

"Did your wife employ a dogwalker?"

"Yes, there was a girl. A cute little thing, used to skate around the neighborhood. I still see her around every so often. Can't think of her name, though."

~

The summons came just as the next day's edition was being put to bed. Logan tapped on the door, then entered to find Lacey Lamar at her desk, on which a huge screen displayed his latest copy, the account of the Ormsby break-in.

She turned, crossed her tightly skirted legs, and gazed up at him over the top of her tortoiseshell reading glasses.

"Close the door and plant yourself right there." She pointed to a nearby chair.

He pushed the door shut and sat. He would much rather have had a desk between them, but Lacey was a big fan of open-plan seating.

"The reason I wanted to see you is, I got a call from someone."

"Are you naming names?"

She ignored the question. "Apparently you had a chitchat with Marcel Gibbon—is that right? How is the Cherub?" She didn't wait for a response. "Now, I can imagine all sorts of reasons why you'd want to sound him out, but I'm guessing it has something to do with this." She jabbed her thumb at the screen over her shoulder, his words set off against the opal luminescence. "I'm also assuming, because Marcel is Marcel, that he gave you some kind of lead to explore?"

Now it was Logan's turn to ignore the question.

"The reason I ask is, I expect to see the fruit of this information in my newspaper. I don't want to read about it for the first time in your forthcoming book. Am I making myself clear?"

"I got nothing from Marcel."

She arched a brow in skepticism.

He could understand her doubt. In the past, Gibbon had been relatively generous with information, as if he had an ulterior motive in passing it along. But not this time.

"Let me make something painfully clear to you, Logan. I realize you have this dream of publishing a book and leaving journalism behind. Up to now, I've been fairly indulgent. But your coverage on the Petrie break-in was thin, and the Sebastian piece, downright pitiful."

"I've been chasing the Sebastian police report, but the whole department is giving me the runaround."

"So you interview the owner."

"He won't return my calls."

"And since when has that stopped you?"

"I've interviewed his dogwalker and have what I need now."

"It's a little late, don't you think?" She whipped off her glasses. "Listen, if I suspect, even for a minute, that you're sacrificing my story so you'll have an exclusive in your book, I'll see to it you leave journalism behind a whole lot sooner than you were planning. You get my drift?"

He did. "Honestly. Marcel gave me nothing. As for Karl Sebastian, I'll do better. The Ormsby piece is good, though. You have to admit that."

She drummed her fingers on the arm of her chair. "I don't have to admit anything. And if the next piece isn't what I want, you're off the story."

―

The Davidsons' gate squeaked, and Rylee turned to see Detective Campbell striding across the lawn, his eyes fixed on her. He glanced at George in the bushes, then paused, checking his stride. But the distraction was momentary.

"Miss Monroe," he said. "I'd like you to come with me down to the station to make a formal statement."

She blinked. "A statement? What do you mean? Am I in some kind of trouble?"

George lifted the handles of his wheelbarrow and moved to the back of the house.

"Not at all. We're just trying to connect some dots, and it would be awfully helpful if you'd come in. Won't take but a minute."

Her first impulse was to hedge and say she had a dog to walk, but Toro was the last one of the morning. She wasn't due at another house until midafternoon. And she had a feeling Campbell already knew this.

Retrieving her bag from the porch, she passed through the gate the detective held open.

"Pendergrass Gardening," he said, pointing to George's truck. "That belong to the fella you were talking with?"

"Yes." She tucked herself into Nate's Mustang.

Unlike Logan's car, the interior was a mess. The upholstery was sticky against the back of her legs, and the entire car smelled like stale food. The seats were splitting at the seams. The floors had no mats. A grease-stained Popeye's Chicken box lay open on the floor. Balancing in the detective's cup holder, a giant Jack-in-the-Box soda pearled with condensation.

He pumped the accelerator several times before turning over the engine. "I guess you and him are pretty good friends, working at the same house and all."

"George, you mean?"

"What was that last name again?"

"Pendergrass."

"Ah." Picking up his soda, he pulled onto the street, his transmission jerking. "How long you known him?"

"I don't *know* him at all. But he's worked for the Davidsons almost as long as I have."

He sucked from the straw protruding out the center of his cup. "That right? He work for any of your other clients?"

"He just started with the Bosticks, and if I'm not mistaken, he's been with the Sebastians a long, long time."

"Good people, the Sebastians—for lawyers." He smiled and gave her a wink.

She turned her face toward the passenger window.

He made several more attempts at small talk, but she kept her answers clipped. She didn't like him, and he didn't like her. She saw no reason to pretend otherwise.

At the station, they rode the elevator to the third floor, then wove through a maze of cubicles. Subdued voices, spurts of laughter, and cell phone ringtones jumbled together.

"Can I get you something? Coffee? Water?" He made the offer without even pausing at the stained Formica counter that held a coffeepot.

She was tempted to accept just to make him turn around, but the sooner she could leave, the better. "I'm fine, thanks."

This wasn't the jailhouse, just the office, but it still felt confining. She took in the generic tile floor, the dropped ceiling, and the windowless walls, then shot a prayer to heaven thanking God for her job outdoors. She'd go crazy in a place like this.

At his cubicle, Campbell motioned her into a chrome-framed torture device masquerading as a visitor's chair and sank into his own ergonomically correct seat, complete with knobs on the side for lumbar adjustments. "Make yourself comfortable, Miss Monroe."

His desk was buried in paper, accented with fast-food wrappers and a half-eaten bagel of uncertain age. He searched in vain for a clear space on his desk, then deposited his Jack-in-the-Box soda atop an uneven stack of files. When he took his hand away, the cup shifted. She braced for the spill, but after sliding a bit, it stabilized.

Opening a side drawer, he pulled out a recorder and placed it near the edge of his desk. "Do you mind?"

She shook her head.

"For the tape, please."

"No. I don't mind," she said, projecting her voice.

"Great." He rattled off his name and rank, repeated her info, then leaned back, his chair accommodating the motion. She'd expected some kind of interview room, but apparently they were doing the statement right here. "Now, if you could list the names and addresses of all your clients."

"I already told you to get a warrant."

He smiled and pulled one from the inside pocket of his sports jacket. Clearly, he'd been prepared to serve it to her at the Davidsons' had she refused to go with him.

She scanned the first few lines. She'd never seen a warrant before, but it looked legit. Still, she didn't want to comply. But it didn't look like she had a choice. Tucking the warrant into her bag, she started with the Davidsons.

"Excellent. And how long have you worked for them?"

His questions continued, all fairly straightforward. All tedious. She glanced at her watch. Thirty-five minutes had passed, but it felt like hours. When she finished the list, she started to get up. But Campbell wasn't through.

"And where were you on August ninth between the hours of four and six p.m.?"

She blinked. "August ninth? I have no idea."

He rummaged around his desk, then handed her a little 3 x 2 flip calendar. August ninth. A Thursday. The day the Bosticks discovered their statue missing.

"I was walking dogs."

"Whose dogs?"

"All the dogs, Detective. I take them out twice a day. Once in the morning and again in the evenings, except for a few special cases."

"And which ones are your special cases?"

"Well, let's see. Lion has special needs, and—"

"You pet sit a *lion*?" His voice rose an octave.

"No. Lion is a cat. He belongs to the Petries." She explained his phobias along with the requirements of other animals that needed extra care. "Speaking of which, I really need to get going. I'm due at the Maceys' in a little bit."

"Just a couple more questions." He checked his notes. "Where were you yesterday right around two o'clock?"

She shifted in her chair, the thin metal arm digging into her thigh. "I would have been on my way to see my grandmother."

He leaned in. "And where does your grandmother live?"

"At Bishop Gadsden on James Island."

"What time did you arrive?"

She shrugged. "Two-thirtyish?"

"And can anyone, other than your grandmother, corroborate that?"

She stiffened as comprehension dawned. According to Logan's article this morning, a violin was stolen yesterday from Mr. Ormsby on Legare Street. Not a current client of hers, but a past one. And if she didn't miss her guess, the violin was stolen somewhere around two o'clock.

"Are you asking me if I have an alibi, Detective?"

"I'm just asking if anyone other than your grandmother saw you."

She gaped at him. "Am I a suspect?"

He didn't answer.

Gripping the armrests, she took quick, rapid breaths. "You cannot be serious. That would be like . . . like suspecting the *gardener*, simply because he works south of Broad!"

"Funny you should mention that."

She shot to her feet. "I believe we're through here, Detective."

"It was a simple question, Rylee. Any particular reason you don't want to answer?"

She snatched the recorder off the desk and held it close to her mouth. "That's *Miss Monroe* to you, Detective."

Slamming it back down, she grabbed her bag and stalked out of his cubicle. It wasn't until she was outside that she realized she didn't have her car. Groaning, she stormed to the nearest bus stop.

~

She was still angry when she and Romeo returned from their walk. As soon as she'd made it back to her car from the police station, she'd grabbed some shorts and sneakers from her gym bag and *run* her first few dogs instead of walking them.

Unfortunately, she was walking the little dogs and couldn't keep up a jog for long without endangering their health. Romeo stumbled to his water bowl and collapsed on the floor while drinking out of it.

Karl stood at the bar sorting his mail. "What happened to him?"

Rylee grabbed a glass from the cabinet and filled it with water from the fridge. "We stepped up our pace a little bit."

He raised his brows. "Everything all right?"

Ripping a paper towel off the bracket, she wiped her face and neck. "Fine."

Giving her a skeptical look, he circled the bar and stepped into the kitchen. "What's going on, Rylee?"

She took a long swallow of water, then fell back against the counter. "I'm sorry, Karl. I didn't mean to snap. I guess I'm not having the greatest day, that's all."

"Want to tell me about it?"

He really was extraordinarily handsome. He wore silver slacks and a pink-striped Bengal dress shirt with the top two buttons undone. The paisley tie loosened. With his tanned skin and white-blond hair, she could stare at him for hours and never get tired of it.

By comparison, she was sweaty, sticky, and blotchy. She took another drink. It was just as well. No chance of being asked to dinner tonight, that was for sure.

"I got taken in to the police station."

He jerked to attention. "You *what*?"

"I wasn't arrested or anything. The detective came by after my last walk of the morning and asked if I'd come in and give him a statement."

He took a swift breath. "Please tell me you told him no."

She shook her head. "Should I have?"

"Of course you should have. What did you tell him?"

"Everything. I answered all his questions, until he got to the part where he asked about my alibis."

"Rylee." The word was soft. Like a caress.

"He suspects me, Karl. He thinks I might be the Robin Hood burglar."

"That is the most ridiculous thing I've ever heard."

"I know. That's what I said, too. But he had a warrant."

He took the glass from her hands and set it on the counter behind her. The movement brought him into her personal space and made every nerve in her body tingle.

"Don't do that again. Okay?" He hooked a finger under her chin and lifted. "Promise me. If any officer of the law wants to talk to you ever again, promise me you won't say a word until you've spoken to me first. Even if he has a warrant."

"I promise," she whispered.

He's going to kiss me, she thought. *And I smell like sweat!*

She lowered her chin, breaking the contact. He stayed where he was for a few seconds more, then took a step back. Edging around him, she picked up Romeo's water bowl, refilled it, and set it back down.

"See you tomorrow," she said, rubbing the dog's head.

Then she slipped out the door, unsure if she had been saying good-bye to the dog or to Karl.

Chapter Eleven

Logan stared up at the ceiling, unable to sleep, his sheets sticking to him like flypaper. On the desk in the corner, his manuscript pages glowed white in the gloom. Not enough of them, though. Not nearly enough. He was tempted to roll out of bed and flip the laptop open. But it was no good. He'd hit a wall—too tired to write more, too stressed to sleep.

Reaching over, he flicked on the bedside lamp. His notebook lay open, turned to a page with a name and number and plenty of underlining. He grabbed his cell before he could stop himself. He'd just leave a voice mail.

"Hello?"

He sucked in his breath. The last thing he'd expected was for her to pick up. "Uh, it's Logan Woods."

"Oh," she said. "Hello."

"Did I wake you?" He glanced at the clock and cringed. Two in the morning.

"No. I have a load of wash I'm waiting on."

Stacking his pillows, he propped up his head. "Listen, you were really a lot of help yesterday."

"I was?"

"Yeah. I guess you heard about the latest break-in? Jamison Ormsby, the violinist?"

She sighed. "I saw your article this morning. I used to work for them—him and his first wife, I mean."

"He told me."

Silence on the line.

"Are you there?" he asked.

"This is awful. I don't know why it keeps happening."

He tried to picture where she was and realized he couldn't. He had no idea where she lived. "Maybe we should sit down and go over a list of all your clients, past and present."

She groaned.

"What's the matter?"

"I just did that with Detective Campbell."

He rose up on one elbow. "Nate took you in? For a statement?"

More silence.

"Rylee?"

"He thinks I did it, Logan. He asked me for an alibi."

"He's only fishing. I can't imagine he really thinks that." But Logan could imagine it. Only too well. He'd assumed the police were dragging their heels on the break-ins, considering how slapdash the follow-up at the scenes had been. But if Nate had pulled her in for questioning, that put things in a new light.

He sat up in bed.

"What are you thinking?" she asked.

"That we need to find this guy. Robin Hood, I mean."

Rylee put the phone down. The clock on her DVD player still flashed from the last power outage, so she had to crane her neck around to see the time on the microwave. A quarter past two in the morning. The television was on, tuned to a network sitcom she never watched, volume muted. She'd fallen asleep on the couch.

Kicking the blanket off her feet, she went into the kitchenette, poured a glass of Kool-Aid, and debated the wisdom of sharing her client information with a reporter. Detective Campbell had a warrant. Logan had nothing but a thirst to find the culprit.

Down the corridor in the laundry room, all the machines had gone quiet. Retrieving her load of wash, she slung it into the back of a dryer, tossed in a softener sheet from the community box, and fed in some quarters.

Back at her apartment, she found the door next to hers standing open. She gave it a tap. "Liz?"

The door swung wide. She took a step into her friend's apartment, as small and bare as her own. As Liz liked to joke, it was lots of shabby, and not much chic. A futon from her college days was draped in a striped sheet. A particleboard coffee table centered on a fuzzy, hand-me-down rug. Thick grocery-store candles burnt low.

"Liz? It's me."

Liz walked in from the bedroom, still in her Bavarian barmaid outfit, blond ringlets cascading over her freckled shoulders. Since last summer, she'd been working full time at Queen Anne's Revenge, a pirate-themed restaurant out on Daniel Island. Lots of tourists, plenty of tips.

"Hey, girl." Liz gave her a hug. "I just got home."

"I was doing some laundry."

Liz scrunched up her nose. "I need to do mine, too. Make yourself at home while I change."

Rylee curled up on the futon, flipping through one of Liz's old copies of *Domino*.

"Have you reconsidered my offer?" Liz called out.

"Not really."

Since they were both looking to economize, Liz had proposed going in as roommates. A co-worker had tipped her off about a run-down duplex in Summerville. "No charm, but oodles of cheap."

If they split the rent, the half-hour commute would be worth it, according to Liz. But Rylee wasn't convinced. She was already putting too much faith in her little car. Moving farther out from Nonie and work, no matter how much it saved, was too much of a risk.

Liz took a quick shower, then appeared in wet hair and a knee-length T-shirt. She arranged herself cross-legged on the futon, buffing her head dry with a towel. "So why are you stalling on my offer? You know you wanna be my roomie."

"It's not that." Rylee continued to flip through the magazine.

"You're still worried about the distance?"

"It's bad enough already. My car's making funny noises, and I'm afraid to take it in."

"That's not the real reason, though, is it?"

Rylee looked up. "What do you mean?"

Liz gave her a sympathetic smile. "You'd be moving in the wrong direction. You want to be closer to Charleston, not farther away." She shook her head. "That crazy rule of yours, only working south of Broad. You like to pretend that's where you live."

"No, I don't."

Liz's tone gentled. "I think you do. You're trying to recapture what you had when you were little bitty and lived there with your parents."

Rylee fingered her pearl pendant. Liz was the only person she'd ever told about her father leaving along with the truth about her mother's death.

She had fleeting memories of her parents. All of them good. Except for her mother's funeral. She'd spent the entire ceremony searching for her father among the towering men smoking cigars. Among the women wearing black dresses and too much perfume. Knowing somehow that he was gone for good. To this day, she hated the smell of cigars and she never wore a fragrance of any kind.

She remembered Nonie most of all, though. Rocking her. Comforting her. Instructing her.

"Men are unreliable," she'd said, resting her head against Rylee's. "They might come through in a pinch, but in the long haul, the only person you can ever really count on is yourself." Her tears dampened Rylee's hair. "Promise me you'll remember that." She pulled back, placing her hands on Rylee's cheeks, looking her straight in the eye. "Promise me."

"I'll remember, Nonie. I promise."

Rylee set the magazine on the coffee table. "I need some advice, Liz."

"Yeah?" She lowered the towel to her lap. "What's up?"

Rylee took a deep breath. "There's this guy—"

Liz squealed. "Rylee, you? You haven't dated in, like, forever."

"No, it's not like that. We're not seeing each other. He's a newspaper reporter who's been investigating these Robin Hood break-ins, and all but one of the houses belong to clients or former clients of mine. It's kind of creepy, to be honest, and people I care about have been hurt."

"People you care about? You mean clients?"

"Yes."

"Rylee." Frowning, she untwisted her legs. "They're clients. Not family. There's a difference."

"I know. I'm not saying they're family—just that we're . . . close." She paused. "Anyway, this reporter guy, Logan. He thinks I can help him figure out who the burglar is. Or at least, what all the victims have in common."

"Besides you."

"Bottom line, he wants my help. First I said yes, but maybe I shouldn't have."

Liz tilted her head. "Why not? I don't see what the big deal is."

"You don't think I'd be betraying my clients?"

"Rylee, what are you talking about? If somebody broke into my house, how would you be betraying me by helping bring them to justice?"

"I guess. If you put it that way—"

"What other way is there, girl?"

"It's just . . . this particular guy."

Liz gave her a speculative look. "Is he cute?"

Rylee smiled in spite of herself. "That's not what it's about."

"That's always what it's about. You're sweet, honey, and I know all you want to do is take care of your grandma. But have you ever thought you might need more than a dog in your life?"

"I have more than a dog."

"More than a pack of dogs. In other words, a man."

"Actually, my new client asked me to dinner."

Liz gasped. "No! The one who knew you as a kid? The hottie lawyer?"

Rylee nodded.

Squealing again, Liz coiled her towel into a turban. "So, when are you going? Where is he taking you? What are you going to wear?"

"I told him no."

Liz gaped at her. "*Ry-leeeeee!* Why did you do that? I mean that's, like, every girl's dream. Handsome, rich, hotshot attorney falls in love with poor overworked, underpaid Cinderella."

Rylee laughed. "I wish it were that simple."

"But it is!"

Rylee pushed herself up off the futon. "How 'bout if I tell him you're available?"

"You're on. And, Rylee . . . ?"

She paused at the door.

"If you want to help that reporter out, do it. It sounds like an adventure. You'd be crazy to pass it up."

"You think?"

"Yeah. And if we were roomies, we could talk about this stuff all the time."

"Tempting."

＝

Rylee and Toro walked along King Street all the way to South Battery, passing the narrowest house in town. A white-haired man in a Navy cap stood outside, guidebook in hand, while his wife fanned herself with a folded map.

"Will you look at that, Martha? Just thirteen feet across. Thirteen feet." He held so much reverence in his voice he might have been beholding one of the Seven Wonders of the World.

This was the city she knew, alive with people overcome by its sights. Liz could talk about this love as if it were a weakness, but she'd never understand how deeply it ran in Rylee's soul.

Glancing at her watch, she headed back. Logan would be picking her up pretty soon. At First Scots Presbyterian, she peeked through the fence to see if Dr. Welch was around. No sign of him. But just in front of Toro's house, she saw flashing lights.

Please, Lord. Not the Davidsons, too.

She recognized young Officer Kirk from the night she'd chased Logan up the monument. He was standing with one foot propped inside the cruiser's open door, his elbow on the roof as he talked into the radio transmitter. In front of his car, a second cruiser had its flashers going. Officer Munn and Nate Campbell stood on the curb next to it.

They'd boxed in a white pickup full of yard equipment. Her pace quickened as she caught sight of the lettering on the door.

"What's going on?" she asked. "Has the Davidsons' house been hit?"

Campbell scowled at her approach. "Not that we know of."

Her shoulders wilted in relief. She glanced through the open window of the truck, spotting a familiar profile. "George?"

The gardener glanced at her, then turned away.

Detective Campbell moved up on the passenger side while Kirk approached on the driver's, his hand resting on the butt of his pistol.

Kirk motioned George out of the driver's seat, making him spread his hands on the hood.

Campbell shooed Rylee away. "Move along, Miss Monroe."

She walked a few yards ahead, then paused at the Davidsons' gate.

Her words to Campbell yesterday rang loud in her ears. *You cannot be serious, Detective. That would be like suspecting the gardener, simply because he works south of Broad!*

Had she inadvertently drawn Campbell's attention to George? The sense of outrage she'd felt at being questioned came rushing back.

"This is ridiculous," she called out.

Campbell turned around, blocking her view of what was happening.

Instead of leaving, she pulled Toro back down the sidewalk. "Why are you doing this to him?"

"I'm not going to ask you again." He warded her off with his index finger.

A black BMW pulled up in front of the pickup, Logan emerging from the driver's seat, his button-down crisp, his sleeves rolled up. "What's going on, Nate? Are you taking Pendergrass in?"

Campbell never took his eyes off Rylee. "His name's not Pendergrass. It's Reid. George Reid." He turned his attention to Logan. "Get her out of here."

Logan eyed the dog. "Go on, Rylee. Take the dog inside. I'll be right here when you come back."

"Logan . . ." She heard the plea in her own voice.

"Go on," he said gently.

She glanced again at George. Officer Kirk had cuffed him and with one hand on George's elbow and the other on his head, assisted him into the back of a squad car.

Whirling, she rushed through the gate and pulled Toro inside.

⁓

"This is all my fault. I served George up to them on a silver platter."

"How do you figure that?"

Logan headed toward Slightly North of Broad, a restaurant on East Bay. His head was still spinning from the scene on the street. He'd been afraid Nate was ahead of him, and he'd been right. George Reid back in Charleston? Masquerading as a gardener? He couldn't believe it.

"Yesterday I was trying to make Detective Campbell see how ridiculous he was being. I told him suspecting me was kind of like saying 'the butler did it.' Only I said it was the *gardener*." She pressed her fingers to her forehead, her thumb ring glinting in the sunlight. "I was being sarcastic. I never meant for him to take me seriously."

He could tell she felt bad, but there was no reason. If Pendergrass really was Reid, it wouldn't have taken an offhand remark from Rylee to arouse police suspicions. "You had nothing to do with it, Rylee."

"But I did!"

"Nate said his real name's George Reid. He was handed a ten-year sentence back in '90 for grand larceny. It was a famous case back then."

She looked stunned. "There must be some mistake."

"I don't think so." He shook his head. "They caught him hauling paintings, jewels, and other valuables stolen from Low

Country estates that had been evacuated due to Hurricane Hugo. If he's the Robin Hood burglar . . . well, it kind of makes sense."

"How do you know all this?"

"I included the Reid case in my book."

"Your *book*? You've published a book?"

Turning on his blinker, he switched lanes. "Not yet. But I'm working on it. It's about Charleston crimes."

"And George, *my* George, is in it?"

"Yep. The thing that made his case so interesting is that only a fraction of the stolen goods were recovered in his trailer. The prosecutors of the day speculated about a whole series of vehicles, a convoy of thieves taking advantage of the disastrous storm. But Reid was the only one they caught, and he wasn't talking. It was a real mystery—and Reid never cracked. He just did his time and disappeared. I had no idea he was back in town."

She fell back against the seat. "Do you really think he's the one? The Robin Hood burglar?"

"I think it's entirely possible." He couldn't keep the disappointment out of his voice. This wasn't how the story was supposed to end.

"But it doesn't make any sense. If he's an experienced thief, why would he donate the goods instead of hocking them?"

He smiled in spite of himself. "You mean fencing."

"Fencing. And why would he steal relatively worthless things when there were bigger prizes to be had?"

"I don't know," he said. "I really thought we were out ahead of the police on this. It's a letdown."

"Assuming he's guilty. Logan, just because the man has a criminal record doesn't mean he's the Robin Hood burglar."

"You really think he's not?"

She paused, biting her lip in thought. "Honestly? I don't."

He turned right onto the brick pavers lining Cumberland Street and then left into the parking garage. He pulled into a space and cut the engine. "I wish I could say the same thing."

Shaking her head, she reached for her cell phone. With sudden resolve, she punched the buttons.

"Who are you calling?"

"I know someone who'll believe me."

"Who?"

"Karl."

He stiffened. "Karl Sebastian?"

Nodding, she brought the phone to her ear. "I'm going to see if he'll help George."

"No, wait," he said. "I think—"

"Yes. Hi. This is Rylee Monroe. May I speak to Karl, please? . . . Thank you."

He tried again. "Rylee. Karl's firm may do both estate and criminal law, but the only one who's good at both is Karl's dad. Not—"

"Karl! Oh, thank goodness you're there."

Logan couldn't help the flash of irritation that whipped through him. He'd called Sebastian, Lynch & Orton half a dozen times trying to get through to Karl. And she managed it on the first try.

"I need your help."

"My help?" The silence of the closed car and parking garage allowed Logan to hear Karl's voice leaking out of her earpiece. Rylee saw him lean closer and tilted the phone so he could hear better. "Has that cop been pestering you again?"

Logan narrowed his eyes. Nate might not be a saint, but Logan still counted him as a friend.

"Not me, exactly," she said, smoothing the hair at the nape of her neck. "But George."

"Pendergrass?"

"Yes. And you're not going to believe this, but his real name is George Reid and he's a convicted felon and has just been arrested as the Robin Hood burglar, but I know he didn't do it, Karl. I just know it!"

A hum of silence.

"Karl?" She looked at Logan with a frown, as if he was somehow responsible for Karl's lack of response.

"Sorry," Karl said. "You kind of took me by surprise there."

"I know. Me too." She yanked on her hem. Her orange halter dress had a band just below the bust and a bunch of long-limbed yellow cranes toeing the hem. "Anyway, you told me to call if the police bothered me again, and since George has worked for your family much longer than I have, it just made sense that you'd—"

"Slow down, Rylee. Slow down. Where are you now?"

"I'm with Logan Woods." She turned those big brown eyes on him and smiled.

"The reporter?" His voice was sharp.

Her smile faltered. "Yes, we've been trying to see if we could—"

Logan shook his head and cut a finger across his throat.

" . . . could, er, find some time to go to lunch."

A beat of silence.

"Do you think that's wise?" Karl asked, his tone strained.

She fumbled with her phone, pressing the lower-volume button on its side, avoiding Logan's gaze the whole time.

Too late, princess.

He could still hear a faint mumble, but he could no longer make out Karl's words. Logan tapped the steering wheel with his thumb. What was wrong with going to lunch with him?

"No, we're just friends." She picked at a snag on her dress, red creeping up her neck. "He's not interviewing me. We're just . . . visiting." She cringed.

Leaning back against his door, Logan crossed his arms.

"Listen." She flicked the bangs away from her eyes. "I'm in a parking garage and I can barely hear you. But you will help George, right?"

She shot Logan a quick look. "Yes . . . I will . . . See you then."

Hanging up, she tossed the phone in her bag. "Well, he's going to see what he can do for George." She gave him an overly bright smile. "So? You ready?"

He didn't budge. "Karl Sebastian is a rich, spoiled playboy who eats girls like you for breakfast."

She hugged her bag close. "He's not like that."

"Really?" He leaned closer. "You must not read the gossip columns, then. My buddy who works in the society section says Karl has a new woman on his arm every week, every day sometimes."

Stiffening, she put her hand on the door.

He reached across and grabbed the handle. "Has he been hitting on you, Rylee?"

She placed her hand on his wrist, removed it from the door, and pushed it back to his side of the car. "You're moving into territory where you don't belong, Logan."

He wanted to argue, but what was the point? If she couldn't see through a guy like Sebastian, nothing he could say would make a difference. He shrugged in surrender. "You're right. I am. But don't say I didn't warn you."

She pushed open her door.

"Rylee?"

She looked at him over her shoulder.

"If you really want to help George, it's not Karl you want. It's his father. Grant Sebastian could get the devil to dance in a courtroom."

"Well, he's in Europe somewhere, so I guess Karl will have to do." Stepping out of the car, she closed the door with a little more force than required.

He sighed. If Reid really was the Robin Hood burglar, lunch didn't make much sense anymore. He wished there was some way out of it. Let her run to Karl Sebastian. Let her go to bat for Reid. What difference did it make to him what she did?

He sat there gripping the wheel, telling himself to make up some kind of excuse and get out of there.

She tapped on his window. "Is something wrong?"

He looked into her eyes. Necessary or not, he'd asked her to lunch. So lunch it would be. Taking a deep breath, he pushed the door open. "Nothing's wrong. I'm coming."

Chapter Twelve

Sitting across from Logan in the nineteenth-century warehouse turned restaurant, Rylee's irritation melted away. Everything he'd said about Karl was true. He was a playboy. And he was out of her league. Maybe Logan thought he was being a Good Samaritan by warning her.

Whatever his reasons, she decided to shake it off and enjoy the meal. "I guess you're a regular here."

"I suppose," he said, with a grin and a shrug. The hostess had greeted him fondly—and given Rylee a speculative look. Several of the waiters stopped by to say hello. Even the chef waved to him from the open kitchen overlooking the restaurant.

For Rylee, though, it was the first time in years that she'd had a meal at a real, sit-down restaurant—particularly with a guy.

Maybe Liz was right. Maybe she did need to get out more.

The waiter served her a sautéed chicken salad and Logan a giant Palmetto Burger, complete with pimiento cheese, before retreating to the kitchen area.

Logan placed his hand next to hers on the table. "Do you mind if I say a blessing?"

Her eyebrows raised. She didn't even know people did that in public anymore. Slowly, she turned her hand over.

He slid his into hers. They bowed their heads.

Warmth immediately spread up her arm and throughout her body, as if she were an electric cord and he was an outlet. The sensation was so new, so foreign, she inadvertently opened her eyes.

His big tan hand swallowed hers. It had prominent veins and a dusting of light brown hair on its knuckles. She could feel calluses at the base of his fingers, most likely from lifting weights.

His rolled-up sleeves showed off well-proportioned forearms and a simple watch with a leather band. His head was bowed, revealing his unruly swirl of brown hair.

After his amen, he squeezed her hand, then released it.

The gesture left her body humming and she was at a complete loss. She hadn't even listened to the blessing.

A pang of disappointment whisked through her. She'd have liked to have heard it. Liked to have heard what this man said in thanks to the great Jehovah.

Bless the food, Lord. Sorry I wasn't paying attention.

Logan took a huge bite of his burger, leaning over his plate in case anything leaked out the other end of his sandwich. He swiped his mouth with his napkin, then nodded toward her salad. "Something wrong?"

She jumped. "No! No. Everything's fine."

Picking up her fork, she quickly jabbed some lettuce, apples, and pecans and took a bite. Incredible. She looked at her bowl in wonder.

"Good?" he asked.

She nodded.

Smiling, he scooped up some coleslaw. "Yeah. The chef here is really great."

She took another bite.

"So where are you from?" he asked.

"Here, actually."

"Yeah? Me too. I grew up on James Island."

She nodded. "Me too."

His eyes widened. "No way. Did you graduate from JIHS?"

"Class of 2002."

A huge grin split his face, making deep indentions on each side of his mouth and lighting up his eyes. "I'm class of '99."

"Ah. That's the year our baseball team almost won State."

He jerked upright. "I was on that team! Played with Brett Spivey. From the Colorado Rockies?"

"I know." *God bless Mr. Lusky.*

Their talk drifted from baseball to teachers they'd both had to some of the old high school haunts.

"What part of the island were you on?" he asked.

"Folly Beach."

"Get out. Are your folks still there?"

She shook her head. "They don't live here anymore. What about you?"

"I grew up in Fort Johnson Estates, just up the road from the high school. My parents are still there."

Lucky you, she thought, unable to fathom what it must be like to have had both parents all this time and to be able to see them whenever he wanted.

"Do you visit them very often?" she asked.

"Not as much as I should, according to my dad. I got called on the carpet a few days ago because I've missed a lot of church due to all this Robin Hood stuff."

She tilted her head. "You gonna do something about that?"

"Yep. This Sunday."

She'd not seen this side of him before. This new, candid animation. He continued talking about his past, how he'd found his calling halfway through college. He'd gone to Clemson, started in Forestry, then switched to Journalism.

129

"What about you?" He took a swallow of iced tea. "What did you do after high school?"

"I went to college for about a year, then decided it wasn't really for me." She wasn't about to tell him she'd quit in order to be the sole breadwinner for the family. That invited way too many questions.

"Nobody offered degrees in dogwalking, huh?"

She smiled. "I was taking Library Science."

He cocked a mischievous eyebrow. "You should have stuck with it, Rylee. If more librarians looked like you, there'd be a lot more male readers out there."

She knew she should stick up for librarians everywhere, but the backhanded compliment caught her off guard. It must have surprised him, too, because he took a sudden interest in his lunch.

Steering the conversation away from the past, she asked him about his current baseball team. He shared his disappointment over losing in the playoffs.

They compared favorite movies and pastimes, discovering they both loved sand volleyball and Indiana Jones. She asked about his book, and he entertained her with stories of Charleston's most notorious shady characters.

They were still talking when she noticed they'd long since finished their meals, the lunch crowd had emptied out, and their waiter was slouched at another table, head propped in his hand.

She glanced at her watch and gasped. "Ohmygosh! I was supposed to be at the Petries' fifteen minutes ago."

Logan blinked and looked around, then quickly paid the bill.

"All this time," she said, "and we hardly talked about the Robin Hood burglar."

"What's to talk about?" His shoulders sank. "I'm afraid Nate beat us to the punch."

130

"Don't be so sure. You may know all about George Reid, but you don't know George Pendergrass."

"Nate wouldn't have arrested him without a good reason."

She rolled her eyes. "You might be giving your friend too much credit."

They cut through heavy midday traffic on their way to the Petrie house, her words still echoing in his mind. Maybe he *was* giving Nate more credit than he deserved. Maybe they had gotten the wrong man. This wouldn't be the first time the police had just rounded up the usual suspects.

"So you really think George is innocent?" he asked.

"I really do." Her eyes glowed with conviction, and he felt himself suddenly captivated.

Finally he glanced away, cleared his throat, and did something he hadn't planned. "Are you busy tomorrow night? Would you like to go to dinner, catch a movie, something like that?"

He pronounced the words as neutrally as possible, underplaying the audacity of the suggestion. And it looked at first like the boldness would pay off.

She brightened, teetering on the brink of acceptance, then froze. "I can't. I have to go check on Nonie."

Exposed. Flayed on a spit. But there were no rocks to crawl under, so he stifled his disappointment. "Is that . . . a dog?"

She laughed. "Nonie is my grandmother."

"Ah. Where does she live?"

"On the island. At Bishop Gadsden."

He nodded. "I've seen it, but haven't ever been inside."

"Oh. Well, she moved there a little over three years ago."

He dragged a hand across his mouth. "I . . . um . . . I could go with you."

She turned in her seat, eyes wide with surprise. "You want to go with me? To my *grandmother's?*"

"Sure. And afterward, you can set the dogs on me and I'll run away for old times' sake. Or we could get something to eat. Your choice."

She smiled, spinning her thumb ring round and round. "Logan, are you asking me on a date or is this to talk about Robin Hood again?"

He stared into her big brown eyes, melting under the scrutiny. "I guess I'm asking you on a date."

She was on the brink again, close to accepting.

Finally she took a deep breath, exhaled, and took another. "All right, then."

"All right?"

"All right." Her smile was Sphinx-like, entirely unreadable.

But it was a smile. She'd said yes. They had crossed out of clearly defined territory into the shadowland of . . . something else.

His inner wordsmith failed him. They sat quietly, less than a foot of distance between them, not touching but each very conscious of the other's proximity.

The easy camaraderie of their lunch conversation was gone, replaced by acute awkwardness. Giddy constraint. Happy with the new development but afraid to stay too long in each other's presence. They both needed to retreat so they could ponder what had just happened.

He dropped her off at the Petries'. She hopped out quickly, still looking at him in wonder.

He powered down the window. "See you Friday."

She opened the Petries' gate, jerked to a halt, then spun around and rushed back to the car. "I almost forgot!"

She fished in her bag and produced a few folded sheets of paper that had been torn out of a spiral notebook. "I wrote this down for you. It's the stuff we were supposed to talk about at lunch. See ya!"

She waved, then hurried through the gate.

He opened the papers. In neat, looping script was a list of her clients' names, addresses, and pets, along with the hours she worked for each. Beneath that, each break-in had been delineated, with her whereabouts carefully recorded alongside.

He looked at the gate where she'd disappeared. Friday night couldn't come soon enough.

＝

As soon as Rylee entered the Bosticks' home that evening, their chocolate Lab, Cocoa, leapt up to greet her.

"You slobbery thing." She rubbed him behind the ears.

"Hello there, honey." Mrs. Bostick rounded the corner wearing a sleek black evening gown and one earring, the twin dangling from her hand. "Guess what?"

Rylee eased the dog down onto the wooden floor. "What?"

"Doug surprised me with tickets to Paris. This whole burglary thing has been so stressful." She rolled her eyes heavenward. "It'll be nice to get away. I'll need you to keep an eye on this boy. We leave next week."

"No problem."

Mrs. Bostick disappeared into the kitchen, and Doug Bostick came down the stairs, struggling with his cuff links. His black tux was livened up by a tartan cummerbund and matching tie. He nodded to Rylee, then gave her a helpless look.

"Do you mind?" he asked, holding his cuff toward her.

"Not at all." She pushed the post through the series of overlapping holes in his cuff, securing the onyx link in place. "So you're off to Paris?"

He showed her a mouthful of nicely capped teeth. "C'est la vie!"

Mrs. Bostick's heels clacked across the parquet floor. When she reappeared, both earrings were in place.

"Where's the party tonight?" Rylee asked.

"We've got two this time." Mrs. Bostick glanced at her watch. "And if we don't get going, Douglas, we'll be late."

On cue, he opened the back door for his wife, then offered a friendly wink to Rylee. "Night."

"Good night. Y'all have fun." She locked the back door behind them and led Cocoa out the front, pausing on the porch to slip her shoes into her messenger bag and clamp her rollerblades on. The Bosticks pulled out in a black Mercedes coupe, lowering the driver's window as they passed.

"Now, you be careful out there," Mr. Bostick said, but the tone of excitement in his voice undercut the warning.

She waved. "Y'all, too."

Then they were gone.

As she moved through the balmy, blossom-scented air, she sensed that the mood of the city was in perfect harmony with her own. She savored the pleasant jolt of her rollerblades on the uneven pavement, all cracks and cobbles, and the warm glow of old-fashioned gaslight. The swoosh of crepe myrtles in the healing westerly breeze. Even the darkening alleys radiated with crystal moonlight. Everyone she met on the streets seemed content and carefree.

Cocoa pulled her along, gasping merrily. He knew their night-time route by heart.

On King Street, they encountered a line of people in evening wear—black tuxes, pink and red silk. Ladies holding their hems high as they crossed from a black limo up a flight of marble stairs, their escorts ushering them into the regal and brightly lit house.

It was just one of the many parties the city always seemed to be hosting.

Cocoa trotted along South Battery toward the Confederate Memorial. She smiled, remembering Logan's superhuman leap onto its pedestal.

She stood under the monument and, for the first time in her life, really looked at the thing. A muscled man in nothing but a fig leaf clutched sword and shield like an ancient gladiator, while a tall Valkyrie in a winged helmet and flowing robe loomed behind him, her hand raised in greeting, or possibly protection, or even to administer a blessing.

She heard footsteps over her shoulder and turned.

A thick, bald man, his round cheek distorted by an upward twist of the lips—his best attempt at a smile. He stood close. Too close. And made no secret of scrutinizing her.

He wore a rumpled, dark linen suit, and a stubby cigar smoldered between his equally stubby fingers. The smell made her stomach churn.

"Do I know you?" she asked.

He puffed on his cigar. "Not yet you don't."

The leash stiffened as Cocoa strained forward.

A group of tourists ambled through the trees, gazing up at the monument. From their laughter and the way they wobbled, she could see they'd had plenty to drink. Cocoa let out a bark.

"Stop that," she said, then took advantage of the new arrivals to break contact with the bald man.

Skating onto Murray Boulevard, she tugged the leash and Cocoa fell into step. Glancing back, she saw the man following, so she put on speed all the way to King Street, cutting the turn sharply. Cocoa charged ahead. The man's silhouette grew smaller, but he was cutting diagonally across the park. Toward her.

Is this the man who's been stalking me? Prickly tingles raced up her spine.

In an instant, the city's vibe transformed. The moon hid behind clouds, plunging the side lanes into shadow. The partygoers were off the street, their doors firmly shut.

She glanced back again and missed seeing the fissure in the sidewalk. Her skates caught, wrenching her foot sideways. She tried to compensate but landed on knees and palms, barely managing to keep hold of the leash.

Cocoa pulled up short, torquing her foot even more.

Gasping, she rolled to a sitting position, grabbing her throbbing ankle.

The man crossed South Battery, still heading her way. As he passed under a streetlight, a cloud of smoke swirled around his head.

Ignoring her ankle and her skinned knees and palms, she scrounged in her bag for her phone.

"Are you all right?"

She glanced up, momentarily dazzled by the streetlight overhead. A pair of teenage girls decked out in party dresses and costume jewelry clip-clopped toward her. One of them hunched over Cocoa, cooing and caressing.

The other one, big-boned and orange from sunless tanner, helped Rylee to her feet. "You didn't break anything, did you?"

Rylee put some weight on the ankle. "No. It's fine."

The other girl started laughing as Cocoa licked at her face, dodging his tongue as best she could. "He's so sweet. What do you call him?"

Before Rylee could answer, the girl who'd helped her up gripped Rylee's arm, staring at something behind them. Rylee whipped around.

Cigar smoke enveloped them, filling the air with the scent of decay and dried leaves.

He stood twenty feet away, a look of satisfaction on his rounded features. "I guess this makes me the tortoise and you the hare."

"Why don't you just leave me alone?" she snapped.

The two girls glanced at each other, stiff as plastic dolls, while Cocoa moved closer to Rylee's unsteady feet.

"You got me all wrong, little lady. I'm not here to stir the pot. I just figured it was about time I got a look at you. And it was quite a look." His eyes sparked, appreciative and threatening. "Now there's a favor I want from you."

"I'm not doing anything for you."

He chuckled. "We'll see." He took a puff on his cigar, cinders glowing in response. "If it's all the same to you, I'd rather not talk in front of these ladies."

The girls backpedaled in baby steps, but Rylee stopped them with a pleading look. The orange one stood firm, her friend cowering behind her.

Rylee adjusted the leash in her hand. "If you have something to say, just say it."

He shrugged. "Last Tuesday, around two o'clock, you were in the yard at the Petries' house, and George Pendergrass was there with you. The two of you had a nice little chat."

She felt a surge of defiance welling up. "Are you asking me or telling me?"

The man turned, flicking his cigar butt into the street, where it sparked into ash and ember. "I'm telling you. You were with George Pendergrass on Tuesday at two. If anybody comes asking, you tell them so."

He disappeared down the street, leaving the three women and the Lab alone. They took a moment to catch their collective breath, nervous smiles all around.

"Thanks for staying."

The girls nodded. "Who was that guy?"

She glanced into the darkness that had swallowed him. "I have no idea. But I bet I know someone who might."

Chapter Thirteen

After returning Cocoa to the now-empty house, Rylee pulled off her rollerblades to examine her ankle. A bit of tenderness, but it seemed okay. Her hands and knees were pretty skinned up, though. Painful to touch.

She'd been afraid at first, but now she was just angry. As soon as she got to her car, she was going to call Logan and find out just who that guy was. After all the criminals he'd told her about at lunch, she felt sure he'd be able to find out.

She locked the Bosticks' door and headed down the street. She'd parked Daisy a block away, thinking nothing of the distance until she was halfway between the house and car. The alley suddenly seemed to stretch indefinitely, the darkness full of danger.

She set a brisk pace, her keys bristling between the fingers of her balled fist, her other hand clutching her phone, ready to dial Logan's number when she reached the safety of her car.

She made it to Daisy without incident, pulling the creaky driver's door open and slinging her bag into the passenger seat. The dome light had long since burned out. When she dropped into the seat, she felt something sharp stabbing against the back of her thigh. She sprang up, brushing a shard of glass off her capris.

Squinting into the car, she saw a jagged hole where the passenger window had been. Someone had broken into Daisy.

She glanced up and down the street. Wind crept through the tree-tops. Otherwise everything was still. Too still. Goose bumps raised along her bare arms. She felt eyes in the darkness, watching.

A song began to silently play in her head. Her go-to song when she had no dog at her side and needed extra confidence. The same one Maria von Trapp sang when she was about to meet her seven charges.

I have confidence in sunshine. I have confidence in rain. . . .

She retrieved her messenger bag gingerly, wiping the studded glass away. The passenger seat sparkled with fragments. Digging inside the bag, she groped for her flashlight.

. . . I have confidence that spring will come again. . . .

With the flick of a button, the flashlight came to life. She pointed it into the neighboring shadows. Nothing but cobblestones and vines. No one lurking in wait. She bathed the car's interior in cold white light. The glove compartment hung open, all its contents strewn on the floor. The CDs clipped to her visor were gone.

. . . Besides which you see, I have confidence in me. . . .

In the backseat, her gym bag was unzipped, its contents dumped. She moved the beam of light over them.

. . . Strength doesn't lie in numbers. Strength doesn't lie in—

The song in her head came to an abrupt end. Something was missing.

She turned the bag over. It was empty. Her underthings were gone.

In spite of the warm night, she shivered on the curb, then glanced back toward the Bosticks. The distance yawned in darkness. She had no desire to plunge into it. Besides, going back would solve nothing.

Every instinct she had was screaming at her to dial 9-1-1. But the detective's words echoed in her mind.

Don't call us. We'll call you.

She thumbed through her saved numbers for Logan's. His phone rang forever before he finally picked up.

"Well, hello." His voice was low. Husky. Pleased.

She found she couldn't speak.

"Rylee?" His tone changed. "Hello? Rylee?"

"Some sick pervert broke into my car." She barely recognized her own voice.

"What? Are you okay? Where are you?"

"Meeting Street. Down the block from the Bosticks' house. Cocoa. And my car. It's . . ." Her words stacked up at the back of her throat.

"Do you have a dog with you?"

"No."

"You're alone?"

"Yes."

"Get back to the Bosticks'. Go to the house and lock yourself in. Now. And don't hang up. Stay on the line." On the other end of the phone, she heard doors slamming and footsteps pounding. His breath quickened.

"Logan, there was this guy earlier—"

"Do it! Now!"

She closed Daisy's door, even locked it, then realized the futility of the gesture. Glancing around, she saw nothing. But that didn't mean someone wasn't out there.

"Are you moving, Rylee? Tell me you're moving."

She hitched the messenger bag over her shoulder and started walking. "I'm moving."

"How much farther?"

She heard his car ding, as if he'd inserted the keys before closing his door. The engine started. A blast of guitar, a crash of drum and cymbal, and then the music switched off. "How far are you from the house?"

"Four doors down." She picked up the pace.

"Anybody behind you?"

She turned around, walked three steps back, then faced forward. "Not that I can see."

Squealing tires on his end of the line. The throaty roar of German engineering. "How many more houses?"

"One."

"What's taking so long?"

"I twisted my ankle."

"You're hurt? You didn't say you were hurt!"

She reached the Bosticks' front door. "I'm here."

"Good. That's good. Now go inside and lock the door. As soon as we hang up, you call the police."

"No."

"Listen, I understand how you feel, but this needs to be reported. That's what they're there for. And most of the guys are really good guys."

"Except for Nate."

"Believe it or not, he's a good guy, too. Just a little rough around the edges."

She wiggled the first key, finally freeing the mechanism.

"Are you inside?"

"They have three new locks now, remember?"

He swore under his breath.

A half-minute later, she pushed the door shut behind her, flipped all the locks, and sank onto the floor. "Okay. I'm in."

He sighed. "That's good. Now call the cops. Okay?"

She slid her eyes closed. "Okay."

"And if anybody shows up in the meantime, you sic the dog on them, you hear? I'll be right there."

"Logan?"

"Yeah."

"Thanks."

A hum of silence. "You're welcome."

Quietly, she hung up the phone and dialed 9-1-1.

Within minutes, she was surrounded. First the police arrived and walked her to her car. Then Logan showed up in shorts and T-shirt. The Bosticks, passing by on their way between parties, stopped to see what all the commotion was, and Mrs. Bostick ended up hugging Rylee so hard she could barely breathe.

All the attention numbed Rylee—apart from her ankle, which felt like an acupuncture experiment gone wrong.

Once the reports were made and the police satisfied, Logan pressed his car keys into her hand. "You drive mine and I'll follow in yours."

Dazed, she stared at the keys. "Where are we going?"

"I'm taking you home."

She blinked. "Okay."

But it was more than okay. She hadn't realized until that moment that she didn't want to go home alone.

They walked to his car, where she settled into the leather driver's seat, cocooned by the flared wings on either side. The swell of the wheel felt firm under her hands. He bent down, raising and lowering the seat with the touch of a button until it was adjusted just right. Then he pushed a numbered button on the door until it beeped.

"What was that?"

"I stored your seat settings in memory," he said.

"Oh." Stored settings. That seemed significant.

Logan snapped the door shut, motioning her to power down the window. As she did, Mr. Bostick appeared at the curb, offering to have his shop take a look at Daisy's busted window in the morning.

"I'll take care of it," Logan said. Then he looked at her. "I'll be right behind you."

He tapped the roof twice, then jogged toward her injured Civic, the keys dangling from his fingertips.

She buckled up, then pulled onto the street, the reassuring burn of Daisy's headlights in the rearview mirror. The dash of Logan's BMW glowed orange in the darkness, the air-conditioning cold enough to freeze lava.

She shifted into third. She'd learned to drive a stick from her grandmother, who'd taken her to the abandoned high school parking lot one summer weekend for some sink-or-swim tutelage. After a gazillion stalls, she'd finally gotten the hang of it.

Remembering Nonie's patience, she smiled. Back then, Nonie had seemed a bit absentminded, nothing more. She'd never have imagined how much things would change. Nor how fast.

Now, she had . . . no one.

Everyone she could have turned to, everyone she could have relied on, they were gone. They'd left her, willingly or not. Her dad was off living a new life, probably never sparing a thought for her. Her mother was in the grave. And Nonie, the way she drifted in and out of sanity, might as well be gone most days. She had friends—she had Liz, anyway—but Liz didn't understand. No, all she had was her clients—and remembering Mrs. Bostick's bear hug and her husband's offer to fix Daisy, she told herself they were enough.

But she hadn't called one of them. She'd called Logan.

He'd come running, too. Rushing from his home, running interference with the police, and now following her home.

She glanced again in the rearview mirror. She had every intention of living her entire life without a man, never again relying on anyone who could walk away. But there was something to be said for a little coddling.

Hitting the blinker, she took the ramp toward Folly Beach, Daisy right on her tail.

His steering wheel had more buttons on it than her entire car. One side managed the cruise control, the other music. She switched on the stereo.

The car boomed with sound, picking up right where Logan had interrupted the song. After a few bars, she still couldn't place it. Nasally vocals charged with attitude, a pounding, unsynthesized beat.

They whizzed down Fleming Road, passing one apartment complex after another—each a bit shabbier than the last. Hers loomed on the right, a two-story brick building modeled on a drive-in motel, with all the doors opening to the outside.

A metal staircase at the end of the building went up to the second-floor porch, which was cluttered with brown ferns and dirty grills, chained bicycles and folding lawn chairs with frayed seats. Thanks to the manager's loose grasp on the concept of maintenance, most of the sconces beside the doors were burned out. Liz and the tenant two doors down from her were the only ones with working outdoor lights.

The gravel crunched beneath the tires as she pulled to a stop. Before she could get the door open, Logan was at her side. He took her hand as she exited, his eyes roaming the apartment block and the empty lot across the street. He frowned.

"Upstairs," she said, looking up.

Liz's curtains flickered.

Logan saw the movement and tensed.

"Wave to Liz, Logan. It'll make her day."

He obeyed, but the gesture was stiff. The surroundings were clearly not to his liking. They weren't to her liking either, but she'd learned to put up with them. Liz pulled the curtain wider, smiled, and waved down at them.

They climbed the stairs, then picked their way through the accumulated debris on the wide balcony. Logan skimmed his hand along the railing, then paused, holding up his fingers for inspection.

"Here we are," she said, stopping at her door. After turning the key in the lock, she had to butt it open with her hip. "It sticks sometimes."

He rattled the doorknob, staring like he'd never seen one before. Crossing the threshold, he closed and opened the door a few times. Before she knew it, he was on one knee, peering into the gap between the knob and door.

"This thing's a joke," he said. "And you don't even have a dead-bolt or a chain."

Dropping her purse on the kitchen bar, she flipped on the lights. "I don't need a deadbolt, Logan. There's nothing worth stealing here."

He closed the door one final time. "Living on Fleming Street, you should have four deadbolts."

She hurried through the den, grabbing her gym shorts off the back of a chair, scooping up a pair of Latisha Petrie's hand-me-down red stilettos.

"Where's your dog?" He still had his hand on the doorknob, ready to flee, perhaps, if the need arose.

"No worries. I don't have one." She scurried into her room, grabbing a pile of dirty clothes from the floor, then dropped every-thing on the dresser and closed the bedroom door behind her.

"You're kidding."

She shrugged. "Much as I'd love one, my work schedule would keep him penned up all the time."

It wasn't just that, though. It was the expense. And if she had any extra money at all—which she didn't—she needed to spend it on her car.

He frowned. "Then you absolutely need a deadbolt. Promise me you'll get one."

"We'll see. You thirsty?"

He sighed. "I guess."

He stood at the threshold, giving the room a once-over. His long navy athletic shorts hung on his hips. His nicely shaped calves belonged to a man who'd climbed a million stairways and run a million miles. On his feet, he wore what looked like the original pair of Reeboks—pieces of them, anyway.

She pulled two glasses from an upper cabinet. "Do you like Kool-Aid?"

"Kool-Aid?" He rubbed his chin. "I don't think I've had any since fifth grade. What flavor is it?"

"Black cherry."

"Sounds great. Can I help?"

"No, no. I just have to pop the ice out of the tray. Make yourself at home."

He took her literally and flipped through CD jewel cases, shook random paperbacks to see if anything would fall out, and then discovered her box of DVDs. *The Sound of Music*—played so often the disc had permanent scratches—got a cursory look, then he went back to the books, pulling out a copy of *Last of the Mohicans*.

"Not one of your favorites, I guess," he announced, holding up the bookmark that had been tucked near the front of the book.

"It's nothing like the movie." She gave him a guilty shrug.

He returned it to the shelf, then eyed her couch as if he feared a stray spring might be lurking under the upholstery.

She smiled. The overstuffed couch was out of date, but he had no reason to fear. It was still in good shape. Most of her furniture was left over from the house she and Nonie had shared. There were a few flea market finds sprinkled in, things she'd intended to repaint or refinish or at least wipe with a damp cloth, only she'd never found the time.

He paused over the shrine of family photos she kept on the top of an old buffet. He picked a frame up and turned it toward the light. "These your parents?"

She nodded. "They're gone now. My dad . . . my dad left when I was a girl. My mom . . . Well, she was very down after that and . . . died shortly after."

His eyes softened. "I'm sorry."

She came around the bar and handed him his Kool-Aid. "It's just me and Nonie now."

He replaced the photo, then pointed at another. She and Nonie on the beach in winter hats and scarves. Maybe six . . . no, seven years ago.

"Is that her?"

"Yes."

"I'm looking forward to meeting her." He touched his glass to hers and took a deep swallow of his drink, his Adam's apple rolling with each swallow.

She sipped at hers.

"Feeling better?" he asked.

"Yeah." To her surprise, she really did. "Thanks for coming out and following me home and everything."

"Anytime." He made no move to go.

She looked at his drink. "You want some more?"

"Sure."

He followed her, leaning on the bar while she opened the fridge and poured another glass.

"Right before I left the office today, I found out that George refused Karl's offer of representation."

She looked up sharply. "What?"

"Yep. Said 'thanks, but no thanks.' "

She gaped at him, stunned. "Why would he do that?"

"Maybe because he knows Karl would bungle the case. I told you, Karl may be licensed to practice criminal law, but I looked it up today—he hasn't handled a defense case for years. Estate law is his thing, and to be honest, I'm not sure he's any good at that. His daddy owns the firm, that's his claim to fame. If I were George, I wouldn't want him handling it, either."

She handed him the refilled glass. "Still, it's better than a court-appointed lawyer, don't you think?"

"Not necessarily." He took a swallow. "So, do you think what happened to your car is connected to the Robin Hood burglar?"

"Actually, I think it might be something else." She told him about the bald, round-faced man who'd confronted her in the park.

He made her repeat the description, right down to the smell of the cigar. His face hardened. "That had to be Marcel Gibbon. You ever heard of him?"

"Should I have?" She settled back against the kitchen counter, keeping the bar between them.

"Marcel's sort of notorious around here. I got a call from him earlier today, which is pretty strange, since it's usually me who has to make contact. And he doesn't like talking on the phone."

"What did he want?"

Logan dug in his back pocket, producing the list of clients she'd given him after he'd dropped her off at the Petrie house. Next to her writing, he'd added some notes of his own.

"He was making sure I knew about George's alibis for the Robin Hood break-ins. I copied them down right next to yours." He offered her the list. "The funny thing is, he said you were with George for the Ormsby break-in, but according to your notes—"

"He told me that, too. *Insisted* I was with him, when I knew perfectly well I wasn't." An involuntary shudder rippled through her. "How is George connected with that man?"

"They go way back. Nobody could prove it, but rumor was that the job George went to prison for was masterminded by Gibbon. He's clean these days, supposedly, but the man's still connected. I guess he's looking out for George for old times' sake. Maybe he owes him one, you know?"

She knew Logan rubbed elbows with a lot of unsavory characters. That's why she'd planned to call him in the first place. Still, knowing it and hearing him talk about it so casually were two different things.

"He owes him one?" she repeated, shaking her head. "He didn't strike me as the kind of person to return favors. I'd be surprised if he cares about anyone but himself."

"And I'd say you're right." He made circles on the bar with the bottom of his glass. "But I don't think he's the one who broke into your car. That's not his style."

Seeing Daisy broken into, her space violated, her things gone through and stolen, she couldn't help but feel the evil of it. "The person who broke into the car . . ." She looked down at her scuffed loafers. "He took some . . . personal things."

"I heard you telling the officer."

"It's . . ." She felt her throat tighten, then looked up. "It scared me, Logan."

And that was just the tip of the iceberg. The stalker. The Robin Hood burglar. The police. All of them frightened her.

He put his glass down and came around the corner. "Don't worry. I won't let anything happen to you."

"You can't make a promise like that."

His voice was firm. "I just did. And I meant it."

The tiny kitchen shrank with him in it. He wasn't a huge man, but he wasn't puny either.

Embarrassed, she slipped her hand into her cardigan pocket, her fingers brushing his car keys. She pulled them out. "These are yours, I think."

"You keep them. I'll get that window fixed for you."

Her lips parted. "You don't have to do that."

"It's no trouble. Besides, I have connections in this town."

She knew she should argue, but the monthly bill from Bishop Gadsden sat in the bill holder. She had enough to pay for it, but not enough for the deductible her car insurance was going to require to get that window fixed. If he knew someone who might do it pro bono, she was just frugal enough to let him call in a favor. "I have insurance."

"I saw it in the glove box."

She slipped his keys back into her pocket. He tracked every move of her hand.

"Rylee." He edged forward.

She drew her hand out.

He touched her, the lightest whisper of contact.

It was a perfect moment to kiss. She knew it, and she could tell he did, too. But she wasn't ready. Just having him in the apartment was huge. No way could she handle a kiss.

Yet every nerve in her body stood at attention. Waiting. Hoping. Anticipating.

He hesitated, then stepped back, giving her a charming, school-boy grin.

Later, that grin seemed to say. *Not like this.*

She let out a pent-up breath.

He moved toward the door. "I'll call you tomorrow."

"Okay."

"Prop something under that doorknob when I leave."

She gave a slight smile. "All right."

She went out on the railing to watch him go, waving at the departing car. As soon as he disappeared from the lot, Liz threw open her door and padded onto the balcony.

"Who was that gorgeous man?"

Rylee turned, smiling in spite of herself.

Liz had on her fuzzy pink sweats. She grabbed Rylee's sleeve. "Come over here and tell me all about it."

Chapter Fourteen

The next morning, Logan found Nate Campbell tapping the last of the creamer into a mug of coal-black police station coffee, looking like he'd pulled an all-nighter.

At the sight of Logan, the detective slowly straightened, his features tightening. "After that article of yours this morning, you've got some nerve showing your face around here."

Logan jerked his head toward Nate's cubicle. "Can we talk?"

Nate led the way, motioning him into the chrome chair opposite the desk. "If you're thinking an apology's gonna make everything all right, you're wrong."

An apology. *Yeah, right.* Logan propped an ankle on his knee. "Maybe if you'd let me see the police reports I've been asking for, I wouldn't have so many questions about your case."

Nate jerked a drawer open and tossed a thick file on top of his desk. "What're you gonna want next? My firstborn?"

Logan reached for the file.

Nate slammed his hand on top of it. "In your dreams, buddy."

Logan slowly retracted his hand. Nate's vehemence took him a bit by surprise. In the past, whenever he'd hinted in print about the shortcomings of police investigations, the detective hadn't batted an eye. He'd even tipped Logan off about some corner-cutting on the part of Sheila Santos, a rival on the squad.

"You're taking this awfully personal," Logan said.

A tic in the detective's jaw pulsed. "Did it ever occur to you that you don't have the whole picture?"

"So give me the whole picture."

"Ask me some questions and I'll answer what I can."

Logan pulled out his notebook. "What's the status on George Reid?"

"He made bail this morning, and we've cut him loose. He refused to make a statement or cooperate in any way. We'll be keeping an eye on him to see if he leads us to the goods."

"Exactly what evidence do you have on him?"

"You mean besides the fact that he's a convicted felon with an almost identical modus operandi, and he just so happens to have been working for a majority of the victims?"

"That's it?"

"Isn't it enough?"

It would have been, ordinarily. For Logan, these types of coincidences usually equated to a strong circumstantial case. When the arrest had first broken in the newsroom, people who remembered back to the George Reid case slapped their foreheads: Well, duh.

George seemed like an obvious suspect. The only thing keeping Logan from joining in was that the same could be said about Rylee—minus the criminal record. If the only thing they had on George was his record and the fact he worked for a majority of the victims, then their case was pretty thin.

He tapped his pencil against his knee. "I hear what you're saying, but I don't remember George Reid giving away the things he stole. Can you actually link him to any of the Robin Hood break-ins?"

Nate rolled his eyes. "The guy has access to every crime scene. He comes and goes through the neighborhood without anyone

paying attention. He's in a perfect position to case the houses."
He shook his head. "The only other person who has that kind of
means and opportunity is Miss Dogwalker Extraordinaire. And
the only reason I haven't arrested her already is because she's got
no criminal record. Not so much as a traffic ticket."

Logan stilled.

Nate leaned forward. "But I can tell you this. Lack of criminal
record notwithstanding, one more client of hers gets hit and I'm
bringing her in. And not to my office, either."

Forcing himself to stay calm, Logan tucked his pencil and
notebook into his pocket. "That's ridiculous."

Nate gave him a knowing look. "You ever wonder if maybe you're
being played, Logan? Maybe this girl's not what she seems?"

Logan shook his head. "She'd have nothing to gain and everything
to lose. Besides, why break in when she already has the keys?"

Nate held up his hand, ticking off each point one finger at a time.
"The Bosticks were out of town when their statue was stolen. Monroe had the house all to herself and could have busted that window
any time she wanted." Tick one. "She was the sole witness to the
Sebastian theft. She could have heisted the jewelry casket, ripped
down the curtain rod, and acted like she'd caught the burglar in the
act." Tick two. "The Petries were in London when their place was
hit. Monroe, again, had the place to herself and all the time in the
world to trash it." Tick three. "She used to work for the Ormsbys.
She knows the layout of that house the way she knows the palm of
her hand. She knows where the violins are. She also would've known
which way to go when Ormsby came up the front stairs." Tick four.
"One more, Logan, and she's mine." Tick five.

Wanna bet? "It's nothing but circumstantial."

"Over ninety percent of our cases are circumstantial. You know
that."

"So she had the means and opportunity. But what about motive?"

"Her father, Jonathan Monroe, used to own one of those big mansions on East Battery—did she tell you that?"

No. She hadn't.

"Those people she walks dogs for? She used to be one of them. The Monroes were Charleston royalty. What about that? Did she happen to mention that little piece of trivia?"

I barely know her. There hasn't been time.

"And get this. The dad cleaned out their bank account and disappeared. The mom ate a bottle of sleeping pills. End of fairy tale, my friend."

Sleeping pills?

Logan pinched his nose between his fingers. "Even if this is true, it's ancient history. She was just a kid. What does it have to do with the burglaries?"

"You asked for a motive, Logan, so I'm giving it to you. That girl has a temper and a lot of anger bottled up inside. I've been given a front row seat on more than one occasion. Now, who do you think all that resentment is directed at, other than the police? Isn't it obvious?"

"Not to me."

"The people who have what she doesn't. What she should've had, in her own mind. She lives in a dump, barely making enough money to pay the bills. I know. I've been checking her bank statements. But she spends every waking moment with the *crème de le crème* of Charleston society, going through their houses, plotting some sick and twisted revenge. Open your eyes, Logan. You're flirting with the scoop of a lifetime. You'd see it yourself if you'd let your brain lead."

Logan slowly rose, furious with his friend. Make that ex-friend.

He knew how these things went. Desperate to pin these burglaries on somebody, the police might stoop to some low-level harassment. Cold-calling Rylee's clients, pulling any outstanding traffic tickets, alerting patrol to keep an eye out for Daisy, pulling her over without cause. From his departmental contacts, he knew how easy that kind of thing was, and how common.

But Nate was trying to put her in the frame as an accomplice to the Robin Hood burglaries, if not casting her as the burglar herself.

"She's not the Robin Hood burglar, Nate. Let it go."

Nate snorted. "No offense, buddy, but I'm not taking orders from you."

Logan closed and opened his fists. "Just remember, I report it like I see it. You arrest her and it'll be no holds barred."

Nate narrowed his eyes. "You threatening a police officer, Woods?"

"Just putting you on notice." Turning, he strode out of the cubicle.

Wash's car sat idling at curbside, the photographer behind the wheel. Earlier, he'd followed Logan to the repair shop, where they'd dropped off Daisy for a new window.

"How'd it go in there?"

"I'll tell you on the way," Logan said. "First, I've got to call George Reid. Now move over. I'm not getting in a car with you unless I'm behind the wheel."

He left a couple of messages for the gardener, but the man probably had better things to do after being bailed out of jail. So he called Marcel instead. Got a recording there, too.

"What do you want from Reid?" Wash asked.

"For starters, I want to know why he refused representation from Karl Sebastian. I need to check my notes, but if I'm not mistaken, Sebastian's firm represented George back when he had that first conviction."

Wash shrugged. "And look how that turned out. Maybe he doesn't want a repeat."

"When a firm like Sebastian, Lynch & Orton knocks at your door, you don't turn them away. Something's not right there. Anyway, if George had been willing to talk back then, they'd have gotten him a deal, I'm sure."

"I thought you said Karl was all smoke and no fire?"

"Even so."

"And Gibbon? What do you want with the Cherub?"

"I want to know why he's running interference for George. That's not his style, coming out of the shadows like that. It's got to be more than just doing a favor for a stand-up guy. Gibbon must have some exposure here, but for the life of me I can't figure out what."

That wasn't all. The things Nate had told him about Rylee's parents still rang in his ears. The father taking off with a fortune, the mother overdosing. If Jonathan Monroe was involved in some kind of monumental swindle, then Gibbon would be a good person to ask about that, too. He knew the city's secrets like no other.

They swung by George's residence, knocked on the door, and tucked a business card under the screen.

"Maybe he's already back at work?" Wash suggested.

Logan called Rylee, thinking she might know the man's schedule. "You haven't spoken to George by any chance, have you?"

She sounded surprised. "Is he out?"

"When I was at the station this morning, Nate said he'd made bail."

"Well, I haven't seen him."

"If you do, let me know." He lowered his voice. "How you feeling after last night?"

A pause. "All right, I guess."

"You working?"

"Of course."

"Just be careful."

"Why? Do you think I'm in danger?"

"No," he said quickly. "I just wish you weren't alone down there."

He heard the smile in her voice. "It's broad daylight. And besides, I'm not alone. Say hi to Sahsha." On cue, a dog barked in his ear.

"Okay, then," he said. "I'll see you tonight."

When he got off the phone, Wash wasted no time. "What's tonight?"

"Nothing."

"It didn't sound like nothing."

"It was nothing."

"Really? Sounded like a date to me."

"I'm just bringing her car back." Logan checked his side mirror, then switched lanes.

"That's another thing that needs explaining. How come you're the one getting her window fixed? Is that a service you're offering on all your stories now?" Wash settled back against the passenger door. "So, are you taking her out tonight or not?"

He sighed. "I am. So what?"

Wash let out a low whistle. "Let me congratulate you, my man, on your fine taste. She's one hot-looking woman—that's for sure."

Logan kept his eyes on the road.

Wash laid an arm along the closed window and drummed his fingers. "I thought you weren't interested in any female entanglements."

"That's not what this is."

Wash laughed. "Really? Well, we're having that crab boil tonight at the beach, if you feel like bringing her by."

"We've got plans."

They pulled into the *Post & Courier* parking lot, flashed their IDs at the door, then parted ways in the newsroom. Logan found his old file on Reid and read through it as a refresher, stalling on one of the pages. When Grant Sebastian had first taken George's case, Sebastian, Lynch & Orton had been Sebastian, Lynch & Monroe.

Logan fell back against his chair. It couldn't be.

He woke up his computer and went to work. Jonathan Monroe had been a prominent defense attorney for the firm until December of 1989 when he suddenly disappeared. Two days later, his wife, Stella, died of an overdose of sleeping pills. Accident or suicide was undetermined.

They were survived by a daughter, Rylee Rachelle Monroe, and Jonathan's mother, Flora Mae Monroe.

Logan stared at the screen. If she'd graduated from JIHS in '02, she'd have been five in '89 when her dad took off and her mother died.

He dragged a hand down his face, recalling the photo of her parents he'd seen at her apartment. *"They're gone now. My dad left when I was a girl. My mom . . . well, she was very down after that and . . . died shortly after."*

He thought about all his uncles and aunts. His grandparents and cousins. Though he was an only child, his dad had six brothers and a sister. Logan was hardly lacking in the family department.

But no one was mentioned in the Monroe obituary other than Rylee and her grandmother. The grandmother who lived in a retirement home. The grandmother she was taking him to see tonight.

Did Rylee know her dad had been a partner in the Sebastian firm? He shook his head. She had to. But she'd never mentioned it. And why would she?

It certainly explained her defense of Karl, though, when Logan had warned her away from him. She'd probably known the guy forever.

Taking a deep breath, he returned to George's file. Not long after the disappearance of Jonathan Monroe and Stella's subsequent death, George Reid refused to testify during his court proceedings, ending up in jail.

Truth was, Nate was right. Rylee probably did have a motive. But he knew she wasn't Robin Hood. Nobody could fake her lack of pretense. Her innocence. Her naïveté. Nate may think she was harboring suppressed anger, but Logan knew better. Still, he had a lot of questions.

He started typing up his notes, planning to shape them into a follow-up piece about the arrest of George. Ordinarily, he'd lose himself in the words. This time, though, he found his fingers falling still on the keyboard. His mind trying to wrap itself around the tragedy that engulfed a young Rylee, and all the little ways her life intertwined with the case.

He finally forced some focus, finished his piece, and gave his copy a final read-through before sending it up the editorial ladder. Just as he sat back, the phone rang.

"You called me?"

It was Marcel Gibbon.

Logan tossed down his pencil and braced his arms on his desk. "Yeah. Did you break into Rylee's car last night?"

"Don't insult me. All I did was introduce myself."

"So I heard." He wanted to put Gibbon on notice, too, just as he had Nate. The dogwalker was off limits, so leave her out of it. But he needed information. "Listen, I need a face-to-face."

"This is getting a little tedious, Woods."

"I'm happy to discuss it over the phone."

Gibbon sighed. "As it turns out, my evening is open."

"I can't tonight." Logan picked up his pencil and drummed it against a stack of folders. "I have plans."

"Change them."

"I can't. It's a . . . date."

"A date? Let me guess. With the luscious Miss Monroe?"

Logan didn't answer.

"By all means, bring her along. If I made a bad impression, this will give me a chance to make it up to the girl."

Logan raked a hand through his hair. "I promised I'd go meet her grandma."

A pregnant pause. "My, Logan. What big eyes you have." His cackle turned into a wheeze, then a lungful of coughing. "I'm a night owl, son. Granny will be tucked in long before our rendezvous. And it's either tonight, or not at all. I have better things to do than cater to your every whim."

Logan rubbed his eyes. "I'll call you."

As first dates went, this one was already teetering on the brink of catastrophe. He was either going to have to end it prematurely or invite her to an evening chat with the man who'd harassed her on the street. Not exactly a recipe for romance.

He checked his watch. Under his desk, his gym bag beckoned, ready for the quick change after work. He dialed the repair shop, then called Wash for a ride over.

Chapter Fifteen

Rylee exited through the sliding doors of the Piggly Wiggly, grocery bags in hand. As soon as she filled up the BMW, she could go home, make herself a salad, and enjoy her day off.

Logan was picking her up at seven thirty, so Liz had insisted on spending the afternoon giving Rylee a facial, doing her nails, and helping her pick out what to wear. She'd given Rylee plenty of warning that she must, without exception, wear perfume.

"It can be light, soft, just a whisper of a scent. I've got tons to choose from. But if I have to hold you down and apply it myself, you *will* wear it."

Rylee crawled into the car, lowering the windows to let out the trapped heat. The soft leather seats enfolded her. The seatbelt hugged her close.

Running her errands in Logan's car gave her a curious, proprietary feeling. As if she was his and he was hers. The thought made her panic a little. What had she been thinking to agree to a genuine walk-you-to-the-door-for-a-good-night-kiss date?

She hadn't. She hadn't been thinking at all.

To settle her nerves, she reminded herself they were starting off the evening by going to see Nonie. Nothing risky about that. She hoped, prayed, Nonie would be her normal self, though.

Please, Lord. Let her be lucid.

Even Nonie's lucidity could be murky, so she wasn't asking for much. Still, it would make all the difference. In one of her good moments, Logan would get to know her. He'd see the woman she'd been before, the one who'd raised Rylee up to be the woman she was today. That was important.

If it was one of the bad times—and they were mostly bad these days, getting worse—he would miss what Rylee wanted to share with him. He'd miss meeting the one person she loved more than anyone.

She pulled into the Exxon station and hopped out of the car.

"Rylee?"

She whirled around. "Karl! What are you doing over here on the island?"

Slotting a gas pump into his silver convertible, he leaned against its side, ankles crossed, sunglasses resting against his neck. He somehow managed to make his rugby shirt and jeans look like something from a high-fashion runway.

"I had an appointment with a client." He lifted his brows. "Did you get a new car?"

She fit a nozzle into the car's tank. "No. I'm borrowing this one. Mine was broken into."

"Broken into! When? Where?"

She told him about Daisy's window and the missing CDs, where the car was parked at the time, but not about the gym bag.

"That's awful. I can't believe it." Finishing his transaction, he slipped between the pumps and nudged her hand away from the nozzle, taking over for her. "So whose car is this?"

She felt a blush rushing up her neck. "Um, it's Logan's. Logan Woods."

He said nothing at first, the censure in his stare speaking for him. Finally he looked out at the street bordering the gas station. "I thought you were going to stay away from him."

She clasped her hands together.

"How did he even know about your car?"

"I called him."

He gave her a sharp look. "Why didn't you call me? I live right there. I could've gotten to you in minutes."

She looked down. "I've asked myself the same thing. There are any number of clients I could have called."

"He's a reporter, Rylee. And I want you to stay away from him."

"I know you do."

"But?"

She shrugged, opting not to answer. Not sure she even could.

Sighing, he slipped the gas nozzle back into its housing. "So how 'bout some lunch?"

She blinked. "Lunch?"

"Sure. Why not?"

Tilting her head, she smiled to take the sting out of the rejection. "You know why, Karl. I don't date clients."

"But it wouldn't be a date." He screwed the gas cap on. "We didn't arrange it in advance. I haven't come to pick you up. We can each pay for our own meal. And I won't be expecting a kiss at the end." Leaning close, he gave her a wicked grin. "But I'm certainly willing, if you want to bend the rules a little."

She glanced at her watch. "I don't know. . . . I really—"

"Come on. You have to eat." He looked around. "How about there? The Souper Sandwich Shop. We'll be in and out in no time."

She bit her lip. She couldn't afford to eat out. But he'd done her a huge favor by offering to help George. He was an old family friend. And maybe she could find out for herself why George didn't accept the offer. Logan might think Karl incompetent, but she knew better. "Okay. But I pay for my own."

Smiling, he opened her door. "See you in a minute."

⌒

It wasn't there anymore. The Sebastian charm. Rylee realized it halfway through the story Karl was telling about the travails of a client trying to recover on a bad investment. It was meant to be funny, and it probably was. He looked good telling it, too. The sparkling eyes, the inviting smile, the tone just this side of familiar, like he was letting her in on a little secret.

Not long ago she would have melted. She wouldn't have trusted herself alone with Karl, would have been afraid of breaking her no-clients dating rule. Not anymore, though.

"You shouldn't be telling me any of this," she said. "What about attorney-client privilege?"

He stopped in midsentence. "Well. It's kind of hilarious, though."

She decided to change the subject. "So have you heard from your dad at all?"

He hadn't, but the longer they talked about his father, the more critical Karl sounded. She hadn't realized their relationship was strained, but clearly things were not good between them.

Grant Sebastian, however, was the closest thing to a father she had. He'd set her up in the house on Folly Beach. He'd attended her high school graduation. Brokered the sale of her house three years ago and went with her the day she admitted Nonie to Bishop Gadsden. She wasn't about to sit here and listen to Karl badmouth him.

"So what's up with George?" she asked, changing the subject yet again. "He turned down your offer of representation? Why would he do something so crazy?"

"What offer? I never made one."

"But I thought—"

"I know I told you I would, but here's the thing. Five minutes talking to him, and I already knew. The man is guilty."

Her heart stopped.

"He's the one you walked in on, Rylee. Breaking into my house. So there was the conflict of interest, for one thing. But that's not why I wouldn't represent him. When I thought about what he could have done to you, if you'd walked in a moment sooner—"

"He would never hurt me," she said, softly.

"Don't be naïve, Rylee. The guy's a low-life. He confessed to everything, and I don't want you anywhere near him."

"Confessed?" She reared back in her chair. "Isn't that a breach of confidentiality, telling me that?"

"Don't stick up for George Reid," he said. "He's a foot soldier for one of the dirtiest crooks in town."

"You mean Marcel Gibbon?"

He gave her a piercing stare, like he was surprised she knew the name. "That's right. The same guy Logan Woods is so chummy with. And because Woods is a foot soldier, too, he's shilling for George in the paper, but it's Gibbon who pulls the strings."

"You're wrong about—"

"Which is why you need to steer clear of Woods. He'll bring you down—don't you see that? He's using you for a story, Rylee. And you're just letting him."

He snatched the bill off her tray, eluding her unsuccessful grab.

"I said I wanted to pay for mine."

He stood. "Listen to me. Whatever he's told you, it's a lie. So, stay away from him."

He strode to the cashier stand, leaving her to clean up his mess.

~

Hair and makeup finished, Rylee padded into the bedroom to confront a dilemma. Liz wanted her to wear the red dress, but Rylee wasn't so sure. The red nipped in at the waist, with cute little button tabs, but wearing it would make it a capital-D date, while her blue jersey not-too-mini dress would keep things a lot more casual.

She held each one up in front of the mirror. She never had much of an occasion to wear the red. And Liz thought that was the one she should go with. She hung the blue back up.

Logan knocked just as she slipped on her high-heeled sandals. She paused, hand on the knob, then pulled the door open.

"Well, hello," he said. "I mean, really."

She widened the opening. "Come in."

Liz's instincts had been dead on. He wore a pair of dark jeans and a white button-up shirt. More importantly, he wore a cotton jacket, midnight blue, that fit him just right across the shoulders. The buttonholes were outlined in crimson thread, which was so cute it just about drove her crazy.

They stood by the half-open door. He leaned close. "You smell nice."

"You, too." She could feel his breath on her skin.

Closer now, his mouth brushed her neck. She stood stock-still. When he pulled back, he gazed at her lips until a tremor ran through them.

He was close enough to touch her with his voice. "We could always . . . stay here."

Well, hello.

She stepped back. "I didn't get all dressed up to stay here. And Nonie's really looking forward to meeting you. She said she had some ground rules to go over."

"Ground rules, huh? I guess we'd better get going, then."

She grabbed a pair of flats off the bar.

"What're those for?" he asked.

"I found out at the last minute that the Davidsons were leaving town. So I have to walk Toro at some point tonight. I can do it after you bring me home, but I thought I'd grab these just in case we end up on that side of town."

He groaned. "Toro?"

" 'Fraid so."

A teasing light entered his eyes. "I was sort of joking, you know, when I said you could sic the dogs on me and all."

Laughing, she held up the flats. "Don't worry. No rollerblades tonight. You'll be safe."

In the parking lot, he rested his hand at the small of her back. Daisy sat next to his car, passenger window intact.

She returned his keys. "Thanks for taking care of Daisy's window and for letting me use your car. I really appreciate it."

Hitting the automatic unlock, he slid his hand to her waist and gave it a squeeze, then opened her door. "Anytime."

She sank into the passenger seat. As he circled around, she said a little prayer. Nothing fancy, just the same mantra she'd been repeating all afternoon, the same heartfelt plea.

Let her be lucid, Lord. Let her be lucid.

❦

When they passed through the Commons, Logan seemed a little shell-shocked. "I'd heard Bishop Gadsden was upscale, but I had no idea. I was expecting, maybe, a hospital with carpet and nice wallpaper. But this is like a resort. I can't wait to get old."

She shushed him with a smile. "It's more like what you're thinking here in The Cloister. Nonie needs twenty-four-hour care now. She has for a long time, but I've been fighting it."

They pushed through a set of thick double doors and approached the nurse's station. Nurse Melanie was on duty. She looked up from a paperback romance, recognition lighting up her face.

"Everything quiet tonight?" Rylee whispered.

Melanie nodded. "Who's your young man?"

Rylee made the introductions. She was showing him off, but he didn't seem to mind. In fact, he turned on the charm, practicing for the main event.

"I brought him to meet Nonie. How's she doing?"

The nurse leaned forward confidentially. "Well, honey, I tell you what. She's just been so sweet today. I was talking to her earlier, and she was like a little girl." Noting Rylee's frown, Melanie patted her arm. "No, baby, in a good way. You go on in and see her. She's been waiting."

They paused outside the door to Room C5.

She took a deep breath. "Ready?"

"Let's do it."

Lord, let her be lucid.

Rylee tapped on the door, then slipped inside.

Lit by lamplight, the room seemed especially cozy. Nonie sat up in bed, the covers arranged just so, the serenest of smiles on her face. Everything perfect. Even the gauze wrap on her hand looked fresh and neat. She raised the good one to beckon them forward.

"Come closer and let me see you."

Logan crouched at the bedside, letting her take his hand. On the nightstand, a stack of photo albums had been specially arranged, showing just how much their visit was anticipated.

"Nonie, this is Logan," Rylee said, her voice trembling. "Logan, this is my grandmother, Flora Monroe. She . . . raised me."

Her hand rested in his, cool and weightless, translucent skin stretched tight over bones of birdlike delicacy. A glance at her other hand, already in bandages, and he applied only the slightest hint of pressure as he squeezed.

"Pleased to meet you, ma'am."

She held him with surprising vigor, using the grip to pull herself closer. Her pink-rimmed eyes inventoried the details of his face, as if she were searching for genetic artifacts from people she might once have known.

"Who're your people, young man?" The timbre in the old lady's voice put him in mind of lace doilies, dust, and chintz. But her eyes were piercing. As if she could see straight through to his soul.

"My people?" The question threw him. Like the voice, it seemed to come out of the distant past. "My last name is Woods, ma'am."

Rylee floated to the opposite side of the bed, her fingertips trailing along the bedclothes. The lamp gave her face a golden hue. She looked across at him with pride.

"Remember I told you, Nonie? Logan works for the newspaper. He's a writer." Her voice rose at the word, as if she'd been reading a children's story aloud and just reached the part about his being a prince.

Writer. The title embarrassed him a little. He didn't feel like a writer. Sure, he filled columns with news copy, but he wouldn't feel like a writer until his book was on the shelves. And it never would be if he didn't get a jump on the Robin Hood story.

But he was distracted. By Rylee. Whom he barely even knew. Nate Campbell had brought that fact into sharp focus for him. He suppressed a sigh.

"A writer?" Still clutching his hand, the old lady eyed him with confusion. "And just what is it you write?"

"Nonie." Rylee sank to the edge of the bed, concern in her voice, and pressed the back of her fingers against the old woman's temple as if she suspected fever. "I told you. He writes for the newspaper."

Nonie drew her hand back. Logan was relieved to no longer be responsible for it.

"Oh, of course," she laughed. "How silly of me. For some reason, I got it in my head he was a baseball player."

"In my spare time," Logan said. "Not that there's much of it these days."

As the grandmother's attention turned from him to Rylee, he settled back into a nearby chair. In the doorway of Rylee's apartment, with their bodies close, everything Nate had said seemed to disappear. But the questions were still there, skulking in the shadows of his mind.

"Someone was asking about you earlier," Nonie said to Rylee.

"About me?" She stole a glance his way, smiling. "Who was it? Are you gonna make me guess?"

"No, you don't have to guess." Nonie's voice trailed off. "I'm trying to remember."

"Was it Nurse Melanie?"

Nonie's hand cut the air. "Wait. I'm trying to think."

Rylee quieted.

"Oh, I know." The old lady's eyes lit up. "It was that man with all the car dealerships. What's he called again?"

"Mr. Lusky," Rylee said. "What did he say?"

"Lusky." Her mouth screwed up, like the name tasted funny. "He was saying you don't take care of that car of yours, and I'd better have a talk with you."

"Easy for him to say! He has a whole service department at his beck and call. I've got nobody but myself."

"Hey," Logan said, seeing his chance to get back into the conversation. "Who took care of that window for you?"

"That's right!" Rylee beamed with excitement, grabbing the old lady's hand. "Guess what happened to Daisy the other night?"

Her version of the story rushed through the potentially sordid parts—no mention of the creep sifting through her intimates for souvenirs, nothing to spark concern in a grandmother's mind. And fixing the window, the way she described it, sounded one step down from turning water into wine. By the end, both women were gazing at Logan in awe.

"I'm a keeper," he said.

Rylee tilted her head as if assessing the validity of his claim.

Then it was time for the photo albums. Nonie kept a tower of them next to the bed, and seemed intent on talking Logan through each one. At first he grew eager. A guided tour of Rylee's past might clear up a few gaps. But one glimpse of the black-and-white photos dispelled any chances of that.

Men with slicked-back hair propped their feet on the running boards of old bootlegger cars, their women sporting boxy dresses and flapper bobs. The Monroe clan went way back, it seemed, and there was no skipping ahead to the current crop.

He saw grand old houses, verdant gardens, slender girls in wicker chairs under shady piazzas, sipping lemonade from little glasses. They looked like genteel Southern aristocrats, pillars of Charleston.

The Monroes had clearly had money. But the first time Logan had been to Rylee's apartment, leaving her in that neighborhood after dark had seemed just short of negligence. Her father must have taken a small fortune with him when he disappeared.

Nonie tapped her finger on a photo of her own parents. They stood outside the same kind of narrow-front mansion the Davidsons lived in today.

"Where was this?" he asked, pointing to the house, afraid he already knew. Nate had told him about the Monroe house on East Battery.

She raised her eyebrows. "Home."

"I mean, where in the city?"

He willed her to say the words.

Across the bed, Rylee leaned closer. "Let me see." She took the album from her grandmother's hands, holding it close to her face. "It looks kind of familiar. But this wasn't our house, Nonie."

The old lady turned to Logan, confused. "We had to sell my house when I came here. It should have gone to Rylee, but . . . I wanted it to . . ." She blinked a few times, then looked around the room as if she was seeing it for the first time.

Rylee put an arm over her shoulders suddenly. "It's all right, Nonie."

"What?"

"It's me. Rylee. We were just talking, remember? You were showing us your album."

Trying to help, Logan reached for the photo book, which had fallen shut against the old lady's blanketed legs. Rylee's hand covered his.

"No," she whispered. "It'll upset her more."

Reluctantly, he let go of the album. He wanted another look at that picture.

"Everything's okay," Rylee was saying, smoothing the old lady's hair with her hand. "This is Logan, remember? We were just talking to him."

The door opened and Nurse Melanie came through, heading straight for a bank of whirring monitors at the back of the room without asking any questions. It could have been a regularly scheduled check, except for the glance that passed between her and Rylee.

"Let me have a look," the nurse said, easing Rylee away.

He joined her at the foot of the bed, where she immediately took his hand.

"Nonie's getting worse," she whispered.

"She seemed all right to me."

She sighed. "It happens so fast. But this was one of her good times, and it really lasted. I'm so glad, too. I'd wanted you to get a chance to meet her. The real her."

"And I did." He squeezed her hand.

They waited while the nurse asked a series of questions, the old lady ignoring most of them. Instead, she sank back against her pillows, inanimate except for the rise and fall of her breathing.

"I think she's going to sleep now," the nurse announced.

Logan peered past her, searching the area where Rylee had been standing a moment before to see whether there was a call button. The nurse had been summoned somehow. As soon as he'd started asking about the house, the place Nonie called home, Rylee had snatched the album away and called for help. Why? Was she trying to hide something?

They said their good-byes to Nonie's reclining form. Her body was still there, but the room felt suddenly emptied of her presence. Logan was happy to escape into the hallway.

Rylee slipped back into the room. "Wait one second. I'll be right out."

A minute later, she reappeared, handing him the photo.

Relief flooded him. His doubts retreated even before it touched his fingertips. She'd not been hiding anything at all.

But no. It was a photo, but not *the* photo. He stared down at a gold-cast color snapshot, a man and woman posing together on a coppery lawn.

The man was lean, dressed in a striped pullover, shorts, and boat shoes. His companion wore a vintage minidress in some kind of brocade-like fabric, though it wouldn't have been vintage when she wore it. Bronzed legs and round white-framed sunglasses, with tangles of brown hair radiating from her scalp. Her smile strangely familiar. He flipped the photo over. *Jon and Stella, November 1976.*

Logan looked closer, then glanced up at Rylee. "Your parents?"

She nodded, fingering a pearl pendant at her neck and bouncing slightly on her heels, almost as if she were awaiting his approval.

"She looks just like you."

"I know." She sighed with relief, then snatched the picture away to have a look for herself. "Isn't it strange? I can hardly remember her, but one thing I do remember is how big she seemed, like a giant almost. But look at her. She was younger than I am now when this was taken."

"You hadn't even been born."

"They had me late."

Looking at Rylee, standing pigeon-toed in a nursing home hallway, clutching the photo as if it might start talking at any moment, he wanted to put his arms around her. She put on a show of self-reliance, but maybe that's all it was. A skill adopted early to cope with the absence of her parents.

"You haven't told me much about them," he said.

She handed the picture back to him. "I was a little girl when she died. But I don't remember any of that. Only what they told me after . . ."

"And your dad?"

She clasped her bare arms together, suddenly cold. "I was pretty young, so I don't . . ." She swallowed. "It's not easy to talk about."

"That's okay." He gave her the photo.

She disappeared momentarily back into Nonie's room.

Bad as he wanted them, he wasn't going to push for the details. Not yet. When she stepped out, he slipped his arm around her and they headed to the exit.

Chapter Sixteen

The sun had gone down during their visit, and now a warm breeze whipped over the asphalt, flapping Logan's jacket. He led her toward the car, checking his watch by the parking lot lights. "There's a crab boil on the beach tonight."

At the mention of food, she felt suddenly famished. "There is?"

"Some friends are putting it on," he said, nodding her forward. "Unless you'd rather eat somewhere else?"

"No, I love the beach."

He opened the door for her, then went around. After starting the engine and putting the BMW in gear, his hand trailed across the seat, finding hers, and they intertwined in the dark. A current traveled up her arm.

"Thanks for coming with me tonight," she said. "Nonie doesn't get any visitors other than me. I know it was hard to tell, but it really meant a lot."

He ran his finger over her thumb ring. "I like her. She's really sweet."

They drove in silence, just the sound of the tires gliding over the road. Their hands parted as he turned on some music, a soft guitar ballad she'd heard before but couldn't place, and then his hand found hers again.

They shared a smile.

"Almost there," he said.

He parked above the beach. They left their shoes and his jacket in the car and advanced through the sand with bare feet. She could hear the water out in the darkness, but couldn't see it yet. The fires on the beach served as beacons. The smell of boiling crab beckoned.

A dozen shadows lingered around a long table laden with crab and corn on the cob, potatoes, longneck beer bottles, and pitchers of sweet tea. After rolling up his sleeves, Logan picked up a hammer and went to work, making introductions over his shoulder—too many people for her to keep track of the names.

He pointed out his photographer friend, Wash, shimmying to music from the iPod player, a blonde in a filmy sundress bobbing in and out of his grasp.

"I'm starving," Rylee said, digging some meat from a crab claw.

"Me too."

They ate while the others swirled around them, everybody getting along with easy indifference, longtime acquaintances who saw each other often enough they didn't need to catch up. She missed the inside jokes and felt the inquiring eyes checking out the newcomer.

"So," Wash said, sidling up to the table. "You're Rylee."

She smiled. "And you're Wash."

"I'm glad y'all came by. I mean, after all, if you two become an item, think what a great story you can tell about how you met."

Heat filled her cheeks. It was hard to imagine this charming, affable man had put such a scare into her by lurking in the shadows while Toro chased Logan up the monument.

The blonde wandered over, catching the tail end of the conversation. "Story? What story?"

"Diane, this is Rylee."

Diane reached across the table. Rylee wiped her hand on the tablecloth before shaking.

"Rylee's a dogwalker," Wash said, a smile breaking out, "and Logan is famously afraid of dogs. He squared off with one when he was a kid and came up on the short end of the stick."

"Match made in heaven." Diane lifted her drink in tribute.

They whirled away, captured once more by the music. Some of the others rolled up their pants legs and ventured out into the dark water.

"You were attacked by a dog?" Rylee asked.

"It was a long time ago." He stood. "Wanna dance?"

"I ate so much, I'm not sure I can even walk."

"Sure you can. Or let's test the water."

"All right."

They went to the water's edge, the cool wet rush enveloping their ankles. Logan tried to coax her farther, but she pulled at his hand, tugging him back. He bent low, scooping his hand under the waves.

"Don't do it!" She scrambled back.

A jet of water leapt up and she ran away, laughing. He splashed more at her, but she kept a safe distance. His jeans were wet to midcalf, his shirt billowing in the wind, blown tight around his muscled chest and flat stomach.

He came out of the water holding his dripping hands out in a conciliatory gesture. The firelight caught his eyes as he advanced. They shared a look, then their fingertips touched, his wet hands trailing up her forearm, cupping her elbows, drawing her gently forward. She, on tiptoes, closed her eyes just as their lips touched.

It couldn't have lasted forever, but it felt that way. She imagined them reclining in the surf like in that old black-and-white movie, their limbs intertwined as waves crashed around them. She pressed her hand to his rough jawline, arching her back as he tightened his arms around her. He lifted her gently off the ground like she was weightless, floating.

Off in the distance, Wash howled in approval. The others gave them a round of applause, interrupting the moment.

She pulled back in surprise, unaware the fire had illuminated them against the dark background of the night sky. Logan allowed her feet to touch down but didn't release her.

His eyes searched hers, as if he'd just discovered something unexpected, as if he wasn't sure what to do in the aftermath. "You're beautiful."

Wash called out, "Come on now. Keep it up and you'll have to get a room!"

They broke off, now bashful, returning hand-in-hand to the ring of light around the fire. Wash came up to Logan, slapping him on the back. His companion Diane gave Rylee a friendly but almost envious look.

"All of a sudden," Logan said, slipping his arm around her waist, "this party has gotten old."

"Yeah, I know what you mean."

They said their good-nights, making their way back up the beach, a few of the others following suit. At the car, he paused to wring the water from his pants, producing a fresh towel from his gym bag so they could brush the sand from their feet. She was almost reluctant. She wanted to keep the sand as a souvenir.

In the car, he curved his hand round the back of her neck, threading his fingers into her hair and drawing her close for another kiss. It felt like forever again, and must have been, because the kiss only ended when Wash, fresh from the beach and unaccompanied by the blonde, tapped pointedly on the driver's window.

"I thought you were leaving."

"We are now," Logan answered, turning on the ignition.

As they drove, he found her hand. She turned toward him, surprised to find him watching her.

"Logan." His name felt different on her lips somehow. More . . . intimate. "Keep your eyes on the road."

She studied the lines of his face. The slope of his nose, his chapped lips, his chin, the pulse in his neck. An undertow of longing pulled against her resolution. Feeling the weight of his hand in hers, she knew she needed to be honest with him.

She turned the radio down. "We've started something."

His thumb traced her hand, exploring every dip, every swell. "Yes."

"I . . . I wasn't planning on it."

He kept his eyes on the road. "Me neither."

Moistening her lips, she took a deep breath. "What I'm trying to say is, I *can't* start something."

"Why not?" He glanced at her. She tried to slip her hand free, but he tightened his hold. "Don't pull away, Rylee."

"I have to."

"Why?"

"It's complicated. I'm not even sure I can explain it."

"Try." He stroked her palm.

"It goes back. Way back."

They rode in silence again, her heart keeping time with the thrumming of the tires. He drew her hand to his lips, tasting, nipping, kissing. Singling out each knuckle like he'd never known a hand before.

A ball of desire she'd kept hidden even from herself shattered into a million pieces, scattering fragments of yearning throughout her body. She shivered, goose bumps covering her arms, her legs, her chest.

"Logan." Her whisper a plea. For what, she wasn't sure.

He lowered her hand, resting it against his thigh.

"I'm afraid."

He frowned. "Of me?"

"Of me."

The car slowed. Whether he did it on purpose, she didn't know.

She pulled against his hand again. This time he released her.

"My granddad, Nonie's husband?"

He nodded.

"Well, he took off when my dad was a teenager, leaving Nonie at a time when single parents weren't at all the norm. Her family had money, so she and my dad were okay financially, but emotionally—from what little Nonie has told me—my dad was never the same."

"I'm sorry. I had no idea."

She looked out the window. They were crossing the Ashley River, leaving the island and heading toward the city. "When I was five, my dad did the same thing to my mom. One day he was there, the next he wasn't." She looked down at her hands. "Two days after he left, she overdosed on sleeping pills. We don't know if she did it by accident or on purpose."

He ran the back of his fingers against her bare arm. "Two days is pretty quick to lose all hope. How could she be sure he wouldn't come back?"

She stared at him, completely taken aback. "I don't know. I never really thought about it. But, yes. That does seem kind of strange."

He turned onto Broad Street. "So now you're afraid of what? That if we get serious, I'm going to do the same thing?"

"It's not you, Logan. It's me." She crossed her arms. "Monroe women can't seem to hold their men. That's all."

He wove through the streets of the historic district, finally pulling up in front of the Davidsons' house. He parallel parked, then turned off the ignition.

"You brought me to Toro's."

"Yes."

"You didn't have to. I could have come over after you took me home." She put her hand on the door handle.

"Rylee?"

She paused.

"Just because you're a Monroe doesn't mean you're an automatic candidate for abandonment."

Her eyes moistened. "You can't tell the future, Logan."

Placing a finger at her chin, he turned her toward him, wiping a tear that trailed down her cheek. "No, I can't, but I can tell you this. I'm not your granddad, and I'm not your dad. When I find the woman I want to spend the rest of my life with, it'll be for the rest of my life. Death do us part, just like the vows say."

Pulling away from his touch, she opened the door and fled before he could say any more.

He leaned against the hood of the car, thinking of the manuscript pages waiting back at his apartment. The book he wasn't writing.

He shouldn't be here. Waiting for her to emerge from the Davidsons' house. Waiting to be near her again. But he was.

He ran a hand through his hair. Her being in CPD's sights might be inconvenient, but nothing he couldn't cope with. This abandonment thing, though. That was a problem.

His phone buzzed in his pocket. The incoming number was blocked.

"Woods." Marcel Gibbon's voice. "Half an hour. Washington Park."

"You sound funny. Is everything all right?"

"Half an hour—"

"No, wait. I can't get there in thirty minutes. Make it an hour."

"You can make it," Gibbon said. "Bring the girl."

The line went dead. Rylee came out of the gate. Toro immediately growled, showing his teeth.

Logan froze.

She gave the leash a quick jerk. "Bad dog! This won't take long, Logan. I'll be back in no time."

"I'll walk with you."

"You don't have to. I know you don't like him."

Pushing away from the hood, he fell in beside her. "Keep him on his side of the sidewalk and we'll be fine."

No response. Not even a smile. He sighed.

They walked in stiff silence. He brushed her hand. A block later, he hooked her pinkie with his. When Toro stopped, Logan intertwined his fingers with hers and tugged her to him.

Nuzzling her ear, he caught a tiny hint of the fragrance she'd had on when he first picked her up. "I'm sorry, Rylee. I didn't mean to make you mad."

She looked up, her eyes luminous, distraught.

"It's okay." He cupped her cheek, brushing her lower lip with his thumb. "We'll just take it slow. One day at a time. Okay?"

Her chest rose and fell with deep breaths.

Moving his hand to the back of her head, he lowered his mouth. They'd barely touched when Toro gave a bark. She pulled back and patted the dog.

The mastiff led them down an alleyway, finally emerging at the waterfront. They climbed the steps and walked along the bulkhead.

The sound of the waves along the wall, the salty, flowery scent of the wind, caught them up in a momentary reverie.

He glanced at the mansions lining East Battery. "Rylee?"

"Hmmm?" A lazy breeze stirred the fabric of her dress.

"I . . . I was wondering about that house, the one your grandmother called home."

"I was wondering about that, too." She looked at him in surprise. "Those old pictures, I haven't flipped through them in years. The ones of my parents and me, I've memorized them all. But the older ones, not so much. I never really paid attention to that house before—just the people in the photo. But, now it's stuck in my head."

"Do you know where your parents lived when you were little?"

"Somewhere around here, though I don't know exactly which house. Nonie hated to talk about anything relating to that time. She'd get really short with me and stay mad for days if I even brought it up. When I got old enough to insist, she was so confused, I never could get a straight answer." She sucked in a quick breath. "Do you think that might be it? Do you think that's a picture of my house?"

He shrugged. "I have no idea. I thought maybe you did."

They turned around and headed back toward the Davidsons'. Her explanation rang with honesty, a fingernail striking crystal. All of a sudden, he felt incredibly stupid. Not for giving credence to Nate's crackpot theories—he hadn't—but for letting the cop bend down and drip poison into his ear.

He slipped his arm around her. As they walked, she tucked her head against his shoulder, her body warm, touching from head to hip.

"Rylee, you need to be careful."

"Careful?"

"Of the police. Of Nate."

"He's a doofus."

"A doofus with a badge. If you give him something—anything—he's gonna use it against you. Understand what I'm saying?"

She lifted her head. "Are you serious?"

"The police seem to think you're some kind of accomplice."

She pulled Toro up short. "Did Detective Campbell say something to you?"

He shrugged. "That's the impression I got from him."

"But it's so ridiculous."

In spite of the dismissive words, her face went pale and hardened. Like a weight had just settled on her, and she had to strain to keep from crumpling. The dog, sensing her mood, gazed up at her.

His warning had hit her harder than he'd expected. "Don't worry. They're keeping tabs on George. If there's another robbery, they'll catch him in the act."

She glanced up and down the Battery. "What about me? Are they keeping tabs on me?"

"What? No. Rylee, of course not. Don't worry, all right? I didn't mean to upset you. I can't seem to say the right thing."

She looked so bereft, he had to pull her against him.

"Don't worry. Okay?"

She nodded, then buried her face against his neck, arms jutting over his shoulders. She hung there limp as a rag doll, breathing hard, her heartbeat thumping so he could feel it against his chest.

Behind them, a woman in a track suit approached, a long-nosed gray dog leashed to her wrist. She passed them, then did a double take.

"Hey, Rylee."

They parted, Rylee turning to face the woman. Toro let out a quick bark, but stayed on his side of the walkway.

"Oh, Belinda. Hey."

The woman trotted away with a salute.

When she was gone, Rylee sighed. "The competition."

He slipped his hand into hers. "Let's get going."

A few minutes later, they made it back to the Davidsons' gate.

Yawning, she ruffled the dog's head. "He did really good tonight. Let me go give him some water and put him in his crate. I'll be right back."

He checked his watch. Still time to get to Washington Park.

When she returned, he had the car door open and waiting. He hustled around to his side and started the engine. "Rylee. There's one thing."

She leaned her head against the headrest, turning toward him. "What is it?"

He glanced at the dashboard clock. She followed his gaze.

"The guy from the other night? Marcel Gibbon?"

"What about him?"

"I . . . He wants to see me."

"Why? When?"

He made a U-turn and headed toward Washington Park. "Well . . . now."

"Right now?" She frowned, then slowly lifted her head. "At, like, one in the morning?"

He looked at her. "This all came down earlier today. I'm sorry. Seriously. But he just called and sort of drew a line in the sand, and I really need to talk to him."

"Right now."

He tapped the steering wheel with his thumb. "I mean it, Rylee. I really am sorry. Tonight has been . . . incredible. I don't want it to end like this, but I think . . . It's about George."

He waited, feeling the distance between them stretch from inches to miles.

"Okay," she said with a sigh. "If we have to, let's get it over with."

"Thanks." He put his hand on her knee, an apologetic touch, and they headed toward the park in silence.

Logan came back to the car, waking her from restless sleep. She rubbed her cheek, feeling the impression left by the leather seat. The clock on the dashboard said three.

"I don't know where he is." He flipped his cell phone shut, tucking it into his jeans pocket. "He said he'd be here."

She yawned. "I don't care where he is, Logan." Fatigue slurred her words. "I don't care about anything but sleep."

"But what?"

"Sleep!"

He closed the car door. "Okay, okay. I'll take you home. It's just weird. He made it sound like it was now or never. "

He'd left her in the car on Broad, telling her he'd ask his questions of Marcel and return to her in short order. Now he put it in gear and headed to her place.

"I'm glad he wasn't there. That guy creeps me out."

He nodded. "Yeah, but I thought he could help."

Her limbs felt too heavy to lift. She let her hand drop. Her eyelids, too. She slid sideways in her seat, her head coming to rest against his shoulder. He put his arm around her, pulling her closer, but the console thwarted his efforts.

"I just want to sleep," she said.

"Then sleep. I'll wake you up when we get there."

So she did. She slept and eventually dreamed, her unconscious mind all rolling ocean and gritty sand.

⌁

When she finally woke, it wasn't Logan that roused her, it was the warmth of an early morning sun. She opened her eyes, her whole body stiff from contortion, awake in the passenger seat as Logan slept deeply next to her, his breathing regular, the clock on the dash reading ten past seven.

They were in the parking lot of her building, Daisy beside them.

She eased back, freeing herself from his encircling arm, then watched him for a while. He looked as uncomfortable as she felt, but there was a faint smile on his lips. His eyelids were troubled, a current of dreams running underneath. Arriving a few hours before, he must have looked at her the way she looked at him now, deciding not to wake her.

She felt the same way. She slipped out of the car, careful to close the door with as little noise as possible. She tiptoed to the stairs. He'd open his eyes and she'd be gone, leaving him to wonder if any of it had really happened at all.

Chapter Seventeen

Pausing at her apartment door, Rylee fumbled for the keys. Over her shoulder, she heard Logan's car start, then listened as he drove away. She felt a pang of separation but knew he'd not been able to see her, even if he'd looked up. Her door wasn't visible from the parking lot the way Liz's was.

She slipped her key into the lock, but the pressure of her hand pushed the door open. She frowned. When they'd left for their date, she'd made sure the door was locked. She was positive.

Prickly tingles went up her back, down her arms.

Pushing the door open slowly, she peered through the ever-widening crack. She stole forward, no sound but her breathing.

Flipping on the lights, she discovered . . . nothing. Not an object out of place.

But looking around, something didn't feel right. Crazy as it seemed, she thought the carpet looked different, pushed against the grain by an alien set of tracks. She bent low to inspect. Maybe she was wrong.

She continued toward the bedroom, pulling up short at the threshold. The bedcovers were tucked in with near-military precision, the surface of her down comforter utterly smooth. Not even the slightest sign of disturbance.

She gripped the doorframe. She'd been running late yesterday. And as a result, she hadn't bothered to make the bed.

On shaky legs, she wobbled to the side where she slept, certain something was waiting for her under those sheets.

She reached out for the edge of the comforter, hardly able to force herself to make the contact. The fabric, soft from a multitude of washings, felt foreign to the touch.

She peeled back the layers. One after another. Her imagination ran wild. Pools of blood. A severed carcass. A smeared threat written in sanguinary finger paint.

But again, there was nothing. The message wasn't under the sheets. It was the sheets themselves. Someone had entered and left a sign that was intelligible only to her.

After making sure once again that the apartment was empty, she checked every window. All the screens were in place. All were locked from the inside.

She went to the front door, dragging a chair over to brace it. Logan had been right. The lock was a joke. With a credit card and a flick of the wrist, she'd let herself in more than once after misplacing her key. That was going to change.

New locks, she promised herself. In the morning, first thing.

Kicking off her flats, she entered the bathroom, its tiles cooling her feet. She reached behind the curtain and turned on the water. Ordinarily, she never bothered to close the door, but now she pushed it tight and thumbed down the spring-loaded lock.

Discarding her clothes in a little pile, she stepped into the tub and let the water drizzle over her, wishing just once it would pound through the rusty nozzle in a constant stream instead of in spurts.

The shower curtain brushed against her skin. She peered around the corner to make sure the room was empty, images of *Psycho* slashing through her mind.

She soaped, shampooed and conditioned in record time, then wrapped her head in one towel and her body in another.

Why hadn't she thought to bring her clothes into the bathroom with her? But she knew why. Because there was never any need. Because the door was never closed.

I have confidence in sunshine. . . .

She whipped open the door, releasing a cloud of steam. Nothing. No sound but the drip, drip of the shower nozzle.

. . . I have confidence in rain. . . .

She padded across the room, the matted carpet coarse under her damp feet.

. . . I have confidence that spring will come again. . . .

She pulled open her underwear drawer and reached inside.

. . . Besides which you see, I have con—

She snatched her hand back.

They'd been returned. The things he'd taken. Laundered, positioned neatly, and left on top.

Chapter Eighteen

Yellow tape fluttered along the perimeter of the historic home like leftover decorations from a Policeman's Ball. Men in white overalls went in and out from the Davidsons' front door. Charleston police officers conducted a fingertip search of the lawn.

Logan's pulse hammered in his head. This was bad, very bad. Just six hours ago, he'd stood on this very spot, waiting for Rylee to emerge from the house.

Nate Campbell stood sentry at the front gate, arms crossed, boring holes into Logan with his eyes. The detective looked like he hadn't gotten much sleep, either. At least he'd managed a fresh pair of clothes, which was more than Logan had.

Logan stopped short on the sidewalk, not liking Nate's expression. "What?"

"You're here pretty fast," Campbell snapped.

"Just doing my job."

"Well, you can park it right here for the time being, 'cause we're a long way from done." He gave Logan's rumpled clothes a once-over, then cracked a mirthless smile. "Long night?" An irritating chuckle. "Did you, uh . . . get to home base?"

Logan rolled his eyes. "Give me a break, Nate."

"So where's your sidekick?"

"Wash? He's meeting me here. And don't call him that to his face."

"I was talking about Rylee Monroe."

"I wouldn't say it to her, either. Now are you going to fill me in on what's happening here or not?"

Campbell jabbed a thumb over his shoulder. "What's it look like?"

It looked like a crime scene.

Logan glanced up and down Prices Alley. No signs so far of the TV news crews. Only a matter of time.

"Could I at least get a statement from you?"

Campbell jutted his chin. "Yeah. I'll give you a statement. At half past five this morning, the neighbors called 9-1-1 to report the alarm was going off. The couple that lives here, the Davidsons, weren't home. First officers on the scene found the door open, went inside, saw what looked like a Category 5 hurricane. Demolition derby on steroids."

"Was anything taken?"

The detective shrugged. "How should I know? It's like ground zero in there."

"Why didn't the security company respond?"

"The owners didn't have the alarm monitored. Pretty stupid, if you ask me. Houses like this go for four or five million these days. It's not like they can't afford it."

"Wouldn't the alarm have gone off as soon as the door was breached?"

"Yeah. The neighbors finally called it in, say, ten minutes later. We responded within ten, and there was no sign of him . . . or her."

"He didn't have a lot of time on his hands, then."

"Unless she had keys. Took her time. Then set off the alarm on her way out."

In the interest of gathering as much info as he could, Logan ignored the veiled reference to Rylee. "So you're treating this as another Robin Hood burglary?"

"What do you think?"

"And George Reid?" Logan asked. "Did you have him under surveillance this morning?"

A woman's voice came from the other side of the fence. "That's what I want to know."

They turned to find Sheila Santos, a middle-aged woman in pinstripes, standing just in earshot. Her jacket was too snug to close, revealing a shiny badge on one side of her belt and a crooked holster on the other. Her dark hair was skullcap short, her makeup heavy as lead.

Nate started walking. "Look, I'd love to stay and chat, but—"

"So he didn't do it?" Logan asked Santos. "Does that mean the police are his alibi?"

"—as you can imagine, I have actual detective work to do."

Nate's hand moved for the gate latch, while Logan gave Santos an inquiring look. But she kept her lip zipped.

"Wait." Logan turned back to Nate. "Can't you get me inside?"

He considered the question, then sighed. "Of course I can."

He opened the gate and went through. Logan started to follow, but the gate slammed shut, blocking the path.

"But I don't want to."

Logan draped a hand over the fence. "Come on, Nate."

A heartless smile. "Tell you what. You just sit tight out here, and once we're done, maybe the family will invite you in. They made it back home just a little while ago. Now if you'll excuse me." He made a beeline for Santos, escorting her inside the house.

After the brush-off, Logan set up shop on the sidewalk, phoning the preliminaries in to the news desk. Then he called and left a message for Marcel Gibbon. He'd called three or four times the night before, when Gibbon failed to appear. It made no sense to insist on a meeting and then not turn up.

Unless . . . He shook his head, dismissing the thought, but it wouldn't go away. Maybe the Cherub had a reason. Maybe he wanted to make sure they were at Washington Park at the prescribed hour. And not at the Davidson place, which was about to be hit.

He checked his own messages, but there was nothing from Gibbon. Instead, he heard the voice of Seth, his agent. "I'm assuming, since you haven't been returning my calls, that you don't have the pages I've been asking for. Well, let me tell you something, buddy. Dora's quit calling for updates. You know what that means? That means I need pages sprinkled with fairy dust. And if you don't get them to me fast, we're gonna lose this thing. Call me. Now."

He rubbed his face. The manuscript was still light. He needed to write up a stack of new notes. Maybe he'd do that now, while he waited to see the Davidsons.

After grabbing his laptop and notes from his car, he spent the next forty-five minutes sitting on the curb, incessantly tapping the keyboard. The TV crews began to arrive, setting up across the street for the wide shot. A kid in a multi-pocketed mesh vest jogged over to shoo Logan out of frame.

He shot the pages off to Seth, then put his laptop back in the car just as Wash strode up, his big camera hanging loose, bouncing against his pecs. The two of them headed for some shade.

"Funny," Wash said. "I could swear I've seen that outfit before." He scratched his head in mock concentration, then lifted a eureka finger in the air. "Hey, wait a second. Weren't you wearing the same thing last night when you left the beach? If I didn't know better—"

"Nate's trying to shut us out."

Wash registered the teeming activity behind the fence. "For real?"

Logan nodded. "I called in some prelims, but until we can get in there and talk to the owners, time's a'wasting."

Making the most of the delay, Wash took some exterior shots. Logan tagged along just to look busy. Like the Petrie house, this one sat perpendicular to the street, with a false entrance leading up to a piazza. As a result, the place looked smaller and more discreet than it really was.

Logan counted two floors, but the attic windows were curtained, suggesting the third might be in use. The piazza was topped by a second-floor veranda trimmed in elegant white woodwork for the complete storybook effect. Although the fence fronting the side yard was screened in thick foliage, Logan caught a glimpse of flowers in full bloom. He heard splashing water, too.

"You know what you could do," Wash said.

"What's that?"

"Your new girlfriend. She knows these folks, right? She works for all of them."

"I don't want her anywhere near here," Logan said. "If Reid didn't do it—and I'm pretty sure he didn't or they'd have caught him in the act—then Rylee is the prime suspect."

Wash shrugged. "But she was with you all night, right? You can vouch for her."

He could, up until about three thirty when he fell asleep beside her. But when he woke, she was gone. He had no way of knowing exactly when she got out of the car. And if the alarm went off at five thirty, then his testimony would do more harm than good.

"Look at that." Wash lifted his camera to eye level, pointing the lens down the alleyway. "Speak o' the devil."

Turning, Logan felt his chest tighten. Rylee. The first time he'd seen her since last night. Since this morning, really. She hadn't seen him yet, hadn't noticed all the commotion.

Unaware of the shock awaiting her, she seemed completely absorbed in the music from the white earbuds whose wires dangled along her throat. She wore a pair of cutoffs and pink tennis shoes. Her pale semitransparent top shimmered slightly in the air, the body printed with a pattern of leaves, the sleeves with peacock feathers. Her short, dark hair framed her cheekbones, her unaware eyes, the lips parted slightly. So beautiful. So innocent.

But was she? He caught a strain underneath the placid lines of her face.

The sound of Wash's shutter punctured his reverie.

"You're always taking pictures of her," Logan said.

"I'll send you some."

"Yes, you will."

She came to a sudden stop, her tranquil expression gone, all that suppressed tension suddenly surfacing. She took in the scene, her eyes widening. Recognizing Logan, she rushed forward, her big canvas messenger bag bouncing against her hip.

She stretched her hand out tentatively, touching him on the forearm. "What's happening?"

But he could tell by the look on her face she already knew.

"I'm sorry," he said.

She backed away, shaking her head. "Not the Davidsons. Not them. We were just here. Everything was fine." Her voice was hollow. Shell-shocked.

"Shhh." Glancing around, he took her elbow. "You need to get out of here."

She pulled away, bolting for the closed gate.

"Rylee, wait!"

Instead of stopping her, Wash jumped out of the way, leaving Logan to fend for himself. He caught up to her just as she threw the gate wide. He grabbed her by the hand. Behind him, he could feel the gathered news teams taking a sudden interest.

"Nate's in there," he said under his breath.

"What about Toro? Is he all right?"

"I'm sure he's fine. But apparently Robin Hood did a real number on the place. They're sorting through the wreckage now. Trying to figure out what's what."

He couldn't tell if she was taking all this in, but at least she'd paused outside the gate. She was breathing heavily, though, and might bolt at any second. "You need to get out of sight."

"Why? I didn't do anything. They can't accuse me just because I work for these people."

"Yes, they can."

Wash strolled up, turning his back to them, screening the action from the other reporters as best he could.

"Rylee," Logan said. "Please."

"They're good people, the Davidsons." She chewed at her bottom lip. "This shouldn't have happened to them."

"It shouldn't happen to anyone. But let's be careful here."

He coaxed her back through the fence, then put an arm around her, the fabric of her sleeve ephemeral. With Wash alongside, he led her down the sidewalk a few steps, closing the gate behind them. Ten more steps and they'd have a hedge of green between themselves and the police. Logan began to think they might make it.

"Hold it right there!" With a couple of uniformed men in his wake, Campbell burst through the gate, bounding toward them with a determined scowl.

Logan sensed a half dozen video cameras limbering up, lenses leveled in their direction. Beside him, Rylee drew a breath, then turned as the cops advanced, meeting them head on.

"Where were you this morning around five thirty?" Campbell asked.

"Five thirty?" She glanced at Logan, then back at Nate. "Sleeping."

Campbell had his notebook out, flipping like a traffic warden though the pages. Behind him, a wall of uniforms had assembled, lending their silent weight to the exchange.

"Can you verify that, Logan?"

"I can."

Nate looked up. "You sure about that? Because in order to corroborate her story, you'd have to have been awake at five thirty and seen her beside you." He leered at Logan. "You sure you didn't wake up alone? Maybe with a little note on the pillow that said, 'Thanks for the good time.' A note that left you to wonder just exactly when she slinked out the door?"

Logan didn't respond, a tic pulsing in his jaw.

"Did you feel used?"

Rylee sucked in her breath.

Wash grabbed Logan's arm, retaining hold of it until Logan shook free.

The photographer let out a long breath, making sure everybody knew how unimpressed he was with police conduct, then moved to the side. Looking through the finder, he began to snap photos.

Logan could've kissed him. The camera had such a moderating effect. The itch of that shutter popping made everybody step back. The uniformed officers assumed a look of professional indifference.

Campbell paused to gather his thoughts. "That's what I thought." He tucked his pad and pencil back into his pocket. "Rylee Monroe, you're under arrest."

She gasped.

"You have the right to remain silent. Anything you do or say may be used against you in a court of law. . . ."

She slipped her messenger bag from her shoulder and handed it to Logan. "Karl's number is on my phone. Tell him I need him."

"You have the right to consult an attorney before talking to the police. . . ."

An officer pulled her hands behind her and snapped on the cuffs.

"I know you don't like him, Logan. But I need him. Will you call him for me?"

He stood flat-footed, uncertain what to do.

"Will you?" she asked, her eyes clear. Unwavering. Determined.

"I will."

Thank you, she mouthed, letting her defenses down just long enough to give him a peek into the panic churning inside her before she turned away.

His heart lurched.

"Knowing and understanding your rights as I have explained them to you, are you willing to answer my questions without an attorney present?"

"I will not." Her glare could have saved the polar ice caps, it was so cold, but Campbell seemed unimpressed.

He jerked his head toward a line of cop cars.

The officer who'd cuffed Rylee escorted her to one, video cameras tracking their progress, reporters shouting questions.

Chapter Nineteen

A swell of police vehicles choked off the street, distinctly out of place in such stately surroundings. The departing patrol car with Rylee inside reversed onto the road, giving a siren squawk to keep the crowd back.

Nate announced to the members of the press that the family would not be making any statements at this time, but the police chief would hold a press conference at the station within the hour.

"I'm gonna head back to the newsroom with these photographs, then." Wash squeezed Logan's shoulder. "Hang tight, man. It'll be all right."

Logan nodded, still trying to take it all in.

The television news crews scrambled into position to film breaking reports of the unexpected arrest. A motley rank of bystanders gathered along the sidewalk. A gray-haired, dark-suited superior walked through the gate, motioning Nate over. They strolled behind the cordon, Nate speaking rapidly, then listening with reluctant deference as the other man replied.

Logan cut across the street, working his way around the edge of the emergency vehicles to the other side of Meeting where his car waited. He dug through Rylee's bag for her phone. A scroll through her contact list yielded Karl's number.

He slipped into the driver's seat of his car, staring at the send button. Karl Sebastian hadn't done George any good, and he didn't think things would be any different with Rylee. Still, she'd asked him to call Karl, and he'd agreed.

The receptionist's voice sounded overly bright. "Sebastian, Lynch & Orton."

"Hello. This is Logan Woods."

She sighed. "Mr. Woods, I've told you—"

"Don't hang up. Rylee Monroe's been arrested, and she asked me to call Karl on her behalf."

A hesitation. "One moment, please."

He thrummed the steering wheel. Finally, they put him through.

"This is Karl Sebastian."

"The police just arrested Rylee. They're taking her in for processing now. The detective in charge is still at the scene, so you might want to move quickly."

If any of this surprised Karl, he hid it well. From the change in ambient sound, Logan could tell he was already in motion, asking questions as he walked. Logan filled in the details. Criminal law might not be the man's specialty, but he seemed to know what he was doing.

"All right," Karl said. "I'll take care of it."

"You can get her out?"

"As soon as I get her in front of a judge so bail can be set."

The weight of the situation pressed down on him, making it difficult to breathe. He'd been with her just a few hours ago, and now she was in jail. Like a common criminal.

He wanted to throw the phone. Kick in a wall. Inflict some kind of damage.

Instead, he sat in his parked car gripping the phone so hard it would leave an imprint on his hand. The hope of resolving the situation quickly, setting things right, did not look good.

"You *can* get her out, though?" he asked again.

"Of course." Karl's tone crackled with defensiveness. "In the meantime, I want you to leave her alone. Whatever story you're after, it ends here. She's my client, and she's off limits to the media. Do I make myself clear?"

Logan bit back his reply. No way was he leaving her alone, but he didn't have to say so to the lawyer. "Thanks for your help, Karl."

Hanging up the phone, he called Lacey Lamar. "Somehow the police have come to the conclusion that Rylee Monroe is the Robin Hood burglar, and now they're processing her at headquarters."

"Maybe she is," Lacey said.

He ignored this. "Karl Sebastian's her attorney. He said he'd get her in front of a judge as soon as possible."

"I thought he wasn't taking your calls."

"He took this one."

She paused on the other end of the line. "This is a big development, Logan. I know you're involved personally. I should have stopped it before now. But I want you to know one thing. If I don't think you're on top of it, I won't have any qualms about putting someone else on the story. My patience is wearing thin. You understand me?"

Involved personally? He almost laughed. Lacey didn't know the half of it. He was dating the prime suspect of the story he was covering.

"Answer me, Woods."

Never in his career had he been pulled off a story. But when Lacey found out for certain he'd been with Rylee at the scene of the crime a few short hours before the break-in, she'd skewer him. "I hear you, Lacey. Loud and clear."

Hanging up, he stared out the windshield. A black-and-white Ford Interceptor was pulling away, edging around the bumper of a news van. Just outside the cone of activity, he spotted Rylee's Civic.

He turned on the ignition but didn't put the car in gear. He needed to find Robin Hood. If he was right about the police surveillance, then George Reid was in the clear. So who was the real burglar? And why had Gibbon stood him up last night?

He leaned his head against the steering wheel. Out of nowhere, his dad's words began to circle in his mind.

I know how it is, son. You think you can do it all. I've been there. The thing is, you can't do it all, not alone.

—

The flashes started popping the moment the door opened, only intensifying as the file of officers advanced. The chief led the pack, in full dress uniform, followed by a series of lieutenants and plainclothes officers, including the gray-haired man Logan had seen outside the Davidsons' house.

Bringing up the rear, Nate Campbell paused in the doorway, momentarily stunned by all the bright lights. Before advancing onto the platform, he adjusted his tie and ran a finger through his hair.

Logan had camped out at the station since coming from the crime scene, trying to pick up more information as his fellow journalists began to congregate. The buzz in the press pool was that the Robin Hood burglaries had been solved.

Logan shook his head. The unstoppable media machinery was in motion, ready to shout from every mountaintop whatever verdict the police announced. Arresting George had set off a flurry, but this was nothing short of an orchestrated frenzy. The trouble he'd been afraid of was here. Nothing he could do would change that.

The chief stepped up to the podium, tapping on the microphone. The thumping sound was nearly drowned out by the *clickety-click* of camera shutters.

"I'm gonna start off by introducing everybody on stage," he said. "Then we'll get this show on the road. We have a brief statement to make, and then I'll take some questions."

The introductions went down the line quickly, the chief devoting less time to each as he descended. Most of the names were familiar. The gray-haired superior from the scene turned out to be the head of the Detective Division. By the time it was Nate's turn, the chief was downright succinct.

Nate squinted at the television lights, his mouth set grimly. If he dared to smile, Logan would go up there and wipe the grin off his face.

"As you know," the chief began, "during the course of the past two months, our city has been plagued by an individual the press has dubbed the Robin Hood burglar, who has targeted residents south of Broad in a series of increasingly destructive break-ins."

Lifting his finger in the air for emphasis, he turned to display his law-and-order profile for the cameras. "Early this morning, the perpetrator struck again. Police were called to the scene, where officers apprehended a suspect. At this time, we are not releasing the name of the suspect."

Logan's pen rested against his notebook. The statement seemed much more guarded than the initial buzz had let on. They weren't taking any chances.

"I want to take this opportunity to thank the team of diligent men and women who have worked this case tirelessly." He indicated the fellow brass onstage, as if they'd been out in the field all this time, tracking leads. "In particular, let me recognize Detective Campbell, who has brought this case to a successful conclusion."

Off the podium, tucked into a corner of the room, Logan saw a disgruntled-looking Detective Santos rolling her eyes at the chief's praise.

"Now if there are any questions—"

The gathered reporters erupted in a volley of interrogatories, their words so intermingled that the chief held his hands up in a gesture of surrender. "Please. One at a time. Gene, let's start with you."

A local television reporter stood, quickly checking his notes. "Is it true that the suspect you have in custody is female?"

The chief conferred with the officer next to him, then leaned into the mic. "We're not confirming that . . . at this time."

Logan's hand shot up, but the chief called on another television talker.

"What happened with the previous suspect, George Reid?"

"We believe that these crimes, while attributed in the newspapers to a single individual, are in fact the work of several."

"So Reid and the suspect in custody are associates?"

"Close associates," the chief replied.

Logan made a mental note to call George again, assuming the police hadn't already reeled him back in.

"Were there any eyewitnesses?" another reporter asked.

Again, the chief conferred. "I'll let Detective Campbell speak to that one."

Nate approached the microphone tentatively, afraid of getting too close. "As to eyewitnesses, we have someone who can place the suspect at the scene, which led to our taking the suspect into custody."

An eyewitness? Who could place Rylee *at the scene*?

Logan's hand shot up. Nate glanced down at him without giving the slightest sign of recognition.

The chief returned to the microphone.

Logan stood, making it all but impossible for him to be ignored and didn't wait for permission to speak. "Sir, when you say 'at the scene' do you mean at the actual house or in the general area?"

No one farther back would have noticed the subtle change in the police chief's expression, but Logan caught the shift. The man had recognized him and had evidently been warned in advance to steer clear of him, yet the slightest hint of relief smoothed his brow. Whatever question he might have feared, it wasn't this one.

"Both," he said, moving on to the next question.

"Following up on that," Logan said loudly, "what exact time does the witness pinpoint?"

Instead of answering, the chief ducked back to confer with the man next to him, and then they pulled in a third officer. The ensuing silence was filled with clicking shutters.

At the far side of the platform, Nate fixed Logan with an incendiary glare.

"For the moment," the chief said, returning to the microphone, "we are not making a statement as to the specifics of the eyewitness testimony."

The other reporters continued to fire off one question after another. The chief bobbed and weaved, finally shutting the whole thing down.

The only person Logan remembered running into last night was the other dogwalker. And if she recognized Toro as belonging to the Davidsons, then the police could place Rylee and him at Toro's house in the wee hours of the morning.

⌒

Passing by Lacey's open door, Logan tried to time his movements just right. Unfortunately she caught a glimmer of motion and called him inside. After peppering him with questions about the press conference, and frowning over his notes, she offered to call Ann Davidson herself, confirming once again just how well-connected she was in these parts.

"And another thing. A little bird informed me that relations between you and law enforcement have become strained."

He didn't answer.

"At the risk of stating the obvious, let me just remind you that in our line of work, we rely on certain relationships. If we take care of people, they'll take care of us. How are you going to cover the crime desk if nobody in the police department will pick up the phone for you anymore?"

"It's not as bad as all that."

She tapped a pencil on her armrest. "My little bird also said you and the dogwalker are an item. Is that correct?"

"You're a regular St. Francis. I wish the birds would talk to me."

"I am not amused, Logan." She leaned forward. "Look, all I want from you—all I've ever wanted—is for you to do the job. Simple as that. Instead, you're losing all semblance of detachment. You're working on this book of yours on my time, you're dragging Wash Tillman down with you, and to make matters worse, you're dating the prime suspect."

"Lacey, I don't think you're being—"

She silenced him with a raised finger. "I'm not finished. Consider this your probation. I'm giving you a week. If I don't see a change, then you're going to pack up your desk and go. Do you understand me?"

He stared at her. Dumbstruck. He'd been with the *Post & Courier* for six years. He'd battled his way up the ranks with painstaking resolve. He'd given this paper way more hours than they'd ever compensated him for. He'd earned his position as a feature, front-page journalist with long hours, sleepless nights, and non-existent vacations.

And she was going to put him on probation? *Probation?*

"You can't be serious."

"Do I look like I'm joking?"

Anger surged through him, but his respect for Lacey kept him civil. "What kind of change is it, exactly, that you expect to see?"

She ticked her points off one by one. "No more chasing after the book. No more chasing after the girl. No more 'borrowing' Wash for hours at a time. And I want you covering the story, not interfering with it. Are we clear?"

"There's nothing in my contract that says the paper can dictate my love life."

"You're inserting yourself into the story. That's a breach—"

"She didn't do it."

"Give me a break, Logan."

"I mean it. They've got the wrong person."

"How do you know? Were you with her when the crime took place?"

He didn't answer.

She slowly straightened. "Tell me you weren't with her."

"We went out last night. Fell asleep in my car at about three thirty in the morning. When I woke at seven, she was gone. But her car was right next to mine. There is no way she could have gotten into it, started it, gone and done the crime, come back, parked, and gone up to her apartment all without me hearing and waking up. No possible way."

"You slept with her in your *car?*"

"Not the way you mean, but yes. And she didn't do it. I'm not turning my back on her, Lacey. I mean it."

"Then you're off the story."

He shot to his feet. "No."

"Yes."

"*No.*"

She lifted a brow.

"Think about it. This is the scoop of a lifetime." He pointed in the general direction of police headquarters. "They have the wrong person. What if we find the real one and splash him on the front page?"

"Would you just listen to yourself?"

"I'm being serious. I *know* Rylee didn't do it, Lacey. You've got to let me finish this."

She swiveled her chair back and forth. "And the book? Wash? Are we clear on those two points, at least?"

He nodded once.

"Say it out loud."

"We're clear on Wash and the book."

She stared at him for a long moment. As stern as she could be, the two of them went way back. This couldn't be easy for her. "Don't make me regret this, Woods."

He slowly released his breath. "You won't, Lacey. I give you my word."

She shooed him with her hand. "Then get. Before I change my mind."

Chapter Twenty

Her jail cell was full of surprises. For one thing, there were no bars. Instead, they locked her behind a door thick as an airplane hatch with a square window to look through, the heavy glass panes pancaked around what looked like industrial-strength chicken wire. The view was gummed up by encrusted filth she wasn't about to try wiping away.

The first hour or so, she perched gingerly on the edge of the bed, which was molded into the far wall, all the corners rounded off. A niche half screened from the window contained a metal toilet and sink, and above that a dented and scratched metal sheet served as a funhouse mirror.

Everything—the bed, the toilet, even the part where the floor joined the wall—had a molded, all-in-one quality, reminding her of a jetliner restroom. Every edge rounded, every surface gritty to the touch.

Whoever did the cleaning wasn't too fastidious. She kept skin contact to an absolute minimum.

If only she could have insulated her mind so easily. As unexpected as the physical details of the lockup were, isolation was the killer. They'd taken no statements, put her through no hostile interrogations. From the moment the cuffs were on, she'd been treated like an inanimate object. Transported in the back of a police car, photographed, fingerprinted, searched, stripped of her belt and shoelaces, and finally stuffed away and forgotten.

The officers in charge of the process ignored her. No one asked for her side of the story. In fact, after Detective Campbell had read her Miranda rights, she'd hardly been spoken to at all.

The woman who'd rolled her fingertips on the input screen—no ink necessary, to Rylee's surprise—kept up a running dialogue the whole time with the man behind the processing counter, discussing their plans for the weekend as if Rylee wasn't there. It didn't matter whether she was an axe murderer or an innocent, everybody was treated the same.

The injustice of the arrest stung her. She wanted to set the record straight. Every time she'd changed hands, passing from one set of officers to the next, she wanted to shake them. Tell them they had the wrong person. She'd been in the Davidsons' house around one in the morning and everything had been fine. She put Toro in his crate, locked the door, and left. The real Robin Hood burglar had come after that.

She wanted to tell them that and more, but she'd never been given the opportunity. Meanwhile, Karl's warning from the last time she'd been questioned rang loudly in her ears.

If any officer of the law wants to talk to you ever again, promise me you won't say a word until you've spoken to me first. Even if he has a warrant.

"Don't I get a phone call?" she'd asked the fingerprint woman, the one charged with escorting her to the cell door. Should she call Logan and see if he'd talked to Karl? Or should she call Karl directly?

It's not Karl you want. Grant Sebastian can get the devil to dance in a courtroom.

She wondered where Mr. Sebastian was. What would he do if she tracked him down? Did she dare to ask him to interrupt his honeymoon on her behalf?

Then she realized she wouldn't be calling any of them. Not without her cell phone. She didn't know their numbers by heart. It would have to be Liz, then, since she'd memorized that one.

The woman gestured her across the threshold, then pulled the hatch until the lock thunked into place. A very permanent-sounding *thunk*.

"Sit tight here for just a minute," she said, her voice muffled through the door.

The minute turned into an hour, and then several hours. Either they'd forgotten about her call, or they never had any intention of letting her make it. She curled on the bed, wrapping her arms around her legs.

She needed to tell Logan about the intruder in her apartment. Was her stalker and Robin Hood one-and-the-same? Had the guy known in advance she wasn't going to be in her apartment the night before nor at the Davidsons' early in the morning? It couldn't all be a coincidence.

She shivered, longing to take a shower. Or better, a hot bath. To clean the filth of the cell from her body, to relax, and ultimately to forget. But that wasn't going to happen. Not anytime soon at least.

Locked in long enough with her frustration, it finally turned on her. Instead of the overeager police and their poster boy Nate Campbell, instead of the anonymous burglar-turned-stalker who'd made sure she ended up here, she began to blame herself.

She could have been less antagonistic with Detective Campbell. She could have put a bolt on her door like Logan had suggested. She could've told someone about the person stalking her at night.

But, no. She was in this impersonal, unsanitary, completely dehumanizing cell. Alone, locked up, abandoned. The story of her life.

She didn't usually dwell on her father's disappearance. Instead, she stuffed it into a little box deep inside, put the lid on, and then sat on the lid.

But now, in desperate need of help, she was too exhausted to fight the rising waves of resentment. She thought about him, relaxing on a beach somewhere with a different name and a different life. A new family, perhaps. Completely oblivious to her existence. Ignorant of what was happening to her.

She rested her head on her knees, a fleeting image of her parents flashing through her mind. A steamy day at dusk. The three of them holding down a blanket on a patch of green grass, sweating in their tank tops while a band on a temporary platform played songs for the setting sun. Mama getting up to dance, pulling little Rylee with her, the hem of her mother's swishing skirt skimming her daughter's bare arms.

Then, a stark, cold casket with a spray of blood-red carnations. Nonie trying to explain Mama was gone. Just like Daddy. Except he wasn't dead. He'd simply left.

It wasn't your fault, darling. Nonie had told her that over and over. But even at five the reassurance rang hollow. If they'd loved her, truly loved her, her daddy would have stayed. And her mama wouldn't have swallowed all those pills. If her own parents couldn't love her enough to stay, how could anyone else?

She thought of Logan. The feelings he stirred within her. The feelings she'd been afraid to have, because she knew they wouldn't, couldn't be reciprocated.

Don't worry. I won't let anything happen to you.

You can't make a promise like that.

His voice was firm. *I just did. And I meant it.*

An impossible vow. A vow that no one could keep. Unless they were God.

God. She scoffed. Even He was gone. She couldn't remember the last time she'd felt His presence. Not here. Not anywhere.

But as she sat in that desolate, barren room, she knew whose fault that was. She might go to church and read her Bible, but she was just going through the motions. On the inside, she'd quit. Quit spending time with Him. Quit telling Him her secrets. Quit saying her prayers.

Oh, she'd fling up a plea for help now and then. But she hadn't talked—really talked—to Him in a long, long time.

She wondered why. Tried to remember some specific moment that she'd walked out on Him and couldn't. It had been more a gradual thing. She had errands to run. Work to do. She was tired. Or hungry. Or not in the mood.

The realization that she'd done to God, the creator of the universe, the very thing her parents had done to her made her sick to her stomach.

I'm sorry, Lord. It wasn't you. It wasn't anything you did . . .

She stilled. It wasn't anything *He* did. *He* wasn't unworthy. *He* wasn't unlovable. *She'd* been the one to just . . . walk away.

The multitude of reassurances Nonie had given her over the years flooded back.

It wasn't your fault, honey. . . . You didn't do anything. . . . They loved you. . . . Adored you . . . You were the apple of their eye.

All the things Rylee was going to say to God just now. All of them true.

She slowly unfolded her body. Could it be? Could it be that it wasn't her—any more than it had been God? That her parents had loved her, adored her, thought the world of her, but they became so inwardly focused they lost sight of what was most important?

Tears clogged her throat. She struggled to take a breath.

Is it true, Lord? Am I worthy of love?

And in the quiet of that dank, filthy cell, she experienced one of the most beautiful moments of her life. A sense of peace, love, and acceptance filled the room. Filled her.

She thought of Christ in that dark, dank, awful tomb, shrouded from head to toe in burial cloths. Ridiculed by His hometown. Betrayed by His best friend. Crucified by those He held dear.

And she knew. If anyone had a right to feel abandoned, He did. Yet He rose. He rose from that grave and changed the world forever.

She dropped to her knees, tears coursing down her cheeks.

I'm sorry. I didn't mean it. I want you back. Will you have me back?

But she didn't need to ask. She already knew the answer. When a sheep returns to the fold, He's happier about that one sheep than about the other ninety-nine who never wandered off in the first place.

≈

The men who came for her must have been detectives, since they were wearing regular clothes. Leaving the jail cells behind, they took an elevator upward, emerging in a part of the station that looked more or less like an office building.

She grew self-conscious about her shackles, but no one they passed in the hallway gave them a second look. The men escorted her through a maze of cubicles, then through a door marked INTER-VIEW #2, outfitted with a table tucked into the corner, a couple of chairs, and a stack of yellow legal pads.

They left her to wait.

Instead of a two-way mirror like on television, the room had a video camera mounted in the corner opposite the table. She yanked on the hem of her cutoffs, wishing for the umpteenth time she'd worn something different this morning.

The red light underneath the camera flicked on. A second later, the door opened.

Detective Campbell walked inside, a thick manila folder under his arm. The door shut behind him with a *click*. "Hello, Rylee."

The last time he'd used her first name, she'd grabbed his tape recorder to correct him, then practically slung it back in his face. Was he remembering that as well?

The back of her chair was to the wall, her elbow propped on the table. Campbell set his folder down, then scooted his own chair to the table's edge. There was nothing between them.

She withdrew her elbow, shrinking back into her personal space. "I'm supposed to get a phone call."

He reached for one of the legal pads, removed a silver pen from inside his jacket, then scribbled a notation, keeping the pad tilted on his lap so she couldn't see. "Now then. We've spoken to the victims of this most recent break-in. We've taken fiber samples from the scene. Evidence is being analyzed this minute by a team of experts. I have to be honest with you." He frowned with concern. "Things don't look very good for you."

The anger he once provoked didn't rise this time. Her sense of calm stayed with her. But that didn't mean she was unaware of her rights.

"I'm supposed to get a phone call."

"Rylee—" Using her name yet again. "I don't think you fully appreciate the gravity of your situation. This goes beyond simple theft. The Davidson home was maliciously ransacked. You won't get a lot of sympathy in front of a South Carolina jury. If you want to have any chance at all, you're going to have to cooperate fully."

At the mention of the Davidsons, Rylee's heart sank.

They pick up strays, she liked to say about them.

And she meant herself—the orphan dogwalker. Then there was Maria, the housecleaner, who bunked in a sober-living facility in North Charleston. The handyman, Ricks, tall and gaunt with a beard like Moses, had been living in his station wagon when Mr. Davidson gave him the job. Now he had a truck with his name on the door and another guy working for him. And of course, George— the ex-con gardener. Even Toro was a rescue dog.

"Ordinarily," Campbell continued, "I wouldn't give someone in your position an opportunity like this. But taking into account your relationship with Logan Woods, who happens to be a friend of mine—"

She couldn't hold back a derisive snort.

"—I'm going to make an exception. This is your chance to tell your side of the story. In fact, it might be the last chance you get. So I want you to take a moment, collect your thoughts, and then tell me what happened this morning."

She took a moment, collected her thoughts, then kept her mouth shut.

"Are you sure that's how you want to play this?" He made another note on the pad. "I know what you're thinking. Maybe the Davidsons won't press charges. Maybe you can sweet-talk your way around a jury. Maybe you can bat those big eyes and make it all go away. But you can't."

The words didn't reach her. "I have the right to an attorney."

"Yes, you do." He wobbled his hands like a scale, weighing the wisdom of her choice. "And if you choose to exercise that right, you won't have a word to say until you're in front of the judge. In fact, even then, you can keep your mouth shut and let your lawyer do the talking. But in the meantime, think about what's going to happen. Everybody in this town, everybody you know, they're all going to hear one side of the story, and draw their conclusions based on that.

By the time your case comes to trial, you won't have a friend—or a client—left in all of Charleston."

She gazed up at the camera, and the red light stared back at her, never blinking. In a nearby room, she knew someone was watching. Campbell's fellow detectives, maybe his superiors. All the mind games were for their benefit. Surely he realized she would never trust him.

"Rylee." His voice hardened. "What was the point of stealing these things? You had your pick, and you went for some relatively worthless items. Did they have some special value? Did they symbolize something to you? Were you trying to send a message?"

She almost felt friendly toward the light, a fellow observer, both of them keeping quiet under Campbell's interrogation.

"I understand why you're angry, Rylee. And why shouldn't you be? After all, you should be the one living south of Broad. The one having your own dogs walked. Not the other way around. I imagine that's a pretty bitter pill to swallow day after day."

She looked at him sharply. A bitter pill to swallow? He knew about her mother's death. Either he was wildly insensitive, or simply cruel. Either way, she wanted nothing to do with him.

"I want my lawyer, Detective. You can sit there and tell me all the lies you want, but I'm not going to say a word until Mr. Sebastian is here."

"Are you certain about that?" He raised his eyebrows, a final entreaty, baffled that she would decline his generous offer of self-incrimination.

Before she could answer, the door opened and an older man entered, one she recognized from the crime scene.

Campbell stood immediately, a deferential tension stiffening his limbs. "Sir—"

"You're done here," the older man said. "Time to wrap it up. Sebastian's outside waiting."

Rylee could have cheered. The boss left the room without closing the door. Campbell deflated. Without a word to her, without so much as glancing her way, he ripped the top page off the legal pad, tucking it into the manila folder, then tossed the yellow pad back to the table.

She willed him to make eye contact, so he could see she wasn't cowed, but he walked into the hallway without giving any sign he was aware of her steadfastness.

Karl slipped through the door as soon as he'd left.

She got to her feet. "Thank you so much for coming. I was wondering if—"

"You haven't said anything, right?" He grazed her arm with his knuckles.

"Not a thing," she said. "Listen, where is your dad now? Do you have a way to get in touch with him?"

He blinked. "My dad? He's in New York waiting for his connecting flight to Charleston. Why?"

"Oh, Karl." Moisture rushed to her eyes. "Are you saying he's on his way home? Right now? Today?"

He gave a nod.

She squeezed his arm. "Would you do me a favor? Would you give him a call? Ask him if he'll represent me?"

He took a step back, breaking the contact. "You want *him* to represent you?"

"Of course. If he doesn't mind, that is. I mean, you know what people say, he can make the devil dance in a courtroom."

"I hadn't heard that, actually." Smiling tightly, he glanced over his shoulder. "Listen, we can't talk here, but I'll do what I can." He looked her up and down. "We have an appointment in front of the judge, so you'll be transferred over to the courthouse late today—unless, of course, you'd rather wait until my dad gets back, but that might mean an overnight stay."

"No, no. Today would be wonderful."

"Fine. We'll talk before then. In the meantime, keep your mouth shut and don't say anything to anyone."

Chapter Twenty-One

Amid the wreckage of her front parlor, Ann Davidson stood tall and elegant, dressed in wide-cut cream flannel pants and a blouse of blue silk to match her eyes. Eyes that held evidence of recently shed tears.

According to Rylee, she was in her early fifties, but her prematurely frost-white hair made her seem much older, and at the same time ageless. Her manners echoed another era, too.

Logan had left his tape recorder in his pocket, opting for the notebook instead. Glancing down, he underlined his final question. "Last, I was wondering if you'd been able to determine if the intruder actually took anything?"

She looked around the devastated room—Nate had not exaggerated in comparing the damage to that of a hurricane—then gave an eloquent shrug. "The police wanted to know that same thing. I wish I could tell."

The chairs had been set right, the sofa cushions put back in their place. But their feet still crunched on a fine rubble of glass, porcelain, the odd splinter of a gilt picture frame. Lampshades lay beside broken lamps, pieces of bulb still jagged in their sockets.

The dining room was much the same. The chairs pounded to pieces on the tabletop, leaving deep gashes in the waxed wood. Over the mantel, the round mirror was shattered. Though the grim-beaked Federal eagle perched atop the mirror had witnessed everything, he wasn't talking.

Mitch Davidson, plump around the middle but with a granite jaw, had loosened his tie and rolled up his sleeves, taking a dustpan to the kitchen. Shards of china and saber-toothed glass covered every surface, blinking in the midday sun filtering through the windows. The police, he'd said, had carried away a bucketful in the hope of retrieving fingerprints, and in the process they'd ground plenty more into the carpets.

"I can't fathom all this," he'd confessed to Logan. "Where did all this glass come from? I never would have imagined there was so much."

Wash came through from the dining room, clearing his throat.

Mrs. Davidson turned. "Have you gotten what you need, Mr. Tillman?"

"I have, ma'am."

He's ma'aming her, too, Logan thought. *You can't help doing it.*

"There's just one thing," Wash said. "If I could take one of you and Mr. Davidson . . ."

Logan winced. "Waaash."

But Ann Davidson nodded her consent. "I think that would be appropriate. A portrait. Though I prefer oil over photographs—no offense, Mr. Tillman."

"I understand."

She turned to Logan. "Do you know much about local painters, Mr. Woods?"

"No, ma'am, I'm afraid not."

She looked confused. "You say you don't? Well, you'll have heard of Charles Fraser at any rate."

He gave an apologetic shrug.

"No?" She stood with one hand on her hip, the other pressed permanently to her neckline in exasperation, fingering her pearls like a rosary. "And you say you grew up around here?"

"James Island, ma'am."

"That's the saddest thing." She spoke in a whisper, shaking her head. "Well, Charles Fraser was famous for miniature portraits, among other things."

She glided past Wash, summoning her husband. He emerged through the kitchen door with his tie flipped over the shoulder, holding the dustpan upright, American Gothic style.

"That's . . . perfect," Wash sighed.

He arranged them at the mantel, the shattered mirror at their backs. As the shutter clicked, the eagle gazed down, impassive.

Mr. Davidson started back toward the kitchen, but his wife reached out.

"Wait." Something was on the tip of her tongue. Her hand fingered the pearls. The men waited quietly for her thought to form. "That must be it."

"What?" her husband asked.

"Charles Fraser." She went back into the parlor, leading him by the hand. Logan and Wash followed. "Help me look."

The couple picked through the detritus, propping pictures against the wall, smoothing canvases on collapsed frames.

"It's a little city scene," she said. "Delicately painted crepe myrtles and live oaks. Whitewashed buildings rising out of the greenery. A reflection on the water—it's very prettily done."

Logan knelt behind the sofa, drawing a large, face-down picture from underneath. He turned it over and found one of those funny children's portraits, where the kid looks like a miniature adult, done up in taffeta and lace.

"Oh no," Mrs. Davidson told him. "The one I'm thinking of is quite small, no bigger than a paperback book." She bracketed the air with her fingers to show him.

"Like this?"

They all turned. Wash held up a Charleston street scene in watercolor.

She smiled. "Like that, yes. But the one in your hands is nothing special, I'm afraid."

"The Fraser is?" Logan asked.

"Oh yes," she said, her eyes troubled. "And no, I don't think it's here."

"So that's it." Mr. Davidson wiped his hands on his pant leg. "I'll give the police a call."

He left the room with a sense of determination, a man never happy without a specific task to perform.

Logan watched him go with a twinge of admiration, then turned to his wife. "Could you tell me something more about the missing painting?"

"I can do better than that," she said. "I'll show you."

Logan and Wash exchanged a baffled look. They went back into the dining room, then through an alcove into a large family room at the back of the house. Robin Hood hadn't made it this far. The room seemed eerily pristine. Through the windows, Logan noticed a lap pool sparkling in the sun, hedged in with slate. Beyond that, a stone fountain—the source of the splashing he'd heard through the bushes earlier.

Mrs. Davidson retrieved an oversized book from the coffee table, handing it to Logan. "The page is marked."

He opened the volume to the indicated section. To his eyes, the little landscape reproduced on the glossy page was no big deal. The same kind of thing graced the postcard rack of many a tourist trap. But he was no connoisseur of art. He nodded at the picture in what he hoped looked like critical appreciation.

"Could I borrow this?" he asked.

"Not that copy," she replied, winging it lightly out of his grasp. "It's inscribed. But you can get one at the Historic Foundation bookstore." She returned the book to its place of honor. "Come to think of it, they have a number of titles that might prove beneficial. For your general information."

His phone vibrated. It was a text from Lacey.

Bail hearing in thirty.

He handed Mrs. Davidson one of his cards. "Thank you so much for your time. And one last thing . . . Is Toro all right?"

She smiled. "He's fine. He was in his crate when all this happened. Rylee must have put him in it last night when she walked him."

He hesitated, surprised she spoke about Rylee with affection. Maybe she didn't believe Rylee did this any more than he did.

He'd planned to feel her out at the end of the interview, but he didn't want to be rushed. And right now, he needed to get to the bail hearing.

Later, though. He'd definitely follow up later.

~

After the long hours of isolation, the packed courtroom was at first a pleasant change. The hum of conversation, the quiet roar of the twittering crowd. It was a relief not to be alone.

Then she registered all the cameras and grew conscious again of her manacles, her cutoffs. Heat rushed to her cheeks. She kept her eyes on the ground.

She passed down the aisle, a bailiff guiding her by the arm. The photographers in attendance called her name. "Rylee, this way. . . .

Look over here, Rylee. . . . Give us a smile, Rylee. . . . Rylee, did you do it . . . ? How do you feel?"

She was pelted by words the way a bride is with rice, only she was heading to the seat of judgment, not to a happily ever after.

"Rylee."

One voice among the many registered. She turned to her left, and there was Logan, half standing in a chair on the aisle, his hand extended. The bailiff moved between them, leading her toward the defense table. She couldn't reach out to him except with her eyes.

When the cuffs were removed and she was seated, she turned in her chair to look at him. He smiled uncertainly, his balled fist telling her to stay strong. He mouthed words that she couldn't make out but that comforted her anyway.

"All rise," the bailiff said.

Everyone stood. She faced the black-robed judge, the man who would decide her immediate fate.

Five minutes had barely passed when the surreal charges—grand larceny and criminal trespass—ended with a very concrete number indeed. Setting bail at fifty thousand dollars, the judge gaveled the hearing to a conclusion, setting off a chain reaction of flash photography in the gallery.

She remained still in the sea of reaction, stunned by the number.

Karl leaned close, his eyes holding none of the warmth she'd been accustomed to receiving from him. "A bail bondsman will require ten percent. Do you have five thousand dollars, Rylee?"

She stared so hard her eyes burned. She had it, but that money was for Nonie's bills. Money she couldn't afford to squander. She bit her cheeks to hold the tears at bay. She'd have to stay in jail until her trial. She had no other choice.

"I don't," she whispered.

The bailiffs moved to escort her out. She stood, trying to hold herself together long enough to exit the room. Just before she passed through the doorway, she glanced over her shoulder. Logan stood in the front row, gripping the railing. Their eyes met.

Don't worry, he mouthed.

The bailiff nudged her across the threshold. The door slammed firmly behind her.

Chapter Twenty-Two

Five grand. The figure took Logan aback. No way would Rylee have money like that at her fingertips. At his salary, given his spending habits, he didn't, either.

But his father did. All he'd have to do was work up the nerve to ask.

He wove his way through the departing crowd, turning his phone on once he reached the courthouse steps.

After a half-dozen rings, his mom finally picked up. "Hi, sweetheart. I have some brisket marinating. You wanna come over for dinner?"

He glanced at his watch. "Dinner? Actually, brisket sounds really good, but I have plans tonight. Can I take a rain check?"

"Of course. You are still coming to church, though, right?"

"Yes, ma'am," he said, trying to keep the anxiety out of his voice. "Eighth row from the front. I'll be there. But, hey, is Dad around?"

"He's right here grabbing for the phone. Hang on."

"Son? I was just watching the local news. They're saying they caught the Robin Hood burglar and it's a woman."

"They've charged a woman, yes. But she didn't do it." He unlocked his car and slipped into the seat.

"How do you know?"

He took a deep breath. "I was with her."

"The Robin Hood burglar!"

"Like I told you, she didn't do it."

He heard a door open and close. He pictured his dad moving to his outside sanctuary on the deck. The place he went when he didn't want to be overheard.

"You'd better start from the beginning," he said.

Driving out to his folks' place on James Island, Logan told the whole story, from his scamper up the Confederate Memorial to the scene outside the Davidson house this morning and the court hearing. He didn't gloss over the fact that he'd spent the night outside Rylee's apartment, but he didn't go into details, either. By the time he finished, he was on the island and only a few minutes from the house.

"You slept with this girl in your car?"

"You're missing the big picture," Logan said. "And anyway, we were just sleeping."

"What were you thinking? Do you have any idea how that's gonna look to people?"

"I know how it looks, but you believe me, don't you?"

A pause. "Of course I do. But it's not me you're going to have to convince." He could imagine his dad on the deck, peering through the glass doors into the kitchen, where his mom was busy preparing dinner. Always a mind reader, Dad added, "I don't just mean your mother, either. Are you gonna go in front of a judge and say, 'Your Honor, she was with me, but don't worry—nothing happened'?"

"At the time, I wasn't expecting to be her alibi."

"No," Dad said. "It's funny how private things have a way of not staying private."

Logan pulled into the driveway and killed the ignition. He cut around the side of the house, letting himself through the gate. He found his dad sitting in one of the teak outdoor chairs, the portable phone still in his hand.

"Have a seat," he said.

Settling in, Logan leaned forward, resting his elbows on his knees and clasping his hands together. "Here's the thing, Dad. About this girl. She's . . . special. Forget about the burglaries, the police, the story, whatever. There's something about her. . . ."

"What are you trying to say?"

"Just that . . ." He struggled for the right words. "I like her, Dad. Only it's a lot more than liking. She's beautiful, yes, but she's more than that. There's a depth to her. The way she cares about people—"

Dad's eyes narrowed. "Are you saying you think she might be the one?"

"I don't know what I'm saying. But yeah, I think there's a chance she is."

"Even if she's mixed up in this Robin Hood case? Because you don't know with one hundred percent certainty that she didn't do it. If what you said is true, she could have left you in the car and had plenty of time to break into that house."

He shook his head. "I *do* know. I just can't prove it."

It was a lot for Dad to take on board all at once. He pinched the bridge of his nose in thought. "Do you think . . . Son, is there any way this girl could be manipulating you? Using you to hide her involvement, I mean? The way she made a point of bringing you to the house last night, maybe she wanted you to be her alibi."

"If you knew her, you wouldn't be saying that."

"Maybe. Maybe not."

"The thing is . . ." Rubbing his hands on his jeans, Logan took a deep breath. "I need some money, Dad."

His eyebrows shot up. "Money?"

"Yeah. About five thousand dollars."

"That's a mighty big chunk a change." Dad templed his fingers over his belly, fixing Logan with a skeptical gaze. "Can I ask what it's for?"

"Bail."

The splash of the water feature over Logan's shoulder underscored the awkward silence between the father and son.

"Why you?" Dad asked finally. "I know you like her, but paying her bail? In my day we never did that kind of thing after only one date." He frowned. "Seriously, why isn't her family bailing her out?"

"She's an orphan. Her only relation is her grandmother, who's not all there mentally. She lives at Bishop Gadsden. Neither of them have money."

"That's a pretty pricey place."

He looked down at his shoes. "That's where all her money goes, I think. She lives out on Fleming Street, Dad."

His father studied him. "And your editor? How's she gonna feel about you getting involved in the story like this? I thought there were rules about that sort of thing."

Standing, Logan walked to the edge of the deck. "Please, Dad. I'll pay you back."

After a long moment, his dad stood. "Let me get online and move some money around, then I'll write you a check."

Logan slid his eyes shut. "Thank you."

⁓

Logan parked on Chalmers Street, then rounded the corner on foot, heading for the People's Building, the city's original skyscraper dating from the early 1900s. The first building in town with an elevator. All office space and high-priced condos now.

He'd browsed in the ground floor of Martin Gallery before but never ascended higher to the mezzanine level, where the offices of Sebastian, Lynch, & Orton LLP were located.

In the lobby, he looked at the check again. Since he couldn't be sure of finding a bank open, he'd asked his dad to make it out directly to the firm. He took the stairs, hoping Karl would be there.

Behind a pair of thick oak doors, he found himself facing a sleek, horseshoe-shaped reception desk, a grouping of tufted leather settees in the corner and an office devoid of life. He glanced at his watch. Six o'clock.

He made his way across the marble-floored lobby and into the bowels of the office. Halfway down the hall, a door stood open, the name KARL SEBASTIAN on the plate. Peering inside, Logan was pleased to observe a tiny slice of office, hardly bigger than his own cubicle.

Tapping on the door, he pushed it the rest of the way open and stepped inside. Nobody home.

"Sir?"

Logan whipped around.

A lanky guy in bike shorts and a canvas messenger bag handed him a brown padded mailer. "This is for you."

Logan took the package without thinking. "Thanks."

He turned it over. No addressee. No return label. No markings whatsoever. Before he could ask who the mailer was from, the courier was gone.

Logan glanced at Sebastian's desk, willed himself to deposit the package there, but his curiosity got the better of him. He worked his finger under the padded envelope's flap and tore it open. An old, dried-leather dog collar tumbled out. He picked it up off the carpet. It was well worn, studded with dainty turquoise rivets. The name on the tag read *Butterscotch*.

I don't get it. He looked inside for some accompanying explanation. A slip of paper rested at the bottom of the envelope. He slid it free. In block letters, the sheet held just two words.

YOU'RE MINE.

His heart rate picked up. What was this? The sharp, heavy writing dug into the paper, as if the author had been angry enough to go over the words many times.

Was this some kind of threat? All he could think was that Butterscotch belonged to one of Rylee's clients—only the collar seemed so old.

"Where did you get that?"

Logan spun around to find Karl at the threshold of the opposite office, his posture rigid, a sheaf of papers under his arm.

Logan shrugged. "Some guy just handed it to me."

The lawyer snatched the collar, then took the note, too. "Well, it's mine."

Everything about Karl—the fit of his suit, his antiqued leather shoes, his too-perfect tan, and especially the fact that Rylee catered to him—irritated Logan. His rudeness was icing on the cake.

Logan smiled. "He said it was for me."

"Obviously a mistake. What are you doing here? This is a private workplace."

Logan didn't appreciate his tone, but he hadn't come here to fight. He might not like the guy, but for Rylee's sake he had to work with him. Fishing in his shirt pocket, Logan withdrew the folded check. "I was bringing you Rylee's bail."

Karl smiled thinly. "I've already posted it. And even if I hadn't, you're the last person I'd let her accept money from. Now get out of this office before I call the police."

Throwing a punch would do no good and plenty of harm. Logan was still tempted. The arrogant, entitled idiot thought he could say and do whatever he liked, and it was about time someone disabused him of the notion.

It couldn't be Logan, though, not now. The important thing was getting Rylee out of jail, and it hardly mattered how that happened. If anything, he should feel relieved, since his dad had written the check grudgingly, sure he was getting his son in deeper when he ought to be getting him out.

"I'll see myself out," Logan said.

"Do that."

"Tell Butterscotch I said hello."

He didn't turn to see the expression on the lawyer's face.

~

You're mine. You are mine. You belong to me. I own you.

Logan turned the words over in his mind, and no matter how they ended up, the menace remained. Someone was threatening Karl Sebastian. Maybe even blackmailing him. Only he couldn't work out why, or what a desiccated dog collar had to do with anything. Maybe Rylee would recognize the name.

He sat at his desk, staring at the legal pad in front of him, where he'd scored the two words into the paper in his best approximation of what he'd seen.

Something buzzed under his desk where he kept Rylee's messenger bag. Lifting the flap, he found her phone, the screen lit to display a new text message. There were three total, all from Liz, who'd also called twice.

He shook his head. After being arrested and plastered on all the news stations, the only person trying to call and check on Rylee was her next-door neighbor. Even her grandmother hadn't bothered.

Of course, the elderly woman probably didn't even know what was going on.

Maybe he should let her know. Would Rylee want that? He thumbed through her contact list, looking for the nursing home's number. Most of the stored names belonged to pets, not clients. To call the Davidsons, Rylee would punch Toro's name. He smiled.

There was an exception, though. Grant Sebastian. His finger paused when he saw the name.

Why not?

He hit the send button.

Grant answered after the first ring, his voice paternal. "Rylee. You've been released, then? Are you all right?"

Logan cleared his throat. "Actually, this is Logan Woods. I'm a friend of Rylee's."

A pause. "Yes. I know who you are, Mr. Woods."

"I was wondering, sir, when you were going to be back in Charleston. Rylee's in hot water, and she could use your help."

"My plane has just touched down in Charleston," Sebastian said, a hint of irritation in his voice. "We haven't even made it to the gate yet."

Logan straightened. "You're back? So I take it you'll be assuming her case?"

"I don't believe this is any of your business, Mr. Woods."

The line went dead. Sebastian had hung up. Suppressing a flare of anger, Logan scrolled through her phone book again. A name caught his eye. But instead of calling, he grabbed his car keys and headed out the door.

In the car, he flipped on the radio. After the tail end of the latest R&B ingénue's hit debut—he'd gotten where he couldn't tell them apart anymore—an evening host started recapping the events of the day. Logan turned up the volume.

"So did you hear?" the host said.

A female radio voice replied, "Hear what?"

"They caught the Robin Hood Burglar this morning, only it turned out to be Maid Marian. The dude was a lady."

"No kidding? I guess sisters are doin' it for themselves."

"And get this, the burglar was actually, like, the neighborhood dogwalker!"

"The dogwalker?"

"You know, the person they hire to walk the dog."

"Huh," the female voice said. "I guess that's what they get for not walking the dog their own self!"

He switched it off.

The sun was on its way down as he made his second trip of the day to James Island. Taking the turn off Camp Road into Bishop Gadsden, he parked outside the Cloister, retracing his steps from the earlier visit.

He told himself Rylee would want him here. As close as her grandmother was, she'd appreciate his reassuring her that everything was fine, even if he wasn't too sure himself.

Or if she didn't know, maybe he should instruct the nurses to make sure she didn't find out. He wasn't certain. All he knew was that being with Flora Monroe would somehow combat his feeling of helplessness. If he couldn't pay Rylee's bail, if he couldn't enlist Grant, if he couldn't find the real Robin Hood, he could at least set her grandmother's mind at rest.

The nurse from last time wasn't on duty. Instead, a kind-faced woman in a floral smock presided. For all her politeness, she wasn't too keen to let Logan pass.

"If you'd like to see Mrs. Monroe, you'll need permission from her granddaughter."

"Rylee's the one who brought me the first time," he said. "I'm here on her behalf."

The woman frowned, reaching for the phone. "Why don't I just call her, then?"

"I guess you haven't heard."

"Heard what?"

"Early this morning, Rylee was arrested. That's why I'm here. She wouldn't want her grandmother to hear about it accidentally and not have anyone to explain."

If he'd have told her he had come from the moon with a special message for earthlings, the nurse couldn't have looked more astonished. "Is this some kind of joke?"

"I wish it was," he said. "Look, there was another nurse here when I visited before. She'll remember me. If you call her, she can verify what I'm saying."

They spent the next five minutes wrangling, but she finally made a phone call and within another ten minutes Nurse Melanie herself appeared, her face filled with concern.

He explained what had happened and then tried to explain why he'd come, though his motives were getting muddier by the moment.

He ran his fingers through his hair. "Maybe I shouldn't even be here. I don't know. I just thought . . . I mean, Mrs. Monroe is the only family Rylee has, and if she somehow got hold of this news . . ."

She made a stop sign of her hand. "Say no more and follow me."

At the door to C5, they paused. In an undertone, Nurse Melanie suggested she enter first, and she'd invite Logan inside if the moment was right. Having no choice, he agreed.

He leaned against the wall, letting his head fall back. This was definitely the wrong move, coming to see a senile old lady he'd only met once before. He'd probably do more harm than good.

Nurse Melanie peered through the door. "Okay. I think she's ready."

When he'd entered before, Mrs. Monroe was sitting upright, anticipating a visit. Now she lay buried in covers almost to the chin, her eyes like dark slits, giving only the slightest sign of following his movements.

He returned to the chair he'd occupied last time, hoping this would heighten her sense of familiarity.

"What is it?" she asked, confused, as if he'd awakened her.

He cleared his throat. "It's Logan Woods, remember? I'm Rylee's . . . friend. From the other night. We stopped by and visited."

Her head craned for a better look. When he stopped talking, she waited, as if for a translation. At the foot of the bed, Nurse Melanie encouraged him with a nod.

"Rylee sent me to tell you . . ."

The old lady blinked.

"She wants you to know . . . everything's fine."

Nurse Melanie shuffled to the door. "I'll leave you two alone a minute."

He wasn't sure that was such a good idea. He almost called after her, but that would have been even more absurd. After campaigning so hard to get into the room, there was no turning back.

Nonie stared at him a moment, then shut her eyes.

Her breathing grew deep and regular. Asleep.

On the nightstand, the stack of photo albums sang to him like a siren. Their leather covers glistened like the skin of the forbidden fruit. He stood, waited, and then moved quietly around the bed. At the far side, he leaned over her, checking to make sure she was asleep. Then he picked up the album on top, opening to the middle.

He couldn't find the photo from the other night. After flipping a few pages, his eyes alighted on a candid shot, a man in a three-piece suit seated in a leather chair, reading a small black book. It wasn't the reader who caught his attention, though.

On the side table behind the man's chair stood a familiar-looking piece of art. A bronze-cast jockey identical to the one that was plucked unnoticed from the Bostick house, later discovered on the steps of First Scots Presbyterian, where Rylee had smothered it with her hands.

Stunned, he turned the page. Nothing revelatory. He continued through the album, stopping on the second-to-last photo.

In the lower corner of the leaf, a sepia-toned boy had a violin propped beneath his chin, bow at the ready. Logan held the album closer, scrutinizing the instrument. He wondered whether the details were clear enough for Jamison Ormsby to tell whether or not this was his Prokop. And though Logan would ask him, he already knew in his heart that it was.

Did Rylee know about these? Of course. She had to. Which meant she hadn't been honest with him. She'd known all along these items were linked to her family somehow, yet she never said a word. He wanted to know why.

"Is she asleep?" Nurse Melanie stood in the doorway, eyebrow raised.

Logan closed the album, tucking it under his arm. "She nodded off before I could explain. So I'd appreciate it if you'd keep her away from any TV or radio." He patted the album. "I'll bring this back when I come check on her again."

Before the nurse could reply, he slipped past her into the hallway. In his hand, the album grew heavy as a stone.

Chapter Twenty-Three

According to the jail's desk clerk, it would be after ten thirty before Rylee would be released. So Logan hit the newsroom, pounding the keyboard like it was his evening workout. His article about her arrest was due within the hour.

He skimmed over the actual arrest, though, focusing instead on the inconsistencies of the investigation. Highlighting what he could about the stolen painting.

A curator at Gibbes Museum hadn't been able to offer much, since the painting was in a private collection. And his calls to Ann Davidson about Rylee as well as the painting's provenance had gone unanswered so far. Meanwhile, he had plenty on the painter, Charles Fraser, to use as filler until he gleaned more specifics.

His phone vibrated in his pocket. He answered without checking the display, thinking Mrs. Davidson was finally returning his call.

"I just read the pages you sent," his agent said. "And this dog-walker character is great. I can't believe all this stuff! The editor went crazy. She wants you to ramp Rylee up a bit, though. Really flesh her out. Give us an intimate look at her background, her fears, what makes her tick."

Logan stilled. He'd e-mailed the raw pages to get Seth off his back, assuming they'd talk before he forwarded anything to Dora. Now, hearing his agent talk about Rylee this way, as if she was just another character in the story, he wanted to take it all back.

"To be honest, Seth . . ." He shifted in his chair. "I was actually going to decrease her role. Maybe take her out completely."

"No, no, no," Seth said. "A beautiful girl is always a good draw, but you've got to play up this Southern Gothic backstory of hers, the victimized girl lashing out at the people living the life that should have been hers, a female Robin Hood. It's fantastic."

Logan cringed. "Where did you hear that? I didn't write that."

"Don't you read your own paper? It's all over the website. Dora's called me twice already."

He fell back in his chair. "Unbelievable."

"What's the matter? This is great. Maybe the national news stations will even pick it up. The bigger the story, the bigger the book deal."

"She didn't do it, Seth. And she's been through a lot. She has no family to speak of. No support system. I'm not about to exploit her further."

Seth took a moment before answering. "Logan, are you, have you . . . What's up with you and this girl?"

And that was the problem with having one of your closest friends as your agent. Not a lot gets by him.

"Talk to me, man."

"I'm not dragging her personal life into this."

Seth laughed. "You're dating her, aren't you? You dog! You're dating the prime suspect. That's not a book proposal, Logan. That's a movie deal."

"No."

"How long have you been seeing her?"

He didn't answer.

"Come on. How many dates?"

One. But it didn't matter. One. A hundred. He wasn't putting her in the book.

"Listen, things like this don't drop in your lap every day, Logan. You should get on your knees and thank the patron saint of publishing. If she's the story, and you're with her, then you're the story. I've got to call Dora with this."

Logan gripped the phone. "Just hold on a second."

"I understand," Seth said. "In terms of the journalism, this is a serious breach of ethics. I'm not going to out you or anything. But once this contract is signed, you won't need to worry about the code of conduct. All your conflicts of interest will be resolved. This girl will be your number-one interest after all."

"The entire book does not hinge on this one girl."

"Maybe last week it didn't, but it does now. And all you have to do is live it, then write it down."

Logan pictured Nonie's photo album. Rylee was somehow connected to the robberies. That much was obvious now. But until he'd spoken to her, he wasn't going to jump to any conclusions—or let anyone else jump to them, either. "No, Seth."

"Why? You can't be in love with her. You haven't known her long enough."

"That doesn't mean I'm willing to take advantage of her. She's a person. With feelings. Who didn't do anything but be in the wrong place at the wrong time."

"Everyone in your book is real. Every single crook you've written about is a person with feelings. Why should she be any different?"

"She's not like them." *I hope.*

Seth groaned. "You're killing me here."

He tried a different tack. "Lacey would have my head. She's already given me an ultimatum. Made it crystal clear that the paper's my first priority. If she finds out otherwise, she'll drop the hammer on me without a second thought."

"You told me you'd make whatever sacrifices were necessary. What's changed, Logan?"

He rubbed his eyes. "Everything."

After hanging up, he took a walk around the newsroom to clear his head, then tried Ann Davidson again. This time, he got through.

"The Fraser?" she said, repeating his question. "Oh, we've had that painting going on twenty years or so. Acquired it from an estate. Well, not directly, of course. It went through a third party."

"A third party?" Trapping the phone between his ear and shoulder, he scribbled some notes. "Do you remember who that was?"

"Grant Sebastian. He handled it all."

Logan froze. "You're kidding."

"Why, no. It came from the home of his former law partner, Jonathan Monroe. Since you know Rylee, I'm sure you're familiar with the family's tragic story. When he left, there was a terrible debt to settle, and Grant stepped in to help. "

He removed the phone from his shoulder. "To help?"

"He didn't have to. He organized everything very discreetly, of course, to protect the family's dignity. If it wasn't for him, I think the Monroes would have lost everything." She paused. "I'm not giving you my permission to use this information. This is strictly off the record, you understand?"

"Of course." Logan was reeling. "So you're saying the painting stolen from your house used to belong to the Monroes? Do the police know that?"

"Not from me they don't. That girl's in a bad enough position as it is."

"So you don't think she's guilty?"

"Let me tell you something, young man. In this country, people are innocent until proven guilty. We trusted her, and until somebody can prove otherwise, I'm going to believe she kept that trust. What happened here would have taken a lot of hate, don't you think? Well, I don't believe Rylee has that in her. Do you?"

"No, ma'am. I don't believe she does." He cleared his throat. "So this private sale, it must have included a lot more than the painting. Do you know if there was a violin, or maybe a bronze statue?"

"I wish I could help you," she replied, though it was clear from her tone she was glad she couldn't. "The truth is, Grant knew about my admiration for Fraser and brought the piece by. I have no idea what else he brokered, or who did the purchasing. Apart from the house, of course—but everybody knows that."

"The house?"

"The Monroe house," she said. "On East Battery."

The photograph from the album came to mind, the familiar-looking façade he couldn't quite place.

"And who bought that?" he asked.

She laughed. "You really do need to brush up on your local history, young man."

"Could you give me a name, ma'am?"

"Grant Sebastian, of course."

~

Logan hunched over in a preformed plastic chair welded to a long series of matching seats, watching the featureless, gray double doors for any sign of movement. From time to time, they'd open to admit an officer or civilian technician, prompting yet another frustrated sigh. If the wheels of justice turned slowly, it seemed the wheels of injustice didn't turn at all.

Grant Sebastian finally pushed through the doors, escorting Rylee by the elbow. Logan jumped up, shaking the stiffness from his legs.

She looked disoriented and pale, as if she'd spent a week locked in a basement only to be thrown out into the light. She gazed at him a few seconds in a daze, before a spark of life touched her eyes.

He stepped forward but couldn't cross into the cordoned-off area, nor could she leave it until the final paperwork had been executed. A woman behind a glass window worked through a series of pointless questions, which Rylee answered without once taking her eyes off Logan.

The moment she'd signed her name to the last document, she flung the pen down and turned toward him. She didn't run to his arms. She flew.

Before he could brace himself, she was there.

"Are you okay? Are you okay?" he kept saying.

He kissed her forehead. Her cheeks. Her nose. Her eyes. Her jaw. Her ears.

She bracketed his face with her hands, and drew his mouth to hers. Her lips were gentle and soft, filled with something unspeakable from deep inside.

"I was so worried," he said. "You're shaking."

"Just get me out of here," she whispered.

Grant appeared beside them holding a limp paper bag. "Is this really all you had, Rylee? What about purse, wallet, keys, money, that kind of thing?"

She stepped from their embrace, glancing into the bag. A coiled belt, a pair of shoelaces, and a paper envelope containing her jewelry.

Logan kept a watchful eye on the lawyer. The man was living in Rylee's ancestral home and brokered the deal for an item—maybe all the items—Robin Hood had stolen.

A few hours ago, he'd wanted nothing more than for Grant to take over the case. Now he wasn't so sure.

"That's it," she said, clipping on the pearl-drop pendant she always wore. "I gave Logan my bag before they brought me in."

Logan forced himself to extend a hand. "Thank you for coming, Grant."

The attorney tucked a sheaf of papers into his litigation bag, then accepted Logan's hand. "I've read many of your articles over the years."

"Yes, sir."

Grant glanced at his watch. "You're taking her home?"

"Yes, sir."

Nodding, he patted Rylee on the shoulder and told her to check in first thing in the morning. Then he was gone.

Logan kept his arm around her as they walked to the car. The balmy night air only heightened the coolness of her skin. She listed back and forth with fatigue.

"Have you had anything to eat?" he asked.

"No."

"How does a Big Mac sound?"

She pushed back her bangs. "I'd rather just go home. Is that okay?"

"You bet." He eased her into the passenger seat, careful that she didn't fall, then went around to the other side. As they pulled onto the empty street, he glanced her way. "Rylee, do you know a dog named Butterscotch?"

She turned her face toward him, leaving her head against the seat. "No. Should I?"

"I just heard Karl mentioning it. Did he or the Sebastians or anyone you know ever have a pet named Butterscotch?"

"Not that I know of. Why?"

He shrugged. "Just wondering."

She let her head loll against the window. "I'm exhausted. But if I fall asleep, you have to stop me. I have too many things to do.

First, I need a shower. Then I need to call my clients. I have to check on Nonie—"

"It's almost midnight, Rylee. Everything but the shower will have to wait until tomorrow. As far as your grandmother goes, though, I already checked on her."

Her eyes grew wide. "You did?"

"Late this afternoon, I went out to Bishop Gadsden. To make sure she hadn't heard. And then to make sure she wouldn't hear."

She reached across the gearshift, cradling his hand. "You really did that?"

"It's no big deal."

"It is." She smiled. "It's a really big deal. . . ."

Leaning over, she kissed him again, a damsel rewarding her knight.

He needed to tell her about the trip to Bishop Gadsden. That he'd taken one of the photo albums and why. He needed to ask her about what Ann Davidson had said, too. But she sank against the window, eyes closed, and he decided it was better to let her sleep.

They drove the rest of the way to her apartment in silence. He listened for her breathing, but the air-conditioner drowned it out.

They paused at a red light, the intersection illuminated by streetlights, and he glanced over to study her gamine profile, the indolent upturn of her nose. The graceful jaw. The long neck. The swell of her chest. The flat waist. The long legs. The fringe around her cutoffs flickering in the A/C.

She'd probably throw the shorts away now, not wanting to be reminded of this day. He looked at her legs again. It was a crying shame.

Reaching the apartment brought memories of their unintentional night together, sleeping side by side in the parked car. This time, he rubbed his knuckles softly against her cheek until her eyes opened.

"Are we here?"

He hoisted her bag from the backseat and came around to open her door. Glancing at the parking lot, he realized they still needed to collect her car, but the errand would have to wait. She wasn't in any condition to drive. Maybe he could phone Wash once she'd settled in and the two of them could make up a convoy.

She got a few paces ahead of him, anxious for home, unsteady as they ascended the stairs. He put his hand out in case she fell.

When she reached her door, she leaned against the wall, eyes closed. "You have the keys."

He dug through the jumble of items in the messenger bag, chasing the sound of clinking metal. Finally, his fingertips hit on the telltale ridges.

He aimed for the lock and missed, but the door cracked open anyway. "Rylee."

"Hmm?" She opened her eyes.

He nudged the door open farther.

"Wait here," he whispered.

Feeling along the wall, he flipped on the lights, then froze.

Some forms of destruction seem random and impersonal. A tornado rips through, leaving carnage in its wake, but inspecting the debris never yields a message from the storm. Nature did what it did but had nothing to say.

The scene in Rylee's apartment was not like that. What he saw spoke. It screamed. And he recognized the voice all too well. Her couch disemboweled, her books scalped of their covers, the shelves upended and some of them snapped in two, as if over a knee.

Every CD case opened, the discs methodically broken. Her DVDs smashed. The kitchen had gotten a good shake, rattling everything, the contents of the fridge still fresh on the linoleum floor. Something viscous and ruby which he hoped was Kool-Aid had dried sticky on the surfaces. Liquid oozed from behind the closed microwave door.

He advanced farther, turning on lights as he went, his body contracting into a crouch.

The rags strewn across the bedroom floor had been clothes once. Now they lay tangled in odd bundles, almost corpse-like, studded with shoes that had gummy scars where their heels had been.

The red dress from their visit to Nonie lay razored across the bed. The sheets themselves had been cut up beyond recognition. A drawer dangled from the nightstand like a cigarette from an ingénue's lips.

He turned, half expecting Rylee to be on his heels. But she stood petrified in the apartment doorway, hands clasped over her mouth, eyes wide. He motioned for her to stay there. He needn't have bothered. She looked like she never planned to move again in her whole life.

The sound of running water came from the bathroom. He approached the pockmarked door, his feet raising water from the carpet. Pushing it open, he peered inside.

The bathtub ran, water pouring over the lip. He sloshed across the vinyl floor and shut off the knobs. The surface of the water stilled.

He saw something floating out of the corner of his eye. He yanked the curtain back.

Near the top of the tub, a soaked bra, striped pink and white, frilled around the edges. Near the middle, the matching thong. As if a woman had been submerged here, and her body dissolved, leaving only her underwear behind.

His gut twisted. Turning around, he recoiled, slipping backward. He grabbed the curtain for support, only to have it and the rod crash to the floor. Cold water spilled onto his shoes and jeans.

The words were inscribed in thick black marker on the toilet lid's underside. The letters emphatically uppercase.

YOU'RE MINE.

Chapter Twenty-Four

Last time he broke in without leaving a trace. Just an unspoken message in the sheets. Now he'd made sure there was no mistake. She stared at the words, not reading but hearing them. An angry snarling shout, the kind that leaves flecks of spit behind.

In spite of the warm draft from the open apartment door, she stood shivering on the bathroom threshold. No matter how tightly she held herself, the tremors wouldn't go. "What does it mean?"

Logan turned at the sound of her voice. "You shouldn't be in here."

His skin was pale as the white plastic tub. She gazed into the water and saw that another message had been left behind.

Her bottom lip trembled. "What does it mean?"

He shook his head. "I don't know."

"Does he think I'm his?" A fit of coughing seized her, threatening to flood her throat.

He reached for the lid, lowering it as carefully as a museum exhibit.

She leaned over to prop her hands on her knees, taking quick, erratic breaths. "Who is this guy? What does he want?" She looked at the water lapping at her feet. Pictured the carnage of her apartment. "It's not my things, obviously . . . because he completely destroyed . . . everything I have in the world."

Suddenly he was before her, his arms around her. And she realized she was shaking. Convulsing with horror. Her throat raw, her eyes burning in the sockets.

She squeezed herself against him, digging her hands into his muscled back, pressing her face into his chest.

She couldn't speak. She could hear a sob in her throat, but couldn't fathom where it was coming from.

He kept saying it was all right, all right—whispering the formula into her ear, a magic spell he kept getting wrong.

Then it all rushed out of her like so much tepid bath water, the emotion spilling onto the floor, leaving her wet and dripping, but also numb.

She slipped out of his arms, not wanting to be touched. In the mirror, the eyes looking back at her were dark and empty and glistening. The skin flushed pink.

He splashed to the side of the tub, staring down. "This I just don't get."

Her hand dipped gull-like through the rippling surface, snatching the bra and thong, balling them in her fist. She ripped them free of the water and, turning, slung them to the far side of the bedroom.

"Rylee." He touched her shoulder gently. "Is it some kind of message?"

"Yeah," she snapped. "It means, 'I'm a sick pervert.' It's the universal symbol."

"Sorry. I just thought—"

"No, I'm sorry. Look. I didn't tell you everything. Remember when he stole those things from my gym bag? That's what he took."

"Ah." He was still treading carefully. "Those exact ones?"

"Not those exact ones. I threw them out. I wasn't going to wear them after . . ." And then she stopped, realizing what she'd just let slip.

"You threw them out? But I thought he took them, that was the whole—"

"He took them," she said. "And last night, he brought them back."

"Last night? While we were on our date?"

"Yes. He broke in and . . . made the bed, and he put them back in the drawer. I was going to put a new deadbolt on today, but before I could, your baseball buddy threw me in jail."

He was silent a long time. Finally he took her by the arm, leading her out of the bathroom, sitting her on the edge of the bed. When he leaned down, she could see how calm and reasonable he was trying to be, from the measured expression to the constraint in his voice. Like he was on the bomb squad and just needed to figure out which of her wires to pull to keep her from exploding.

But she wanted to explode. To kick and claw and spit and curse and—

"We have to call the police," he said.

Wrong wire.

"We have to do *what?*" She jumped to her feet, letting him have it with a glass-shattering voice, a radioactive glare.

He didn't flinch. "What choice is there?"

"You're talking about the people who wanted fifty thousand dollars to let me out of jail? The ones who think I pulverized the Davidsons' house and trashed my own car? What are they gonna do when they get here? Arrest me for vandalizing my own place?"

Breathless, she took in the destruction around her. No, the desecration. The remnants of her life with Nonie at Folly Beach. Pretty much everything she had in the world. In tatters and rags. Torn apart.

And for what? To send some twisted message? A message that was supposed to mean something?

"I'm sorry." He slipped his hand into hers. "We have to call them, Rylee. You don't see what I see. There's no way they're gonna walk in here and think you did this to yourself."

She started to argue, but there was a squeak at the door.

"Rylee?"

It was Liz.

"Tell her I'm in here," she said, pulling her hand from his.

Logan turned, but before he could get a word out, Liz was already rushing through the doorway to the bedroom, her hands glued to her face like that painting of the Scream.

"What happened?"

She didn't wait for an answer. She flung herself at Rylee, wrapping her arms tight. Cooing, shushing, rocking until Rylee again broke into sobs. Straight from the gut.

⌐

They went to Liz's apartment after Logan called the police. Rylee curled up on the futon, wrapped an afghan around her shoulders, and buried her head in her hands. The thought of detectives going through her shredded things was just as repugnant as the monster who'd done the original damage.

Liz hovered like a timid hummingbird. "Can I get you something? You hungry? Or how 'bout a shower? You wanna get cleaned up?"

Rylee got tired of shaking her head. "We need to call Mr. Sebastian. He won't want me talking to the cops without him here."

As she spoke, she looked to Logan, expecting him to fly into action. But he was strangely still.

"What's wrong?"

He ran his fingers through his hair. "I don't know. Nothing, I guess."

She sighed. "Would you rather I call Karl?"

"No." Picking up her phone, he scrolled through it and stepped outside, shutting the door softly behind him.

When the police arrived, she stayed with Liz. At the thought of all the damage, her eyes started to melt again. Liz put an arm around her.

"I'm just glad you weren't home when it happened," Rylee said.

A knock at the door, and a middle-aged lady slipped through. Her short black hair and unflatteringly tight pantsuit meant business. A badge dangled around her neck. She introduced herself, but Rylee missed her name. She expected the woman to be gruff, but instead she spoke to Rylee in the softest of tones.

"Is Detective Campbell going to be here?" Rylee asked.

At the sound of his name, the woman detective gave the thinnest of smiles. "Any minute now."

Rylee nodded, then clasped her hands together. "Don't take this the wrong way, but I've called my lawyer, and I'd prefer not to say anything until he arrives."

The woman nodded. "Under the circumstances, I understand."

After she left, Rylee heard her lecturing another officer out on the walkway.

"You know something?" she was saying. "I don't believe everything I read in the papers or see on TV. I look at the scene. And until the scene tells me otherwise, that girl in there is a victim."

A spark of warmth entered Rylee's heart. She caught Liz's eye. "I like her."

Logan appeared at the door, ushering Grant Sebastian through.

Judging from the lawyer's stricken expression, he'd already looked in on the apartment. "I'm so sorry, Rylee. Are you all right?"

Before he spoke, she'd have bet money all her tears had dried up. But the well turned out to be inexhaustible.

"I'm sorry," she said, dabbing her raw eyes. "Anyway, who's the lady detective?"

Logan jumped in. "Sheila Santos. Nate can't stand the woman."

That's enough for me, Rylee thought.

"You haven't made a statement, have you?" Sebastian asked.

She shook her head.

"Good. Then I'm going to go out there and see if I can learn anything. If you need me, I'll be right outside."

He excused himself, and Logan followed. After several moments, Rylee stood.

"Where are you going?" Liz asked.

"Out there." She paused at the door, reluctant to go.

"Why?"

"Because it occurred to me that all of a sudden I've been letting Logan and Mr. Sebastian handle all my problems for me."

Liz gave a sniffly laugh. "Girl, in the last twenty-four hours you've been arrested, vandalized, and threatened. Under the circumstances, I'd say it's okay to coast a little. So just sit yourself back down and chill."

Rylee compromised by posting herself at the door, listening to the activity outside through the narrow opening. Logan and Sebastian were conversing in hushed tones.

"I spoke with Ann Davidson earlier," Logan said. "She claims her stolen painting was originally acquired through you. That you were selling it for Flora Monroe."

Sucking in her breath, Rylee adjusted the window curtain slightly so she could peer through with one eye.

"It was a confidential transaction. I'm not at liberty to discuss it."

"Well, I have reason to believe that some, maybe all, of the things the Robin Hood burglar has stolen were originally in the Monroe family."

Sebastian's whole face—from his crow's feet to jowls—suddenly collapsed. His body staggered visibly, his hand gripping Logan's bicep for support. "Are you serious about that?"

He nodded.

The old man's voice was little more than a whisper. "What reason do you have?"

"I'm not at liberty to discuss it."

Drawing up to his full height, Sebastian fixed him with a steady glare. "I thought you were on Rylee's side."

Logan stiffened. "I am."

"Then I shouldn't have to tell you how prejudicial the statement you just made could be to her case, assuming it were to be repeated. Your theory would give the police precisely what they lack, a plausible motive. You realize that, don't you?"

"Of course I do."

"Well, if you are on her side, I hope you'll keep that in mind from now on. If you don't, it's Rylee who will suffer. This may be just a story to you, but it's *her* life."

They moved farther down the walkway, taking their conversation with them.

Rylee eased the door closed and flattened a hand against the frame. Pulse pounding in her temples, lungs filling, she could hardly catch her breath.

Liz came over to her. "Are you okay?"

"I don't know."

You were selling it for Flora Monroe. . . .

"Maybe you should sit down. You look—well, never mind how you look."

Some, maybe all, of the things the Robin Hood burglar has stolen were originally in the Monroe family. . . .

She leaned her head against the door. The things Robin Hood had stolen were connected to her? How? And why hadn't Logan said something to her?

This may be just a story to you, but it's her life. . . .

Was it just a story to him? Karl had warned her time and again. But she hadn't believed him. Didn't want to believe him.

Yet, Logan had acted funny when she'd wanted to call Mr. Sebastian and he'd no more gotten her into his car tonight than he began asking her about some dog. Butterscotch. Something was definitely going on. And he was obviously keeping it from her.

"Rylee, I'm serious." Liz pulled her by the wrist. "You need to sit down. I'm going to get you some Tylenol. I guess everything's finally catching up to you."

"Yeah." She allowed Liz to lead her back to the futon. "I think it is."

～

"I'm heading out, my dear." Mr. Sebastian pulled an envelope from inside his jacket and handed it to Rylee. "Now that Amelia and I are back, there's no reason for you to worry with Romeo. I really appreciate you taking care of him while we were gone."

She set the envelope on Liz's table. "It was no trouble. He's a real sweetie. You can call me anytime."

The door opened. She'd expected Logan, but the first one over the threshold was Nate Campbell. Detective Santos followed on his heels, then Logan. The little living room could barely hold them all. They shared an uncomfortable look, uncertain who was going to take the lead.

"Miss Monroe." Campbell had to clear his throat before continuing. "I'm going to have to request a handwriting sample from you."

Logan threw his hands up. "Give us a break, Nate. What, are you blind?"

Santos leaned in the doorway, arms crossed, enjoying the moment.

"My client isn't obligated to give you anything," Mr. Sebastian said. "And under the circumstances, this is starting to look like harassment."

Campbell ignored them both, crouching down to Rylee's eye level. "Listen to me. The best thing you can do is cooperate with my investigation."

"Detective—" Mr. Sebastian began.

Rylee stopped him. "It's all right. I'd give you a diary or a letter or something like that, but it might take too long to reassemble all the confetti. Why don't I just write something for you, and then you can go have it analyzed."

He handed her his notebook and pen. She didn't even hesitate before leaning over the pad to write.

After one look at the sentence, Campbell snapped the notebook shut and walked stiffly out of the apartment.

Before following him, Detective Santos put a card in Rylee's hand. "If you need anything, I want you to call."

"Thanks." She slipped it into her pocket.

Logan watched them go, then closed the door. "What did you write?"

She smiled for the first time since arriving home. " 'Detective Campbell is a doofus with a badge.' "

She took a shower first, then a bath, then another shower. By the time she was finished, her skin had pruned up, but she felt clean. Wonderfully, blessedly clean.

Pulling on a pair of Liz's sweats and a T-shirt, she toweled her hair dry, and padded out to the living room. Liz was nowhere in sight. She'd left to get takeout, but not before insisting that Rylee stay with her as long as necessary.

Logan was asleep on the futon. Her messenger bag lay on the coffee table.

Sitting on the edge of the table, she riffled through the bag for her phone. Dialing her voice mail, she set the phone between her ear and her shoulder, and began to clean her nails.

"Rylee. This is Doug Bostick. I can't begin to tell you how shocked and disappointed I am. You are obviously relieved of all duties. Effective immediately. You can put the keys in the mail."

Beep.

"It's Latisha. . . . I don't even know what to say. Please . . . don't bother coming back. I'm so . . . speechless. I just—"

Beep.

"Rylee. It's . . ."

She put the phone on her lap and let the messages run. She recognized the voices, though she couldn't understand the actual words. But there was no need. She knew what they were saying.

She fished inside her bag for the big ring of color-coded keys. She unclipped one after another, dropping them on top of the growing pile beside her.

"What are you doing?"

She looked up. Logan sat staring at her.

"What does it look like?"

"Looks like you're crying."

"Am I?" She touched her cheek. "So I am."

He pulled away from the futon, scooting forward until his legs formed a bracket on either side of her. He picked up her phone, listened for a minute, then silenced it with a push of a button. "You don't need them."

Oh, but she did. She needed them all, now more than ever. She started to say so, but her lips trembled violently.

He placed his hand over hers, stilling her movements. "Rylee."

She blinked. A tear splashed onto his hand.

He tugged gently until she released the key ring.

"I love them." She looked at him. "They're . . . they're my family."

"The animals?"

She nodded. "And they love me, too."

He pulled her closer, tucking her legs up so he could wrap her completely in his arms.

After a while, once she was breathing normally again and the sharp edge of the voice mails numbed to a dull pain, she slid away. "I heard you on the walkway earlier," she said. "Talking to Mr. Sebastian. You said the things Robin Hood stole belonged to my family. That Mr. Sebastian had sold a painting for Nonie. What was that about?"

"You don't know?"

She pulled back. "Would I be asking if I already knew?"

"We don't have to talk about this now."

"I want to talk about it."

He rubbed her arms. "Tomorrow, okay?"

"Are you keeping something from me, Logan?" She finger-combed her damp hair. "You can't. Don't you see? If I'm going to trust you—and I need to trust you—then you have to trust me, too. You've been acting . . . differently. Ever since . . ." Her lips trembled. "Ever since I was arrested."

He pushed his palms against his eyebrows, willing the conversation away.

"You have to tell me."

He sighed. "All right. Wait here and I'll be right back."

Before she could say anything, he was on his feet, jogging for the door. She heard his footsteps on the walkway, then a distant pounding on the stairs. A car door opened, then closed. More pounding. A moment later, he was back at the door. In his hand was a maroon leather photo album.

It was one of Nonie's. He sat down next to her, flipping through the pages, then handed the book over, marking a spot with his finger. It was a snapshot of her great-grandfather reading a book.

"I don't understand."

He flipped to another page, pointing out a picture of her great-uncle as a boy during one of his music lessons.

She grabbed the album away. "What are you even doing with this?"

"Just look. Are you telling me you've never seen them before?"

"Of course I have." A sick feeling came over her. "Logan, did you take this from Nonie's room? I thought you went there to tell her I was okay."

His face reddened. "I did."

"She would never have let this leave the room."

"Well . . . she was sleeping. I didn't want to disturb her." He wouldn't look her in the eye.

She swallowed. "I don't believe you. This is for your story, isn't it? That's been it all along. The lunch at North of Broad. The visit to Nonie. The beach."

"No, Rylee, I can—"

"Stop." She touched her hand to his mouth. "Just stop talking, all right? You're going to keep lying and it's going to break my heart, so just . . . just shut up. And go." She withdrew her hand. "I'm too tired for this. I'll say things I don't want to say. Just get out."

He didn't budge.

"I'm serious." She clutched the album. "You took this."

"I had to, Rylee. You didn't give me much of a choice, did you?"

She stared at him. Same chocolate eyes. Same unruly hair. Same square jaw. But it was as if she didn't know him at all.

"Just go," she whispered.

"I'm sorry, okay? I shouldn't have done it. But that's not the point. I—"

"It is the point. It's the only point. You stole this from her. You did it behind my back. When I was in jail, no less. So don't sit there and tell me what the point is. You betrayed me. You and everybody else."

He tried to loop his arm around her.

She recoiled.

Her vehemence seemed to shock him into awareness. Did he think he could talk his way out? Not hardly.

He stood. "I am sorry. Just look at the album, okay? Everything's in there."

"Good night, Logan," she said.

At the door, he tried to say something more, the words dying on his lips. He threw it open. She followed, holding the album tight to her breast, making a promise to herself not to cry.

Liz crossed Logan on the walkway, fast food dangling from her hands. She did a half-turn, saying something as they passed. But Logan just sulked his way to the stairs.

"He's leaving?" Liz asked. "I got enough for everybody."

Rylee shut the door. "I'm not hungry."

"Are you sure?"

Without answering, she crossed to Liz's room. "I'm gonna lie down for a few minutes."

Liz frowned. "Okay, honey."

She gently closed the door behind her, then threw herself on the bed.

She buried her face in her arms and pictured her junk pile of possessions next door. But that wreck was nothing compared to the condition of her heart.

Chapter Twenty-Five

Lacey looked like a woman who'd made a decision and intended to stick to it. Her eyes followed Logan to the chair, and once he sat, she handed him an envelope.

"What's this?"

"Your invitation."

He slid a card from the envelope. Some artist he'd never heard of was having a reception over the weekend, to be hosted in a swanky People's Building penthouse. The invitation was inscribed with his name. *Logan Woods and guest.*

"I don't understand," he said.

"Your new assignment. I've decided to take you off the Robin Hood story. It's not like you've given me much of a choice."

He stared at her, unable to believe she really meant it. But there was no mistaking the steel in her posture. The resolve in her eyes.

He waved the card in the air. "So this is my punishment?"

"It's out of my hands, Logan. And to be honest, you're lucky to still have a job. Getting you this wasn't exactly easy."

"So you went to bat for me?"

She smiled at his sarcasm. "You're angry now, but give it some time and you'll thank me. Now make yourself scarce. And be sure your piece on the reception is fit for print."

Out in the hallway, he started to breathe again. So that was it. He was off the story. Yesterday, he was the story. Now Rylee wasn't returning his calls, and his paper thought he was better suited to writing society fluff.

Seth would be livid. But deep down, there was a part of Logan that felt relieved. He looked at the invitation again. *Logan Woods and guest.* He'd ask Rylee to join him. In spite of their strained relationship, in spite of the half-dozen unanswered messages, he wasn't giving up.

Taking the album was wrong, he knew that. But if she looked at the photos, she'd understand. She would forgive him. He had to believe that.

He was certain she didn't know the identity of the burglar. Maybe she didn't even know the stolen objects had been in her family. Didn't know Grant Sebastian was living in her ancestral home. But no, she had to.

In time, she would trust him enough to talk. He'd been a fool to let her bring up the subject yesterday, after all she'd been through. Bad move. Very bad move.

Lacey's door opened. "One more thing."

"Yes?"

She glanced at his Abercrombie T-shirt and faded chinos. "You've got to promise me you won't show up at the reception dressed like that. Remember whom you're representing."

He tried not to smile but couldn't help it. "I promise."

Ever since Lacey had taken him under her stylish wing, Logan had treated the Ben Silver shop on King Street as his walk-in closet. Although he hadn't embraced the look fully—no seersucker suits or regimental bow ties—he'd blown many a paycheck on wool sport coats, cotton shirts, and a pair or two of handmade English shoes.

The results hadn't satisfied his mentor fully. Whenever she saw him wearing his tobacco suede boots and glen plaid linen jacket with a pair of frayed, distressed jeans, she would roll her eyes and mumble something about the impending apocalypse.

But with the new assignment, he wasted no time in making his way to Ben Silver. As soon as he passed through their door, one of the soigné shop girls took charge of him. In the space of ten minutes, she picked out a crisp white shirt, a black silk knit tie, and gray suit. Then she pulled a linen handkerchief from a display, folding it into the jacket pocket until just a thin white strip showed.

"Like Cary Grant in *North by Northwest*," she said. "Perfect."

Looking in the mirror, he hoped she was right.

She handed him a pair of black Wayfarer-style shades. "These too."

He slipped them on, then made a point of not looking at the price tag. Whatever it took. Whatever it cost.

He changed back into his street clothes, then lowered his voice. "There's something else I need help with, but it's going to take a little guesswork."

A half hour later, he emerged on the street, his purchases in a suit bag over his shoulder. Under his arm, he carried a large white box.

⁓

"He keeps calling," Liz said.

"And I'll answer when I'm ready."

Armed with trash bags, they steeled themselves for the inevitable clean-up. Sorting through what was left of her things, separating the whole and the maimed from the utterly destroyed.

"We should keep a list of everything," Liz said. "For insurance."

Rylee forced a laugh. "What insurance?"

They spent an hour on the living room. Liz held things up for inspection and Rylee declared them either "good" or "trash." Mostly the latter.

At first, every splintered picture frame and broken appliance made her want to cry, but soon she developed a crust around her heart. Instead of thinking how much she'd miss, say, her television set, she'd resolutely declare how happy she was to be rid of the thing, how she'd meant to replace it long ago.

When it came to the things from her childhood, though, her optimism took a nosedive. She paused over the cotton guts and strips of fur left over from her junior-high teddy bear collection. Every birthday, Christmas, Easter, and Valentine's Day, Nonie would gift her with a new bear. Not one was left intact.

She cradled the stuffings in her hands. "What kind of sicko destroys teddy bears?"

Liz came out of the bedroom, plastic gloves and Lysol in hand. "I'm working the lunch shift, sweetie, so I need to change. You ready to take a break?"

Rylee took a deep breath, and pushed the teddy bears' remains into the trash bag. "No, I think I'll keep going for a while."

Liz squatted down beside her. "No, Rylee. I really don't want you here all by yourself. Not just because it's dangerous, but because you need a break. Now, come on. There's no need to do it all in a day. Okay?"

Rylee looked at her friend. Her long blond hair was twisted up on her head, the ends sticking out in every direction.

"You think I should grow my hair out?"

Liz blinked. "That would be a fresh start. But I like it short."

Rylee ran a hand across the nape of her neck. "It's definitely low maintenance."

"Come on. Let's call it quits for a while. Besides, I thought you were going job hunting."

She cringed. But what choice was there? With so many holes in her schedule, the money would dry up quickly. Officially, she'd always required a cancellation period, but there was no way she'd call her ex-clients to read them the contracts they'd signed.

The Davidsons—the ones who'd suffered the most damage—were the only ones who hadn't fired her. So there was still Toro to walk.

She pushed to her feet. "Yeah. Okay."

"You could always work with me at Queen Anne's Revenge. There's always room for one more lusty wench, you know."

She put a concerted effort behind her smile. "We'll see."

She went into six different shops, completed six applications. At least five of the six managers recognized her name from the news—the sixth, she figured, was probably just rude to everyone, whether they were suspected of robbing houses or not.

Nobody was hiring. At least, they weren't hiring her.

Giving up for the time being, she retraced her steps to where she'd left Daisy, retrieving Nonie's album from the backseat. She decided to take a walk, maybe clear her head a little.

She thought of her time in jail. That brief moment she'd climbed to the mountaintop and seen for the first time all that lay behind her. And the possibilities that lay before her.

Never, however, did she foresee the vandalism of her apartment. The swiftness with which her clients would sever all ties. The truth behind Logan's interest in her.

Her clients, she could somewhat understand. But Logan.

She swallowed. The thought that everything he'd done or said or shared had been motivated by a desire to write some newspaper article kicked up all the emotional dust of her past.

And though she knew the Lord was with her, wouldn't abandon her, was trustworthy, it still would have been nice if she had real live parents to go to. Much as she loved Nonie, it just wasn't the same.

Thinking of her parents drew her inevitably to Marion Square. Most of her early childhood was lost to her. She'd close her eyes and concentrate, trying to summon up images of her early days, but her memory wouldn't cooperate. Even the pictures in Nonie's photo albums didn't trigger much. Sometimes she thought the wiring in her brain was faulty, the essential coupling having fallen away.

But at Marion Square, her parents' spirits abided, prompting her to treat it a little bit like sacred ground. As an adult, she never went there for mere recreation. She only entered when loneliness overcame her, and never left still feeling alone. She couldn't venture within a block of the square without feeling her mom and dad there with her, the way they'd been at the picnic that one steamy dusk.

In time, had the relationship with Logan gone well, she would have taken him there, preparing him in advance to appreciate the significance.

But it now looked as if that would never happen.

When she reached the green, she slipped off her sandals, slowed her pace, and let the grass push through her toes.

"What kind of parents would you have been?" She let her voice carry off on the wind. As always, the square worked its calming magic. She avoided the crowd near the fountain and settled under the shade of an old oak, watching two young mothers wrestling their toddlers onto a blanket. The children squealed. They were a bit younger than Rylee had been when her parents brought her here, when the music played and her mother's skirt swished through the air.

Jon and Stella. For all practical purposes, perfect strangers.

She let the album fall open in her lap, flipping listlessly through the pages. If Logan had to go stealing a photo album, he could at least have chosen a more recent one. She wanted to see her parents, but instead she got page after page of stiff, old-time Monroes in detachable collars and starchy lace. This had gotten him all worked up? She couldn't see why.

She hesitated over the first picture he'd pointed out. Her great-grandfather reading in his library. Then her eyes widened.

There, peeking over the back of his chair, was that knowing bronze grin. The jockey with his hand on his hip.

The downy hair on her forearm stood on end. No wonder the statue had seemed so familiar to her. She'd noticed it at the Bosticks' house and assumed that was it. But maybe the reason she'd noticed it was that she'd seen it before. Here in Nonie's album, without even realizing. The image had gone straight into her subconscious mind.

But that couldn't be. She'd never taken any notice of the picture until now. Had hardly even glanced at these older albums.

Had she seen it before . . . as a child?

She turned the page, scrutinizing each picture. Stopping on yet another one. On a sideboard in the hallway, an ornate box shaped like a tomb with painted panels and Roman figure finials. Could this be Karl's jewelry casket?

She shook her head. He'd said it had been in his family for years. A few pages later, the other picture Logan had pointed out. Her little ancestor playing the violin. Mr. Ormsby's violin?

This was what Logan meant. This was the connection between the Robin Hood burglaries and her.

And if she went to Bishop Gadsden and pulled out more of the albums, she felt a growing certainty the ormolu clock, the Charles Fraser painting, and the mourning brooch would be there, too.

She looked up, squinting into the sun. No wonder he'd acted so strange. He had asked if she'd seen the albums and she'd said of course she had. So when he discovered the connection, he must have wondered if she already knew.

She snapped the album shut, rising to her feet. She'd wasted the day looking for a job. But now that was over. Now she wanted answers.

≃

When he tried Rylee's phone this time, she answered.

"Are you all right?" he asked.

"Everything's fine."

"Listen, Rylee, about yesterday. I'm sorry for springing all that on you. That was the last thing you needed—"

"Logan."

"What?"

"I looked at that album."

"About that," he said. "I had a lapse of judgment. I knew it was wrong, and I did it anyway. I'm really sorry. I know I should have asked you—"

"I looked at it."

He paused. "And?"

"I saw . . . I don't know what to say."

He shoved his chair back and stood, the phone cord keeping him tethered to his desk. "Listen, let's not talk over the phone. Where are you? Let me come and see you. I have a favor to ask anyway."

"What favor?"

"Not over the phone," he said. "Can I pick you up?"

Silence. He listened acutely for background noise, trying to place where she was. There was nothing but the hum of dead air.

"Are you still there?"

She cleared her throat. "I'm with Nonie. She's sleeping. There's a picture of her as a teenager right here on my lap. She's wearing a mourning brooch, Logan. A mourning brooch. I can't be sure, but . . ."

"Sit tight. I'm on my way."

"No."

He slowly lowered himself back into his chair. "No?"

"I'm sorry. I didn't mean to be so sharp. I'm just trying to absorb it all. I spent the morning cleaning my apartment and looking for jobs, the afternoon going through these pictures. And I . . ." She took a deep breath. "I still need to return all those keys to my clients."

"Let me do that for you."

"No. I've done nothing wrong. I'm not going to cower in the corner with my tail between my legs."

He smiled. She even spoke in dog metaphors. "Then let me go with you, at least."

"No. I need to do it. I . . . I want to do it. And tonight I'm going to give Toro a nice long walk. At least I still have him to take care of."

"Okay," he said. "But I want to see you. I have something for you."

After they hung up, he stared at an e-mail from Seth asking for an update.

His phone rang. He grabbed it before the ring stopped.

"Honey, it's Mom. I'm watching the news. It looks like the girl you told your father about has been released from jail."

"Yeah." He should have thought to call them earlier. He looked at his watch. "How 'bout I come by for dinner and get ya'll caught up?"

"I'll set you a place."

⌒

After dinner, Dad pushed back from the table, leading Logan through the sliding doors out to the backyard. The cicadas outside were loud enough to drown out his thoughts. He wondered how he'd grown up without really hearing them. Maybe his brain had tuned out the familiar frequency. Now he couldn't block them out.

"That was some pretty heavy stuff you laid on us," Dad said. "I'd be lying if I said I still wasn't a little concerned about this girl."

Logan looked down into a sweating glass of iced tea.

"But if you're serious about her . . ." Dad gave him a sideways look. "You are serious, aren't you, son?"

He didn't hesitate. "I am."

Dad nodded and they wandered over to the fire pit, one of Dad's more recent improvement projects. Logan sat on the stone wall ringing the pit, while his father gazed up at the pinprick of stars overhead. For a while, the communication was nonverbal.

Logan sensed Dad's anxiety. Through the kitchen window, he could see his mother clearing the table, her movements sharp and deliberate. He couldn't tell for certain, but he imagined her lips moving. Was she talking to herself or praying?

"What about Mom?" he asked.

"She'd like to meet the girl. We both would. And she's naturally worried that you might be in over your head."

Logan studied the ice in his glass. "Is that what you think?"

"Well, the days when I could just tell you what to do are long past. But I trust you to do the right thing, son. And whatever you choose, you know we'll always support you. Just be careful, you hear?"

"I hear."

When they went back inside, they found Mom standing at the kitchen island, a dish towel in her hands. "I meant to tell you how good it was to see you at church again, Logan. And you seemed to enjoy the message and seeing all your friends afterwards."

"Yeah. Pastor Anderson's sermons always challenge me. But I wasn't visiting afterwards so much as drumming up some business for Rylee. Since the news broke, a lot of her clients bailed on her. She's got her grandmother to support, and I know things have been tight. So I was seeing if anyone was looking for a dogwalker or pet sitter or something."

Mom gave Dad a quick glance, then brushed a lock of hair from her face. "And you're, um, sure she's trustworthy?"

Leaning over, he gave her a peck on the cheek. "I'm positive. Don't worry, Mom. She really is a good girl. You're gonna love her."

~

He parked on South Battery and walked along to the monument where he'd first met Rylee. The time was right, more or less, assuming she hadn't deviated from her schedule due to the sudden dearth of clients. He set the white box from Ben Silver on a bench. Then waited.

A couple passed by arm in arm, oblivious to his presence. Some time later, a group of men in Hawaiian shirts and straw hats strolled past, cigars trailing smoke behind them. He checked his watch again, suspecting the errand was in vain.

But the sound of rollerblades on uneven cobbles caught his attention.

He turned as she emerged into the light, the big dog charging ahead on its leash. Her cotton dress flapped in the wind, outlining her strong thighs. Her earbuds were in, and she gave no sign of recognition. As they drew closer, he expected her to pass him by. At the last minute, she gave the leash a graceful tug, then circled to a halt just in front of him.

"I've got half a mind to sic my dog on you—for old times' sake," she said.

"I've got half a mind to let you."

She jutted out her bottom lip. He was tempted to snare it in his teeth. Not the most appropriate of icebreakers.

"You been waiting long?"

"I would've waited all night if I had to. Like I said, I have something for you." He leaned over and opened the white box, turning it so she could see.

She rolled forward, eyes wide, hands pressed together, fingertips resting against her lip. "What's that?"

"What does it look like?"

"It looks like a dress. What's it for?"

"This weekend, I'm going to a reception. I have to bring a date."

She looped the leash around the bench's arm, then bent over the box to take a closer look. She ran her hand over the green dupioni silk, then drew back. "This is for me?"

"Who else?"

She gave her mouth a skeptical twist. "How would you even know my size?"

He smiled. "I thought I could just sort of describe you." He drew an hourglass in the air. "But that didn't work out so good. So I called Liz and she told me. I hope you like it."

She tucked her hands under her armpits, as if she were afraid to touch it. "No one's ever given me a dress before."

"I've never given anyone a dress before. Do you like it?"

She fixed her big eyes on him, saying nothing.

He angled the box toward her. "Have a look."

After another few seconds, she finally reached for it, shaking the fabric free and pressing it daintily against her body. She pushed it close around the hips, imagining the fit. The silk shimmered in the dim light, swishing softly in the breeze.

"So what do you think?" he asked.

She rolled toward him, a smile on her lips. "I think we're going to a party."

Chapter Twenty-Six

Instead of the stereotypical red roses, he chose a dozen pink ones, the petals delicate as hand-painted china. The aroma filled the car, making him light-headed.

Liz opened the door when he knocked. "Look at you. So dapper. And you brought flowers—they're beautiful!"

She turned toward the bedroom door and shouted. "Rylee? Logan's here."

Liz stepped back, allowing him in. Also giving him his first glance of the fabled pirate barmaid outfit, consisting of a short, clingy shift and a bodice cinched tight enough to squeeze cleavage out of a tree trunk. There were knee-high boots, too, with skyscraper heels and a hundred yards of lacing.

She plopped onto the futon and started tying the laces. "The dress you bought her is perfect. She's been so discouraged because no one would hire her, but now she's floating on a cloud."

He glanced toward the closed bedroom door, wondering whether Rylee had heard her shout.

"I told my manager about her," Liz said, "and of course he said he'd hire her in a minute. Always room for another Yo-Ho-Ho."

Logan gave the outfit another glance. *Over my dead body.*

The bedroom door opened and Rylee glided toward him. Her lips glistened, her hair shone with a dark gloss. The green silk dress wrapped her body with glove-like grace. Over the skirt, a filmy gossamer layer floated about her hips, shimmering as she moved. She'd gathered the sash to one side, the ends hanging down in a waterfall.

"You brought me roses?"

"I hope you like them."

She gathered the flowers with a serene smile, inhaling the scent. "I love them. Thank you, Logan."

"You look . . . amazing."

She held the flowers to one side and twirled for him. "You like?"

You have no idea. He nodded.

"I'll put these in some water," Liz said, exchanging the flowers for a clutch purse. "You two get going."

Rylee tugged one rose free, then touched her cheek to Liz's. "Thanks for everything."

"It was fun. I love playing beauty shop."

Logan opened the door, waited for Rylee to pass through, then turned back to Liz.

"Thanks for helping with the dress," he said, giving her a thumbs-up.

"Thanks for helping with the friend."

Her first five minutes in the condominium redefined the meaning of the word. Two stories connected with a sweeping staircase, a wall of windows looking out over the harbor at twilight, glittering dresses and clouds of perfume, air kisses and peals of laughter.

Live music wouldn't have surprised her, but instead the party's soundtrack came courtesy of a disc jockey by the impromptu bar, who spun the same throbbing European techno heard in the King Street designer boutiques.

The hostess greeted them with the kind of placid facial serenity that betokens an excellent plastic surgeon, living out her early fifties like a porcelain doll of herself at thirty, blinking eyes and a fixed smile. "Any friend of Lacey's," she said, patting Logan with an incongruously veined hand.

Rylee smiled, relieved the woman hadn't recognized her from the news accounts.

Moving through the partygoers, she felt like Cinderella in the most beautiful dress at the ball. Hopefully, no one else would recognize her either. She clung tighter to Logan's arm.

Talking over the music, catching half of what was said but nodding at everything, they wound their way deeper inside, heading toward the windows for a better look at the view.

"This is incredible," she said.

He leaned closer, cupping a hand to his ear.

"I said, it's incredible."

"It's funny to live here all your life, then feel like you're seeing the place for the first time."

She squeezed his hand in agreement.

He bent to her ear. "You having fun?"

She nodded. "I am."

"Well, I tell you what." He settled his hand at the lower curve of her back. "When all this is over and we can breathe again, I'll take you to lots of parties—and not because I'm on assignment."

She smiled. "I just might take you up on that."

A hint of cigar smoke tickled her nose. She glanced over her shoulder. "Logan, look."

He turned around. A group of men had circled up, all in tuxedos, with an assortment of cocktails in their hands. Among them was Marcel Gibbon.

"What's he doing here?" Logan asked.

Gibbon looked up and narrowed his eyes at Logan, then cut them sideways for a leer at Rylee.

She brushed at her dress, pretending she hadn't noticed.

Gibbon slapped the man beside him on the shoulder, then excused himself and made his way over, a cigar and whiskey pinched between the fingers of his right hand.

"They let you smoke in here?" Logan asked.

Gibbon ignored him. "Well, Miss Monroe, it's always a pleasure."

He stopped directly across from her, his eyes working their way from the ground up, as invasive as a touch.

She gave him a disinterested glare.

Grabbing her hand, Logan pulled her just behind his shoulder. "You ditched us the other night. I want to know why. I'm guessing you had a reason to want us at the park?"

Gibbon stuck the cigar in his mouth, a glimmer of satisfaction in his eyes. He obviously enjoyed the effect he had on her and the protectiveness he evoked in Logan. "I'd really like to be forthcoming and all, but I've learned over the years to be circumspect in my dealings. In other words, I don't go shooting my mouth off. Who's to say you're not wearing a wire?"

"You want to check?" Logan started taking off his jacket.

Gibbon turned his full attention to Rylee. "How about you, Miss Monroe?"

Logan froze. "We're not wired and you know it."

"Maybe not, but you are writing a book."

"Yes, I am. And you need to decide whether you want to be one of the good guys or the bad guys."

"One of the bad guys, certainly."

"The kind people love, or the kind they hate? Or the kind they love to hate?"

Gibbon gave him an indulgent smile. "If you think I'll spill everything out of a desire to come off well in this book of yours, well . . . you've got a pretty high opinion of yourself."

"You told me if I connected the items Robin Hood is stealing, I would find the perpetrator. Well, I've connected them. They all belonged to Jon Monroe and were sold off by Grant Sebastian."

Rylee gave Logan a sharp look.

Gibbon swirled the drink in his hand, clinking the ice against the glass. "Ah. We're getting warmer, I see."

"Grant's also living in the Monroes' house."

Rylee sucked in her breath. Logan squeezed her hand in reassurance.

Gibbon gave him a speculative look. "Well, well. I'm impressed."

"I can't help thinking you're mixed up in this. First, you were running interference for George. Then you set up this bogus meet—"

"Bogus?" Gibbon smiled. "I'd have kept our date, Logan, if you'd shown up alone."

"You told me to bring her."

Gibbon looked at Rylee. "It's not her I'm talking about."

"Then you'd better enlighten me."

He took a pull on the cigar, his eyes piercing Logan's with a meaning Rylee couldn't hope to decipher.

Logan reared back. "Are you saying we were followed?"

"I'm not saying anything." He started to walk away, then paused. "By the way, I'd prefer to be the kind of bad guy people love to hate."

He made his way up the stairs, slipping past the guest of honor, who gazed moodily into his champagne glass, looking as if he would have preferred to be anywhere but a society party. On the second floor, Gibbon lost himself in the crowd.

"What did you mean about Mr. Sebastian living in my house?"

Rylee asked. "You can't mean the one on East Battery. The one he's lived in for as long as I can remember. The one I've been in and out of this whole time I was walking Romeo. Was that *my* house, Logan? The one I was born in?"

"Logan?" The curator from Gibbes Museum approached with a smile, her brown hair bouncing attractively at her shoulders. "Have you decided to give up crime reporting for the art section?"

"Angela. Good to see you again." Logan introduced Rylee to the young brunette who'd given him a crash course on Charles Fraser.

They spent the next hour mingling and gathering sound bites for the article Logan had been assigned. Rylee smiled and nodded, but heard nothing other than Logan's words to Gibbon whirling round and round in her head.

She constantly scanned the crowd for Marcel, but the man had completely disappeared.

When they finally broke free of their obligations, she steered Logan toward a quiet corner. "I want to know what's going on."

He pulled her close for a quick kiss, concern creasing his face. "Let's get out of here and I'll explain everything."

Emerging into the balmy night, he pulled her down the sidewalk, looking at her every few seconds.

What did he expect to see, she wondered. Her breaking down and crying, shrieking at the moon, confessing she didn't know who she could trust anymore?

She slowed her stride. Slower, slower, until they were barely moving.

"Are you okay?" he asked.

She inhaled the sultry night air. "Is Mr. Sebastian involved with Robin Hood?"

He stopped and pulled her against him. Held her.

"Logan?" Her voice came out in a squeak.

His hand touched the back of her neck, her head, pressing her tight into his shoulder.

How much time passed? She didn't know. When she pulled away, his jacket was wet.

They walked to his car, fingers twined together, bodies swaying side by side. She could feel him thinking, searching for words. Instead of opening her car door, he settled against the hood, drawing her between his knees.

"How much do you know?" he asked.

"That the statue for sure and possibly the violin, the brooch and maybe even the jewelry casket are pictured in Nonie's albums."

"The jewelry casket? Are you sure?"

"I'm not sure of anything. I have the album in my trunk. I can show you."

He brought their hands to his mouth, kissing her knuckles. "Did you know Grant brokered the estate sale for your grandmother after your parents . . . were gone?"

"Yes. But I didn't know he was living in my house. Nonie never said a word. Maybe she was waiting until I got older and by the time I was, she'd stopped making sense. Whenever she does talk about the past, though, it's always the distant world of her own childhood, not mine."

The party began to break up, guests streaming past, paying them no mind.

She pressed her fingers to her forehead. "Surely you don't think Grant Sebastian is mixed up in all this? He wasn't even here."

"He's got something to do with it, Rylee."

"He's been nothing but good to me, Logan. He's taken care of me when there was no one else."

He said nothing.

She smoothed the silk at her stomach and hips, obsessively stroking the shimmering fabric. "Do you think that, that my dad is involved?"

He reared back. "Your dad? I don't know. The thought hadn't occurred to me."

She nodded. "Logan, Marcel mentioned your book. He made it sound like it was about the Robin Hood burglaries. I thought your book was already written. That it was about past crimes and you were shopping it around for a publisher."

He stroked her hair, rubbing its short ends between his fingers. "The Robin Hood burglaries play a role in the book." He moved his gaze to hers. "A pretty big role."

"And me?" she asked, holding her breath. "Do I play a role in your book?"

"No. No, you don't."

"But I've been accused of being the Robin Hood burglar. All the items he's taken belonged to my family. How can you leave me out of it?"

His Adam's apple bobbed. "I haven't figured that out yet."

"I see." She took a step back.

"Rylee—"

"I think I'm ready to go home now."

Pushing away from the car, he opened her door. A manila envelope rested beneath the wiper blades on the passenger side.

"What's that?" she asked, pointing at it.

"Let me see." He slid out the top portion of the papers, trying to read in the golden streetlight. "Looks like some kind of background information. Maybe from that curator or something. I'll take a look at it later when I have more light. "

He tossed the envelope in the backseat, tucked her in, then went around to his side.

Once she had her seat belt attached, he took both of her hands in his, fixing her with the sincerest, most earnest of looks. "Don't go back to Liz's apartment. Let me take you to my parents' place. They'd be happy to have you."

She shook her head. "I'm still borrowing everything but my toothbrush from Liz. And I've never even met your parents. What would they think of me?"

"They won't judge you, Rylee. And my mom will feed you home-cooked meals. Dad will tell you bad jokes. How can you pass that up?"

She smiled, but held firm. "No, really. Liz is my best friend. Everything's familiar. That's where I feel safe."

He relented with a sigh, then produced a folded piece of paper from inside his jacket.

"What's this?"

"Some folks in my neighborhood who need a dogwalker." He put the car in gear and pulled out into the street.

She punched on the reading light. His neat masculine script catalogued names, addresses, and phone numbers.

"What about this?" She pointed to various times of day written by each name.

He glanced over. "That's when they're expecting you tomorrow. So don't be late."

The parade of disastrous interviews shuffled through her mind. "Do they know who I am? That I've been arrested?"

Without taking his eyes off the road, he nodded. "They do."

She swallowed. "And they're still willing to trust me in their homes? With their pets? Why would they do that?"

"Because I asked them to."

Carefully refolding the paper, she ran her fingers over each crease. His book had set alarm bells off in her head. But now, those concerns began to fade.

She tucked the list inside her clutch purse and turned off the overhead light.

Chapter Twenty-Seven

"Who's seen this?" Lacey asked, flipping to the last page of the affidavit.

"No one but you." Logan still clutched the empty envelope in his hands, the one he'd found under his windshield wiper the night before. "Tell me I'm not crazy. Is that what I think it is?"

She lowered her tortoiseshell reading glasses. "You didn't show it to Rylee Monroe?"

"She was with me, like I said. But when I saw her father's name on it, I just put it aside. She's pretty sensitive about him."

He'd played it off as best he could, and Rylee was so distracted by the encounter with Gibbon that she hardly noticed. Once he'd tossed the envelope in back, she seemed to forget all about it. But he didn't. What little he'd read burned in his mind.

"Who do you think left it?" Lacey asked.

He shrugged. "I assume it's a gift from the Cherub, since we'd just been talking to him. But I can't be sure."

"Well," she said, tapping the page with her finger. "If this is legit, then Jonathan Monroe created this affidavit to expose Grant Sebastian."

"Only he disappeared instead. It doesn't make sense."

She put the affidavit on her desk, then started digging through one of the cavernous drawers in her file cabinet. "I thought I took you off this story."

He held his hands up in surrender. "This was dropped in my lap."

From the back of the drawer, she hauled out a thick manila folder so stuffed with mismatched paper that bits were sticking out from the sides. Spreading it out on her desk, she dug through the stack, setting aside whole chunks of paper at a time. Logan saw printouts, older typescripts, and a sheaf of handwritten notes.

"I covered Monroe's disappearance," she said. "Years ago."

"I know. I dug up all the old stories."

"The thing that always bothered me was, I knew Jon. Knew the family. After the way he felt about his dad leaving, Jon was the last person I would have imagined abandoning his family like that. He and Stella, they were in love. But it was all there on paper. Grant showed me their financial statements."

She found what she was looking for, an old spiral-bound stenographer's pad with half the pages torn out. Flipping through the remainder, she handed the relevant notes to Logan. A report of Jonathan Monroe's cleaned-out bank account.

"What about Stella? Did you manage to talk to her before she died?"

"I scheduled an appointment. Through Grant."

"And she was dead before it came?"

She smiled grimly. "This affidavit changes everything."

"No kidding. You don't draft a document like that and then disappear with the family fortune. He was planning to go to the police."

"Maybe," she said. "Or he thought he could force his partner to make restitution. He could have drafted this as some kind of bargaining chip. 'Give these people back their money, or I'll go to the authorities'—that kind of thing. Only he never got the chance."

"Meaning what?"

"Meaning it's not as easy to disappear as you might think. Did you know that Flora Monroe hired a private investigator to find her son?" She looked him square in the eye. "They never found a trace of him."

"You think he was murdered?"

She didn't answer, but he could see that was exactly what she was thinking.

"By *Sebastian*?"

"Not him personally. He wouldn't get his hands dirty. But he's always had the right kind of connections for that kind of thing. Our friend Gibbon, for example."

"And what about Stella?"

She fingered the pearls at her throat thoughtfully. "If she did kill herself, that suggests grief, doesn't it? Like she knew Jon wasn't coming back. Ever. But if she had any hope at all, then it seems a little convenient—and suspicious—that Stella overdosed, leaving her daughter behind like that."

Logan's mind raced. The puzzle he'd been putting together didn't fit the way he assumed. Now the pieces all looked different, and he had to rearrange his mental map. Grant's whole career was built on a lie. He'd posed as a father figure for Rylee, but only after getting rid of her real parents.

"At least now we have the proof," he said.

"No, we don't." Lacey handed the affidavit back. "If that document can be authenticated, all it proves is Grant Sebastian's guilt in defrauding people whose estates he was executor of. Nothing else. The rest is speculation."

"Wait." Logan stared at the envelope in his hand. "There's something else. I don't know how it connects, but I think Karl Sebastian is being blackmailed."

He quickly outlined the episode at Sebastian's office, where the courier handed him the mailer by mistake. The note inside read the same as the message left in Rylee's apartment.

"You think the blackmail and the Robin Hood burglaries are connected?" she asked. "And it's something to do with the affidavit?"

"I'm not sure what I think yet. But somebody's delivering an awful lot of unmarked envelopes."

"The Cherub?"

"That'd be my first guess."

She nodded. "Well, whoever it is clearly wants this thing plastered across the front page—which is exactly what he's going to get."

"I thought I was off the story." Logan tensed. "Besides, I'm not sure that's such a good idea."

She narrowed her eyes. "Because you want to save it for your book?"

He shook his head. "It's not that. Before we do anything with this, I need to talk to Rylee first. I owe her that, don't you think?"

Swinging her leg, she scrutinized him for a long moment. "I'll only wait long enough for you to talk to her. And leave the original here with me."

"I expected as much, so I made myself a copy. But it's more than just talking to her. I want her consent."

"Logan, it's not like she'll want to keep this a secret. She's grown up thinking her dad cleaned out the bank account and abandoned his wife and daughter. This is good news for her."

"I know. But I still want her consent. I'm not going to exploit her, Lacey."

He expected more of an argument, but she conceded with a wave of her hand. "She'll agree. In the meantime, consider yourself back on the story. You know what that means."

"What?"

"I want a reaction quote from Grant Sebastian."

He left Lacey's office, his mission clear. Before, he'd been uncertain. He had no legal experience. No firsthand knowledge to confirm his suspicions.

But Lacey did. And if the affidavit rang true to her, then there was no reason to doubt. He could reveal the truth to Rylee.

The thought thrilled him. Her whole idea of herself, her conviction that the people she loved would ultimately abandon her—a belief borne out by the mass exodus of clients—would be suddenly overturned.

Her parents had loved her. Her father hadn't left her. Her mother hadn't killed herself—at least, it didn't seem likely. Thinking of it all, he could imagine her face lighting up, the weight she'd been carrying since childhood abruptly lifted.

At his desk, he paused, examining the affidavit again. Suppose she didn't light up, though. He was proposing to tell her that her parents had been murdered, after all. That her inheritance had been stolen from her. And that the man responsible was the one person through all the years she'd believed she could rely on.

Maybe he needed to think about this.

But no. His prevarication of the night before had not sat well with him.

What Rylee needed was the truth, and that was the one thing only he could give her. The book didn't matter. The paper didn't matter. All that mattered was her.

But first, he had to go to Grant Sebastian.

And he'd wring more out of the man than just a reaction quote.

~

Rylee's new clients had one thing in common. They were all members of Logan's baseball team. Some of them were married with kids. Others were single and asked if she cooked.

Only three actually had dogs. The rest offered an assortment of cats, hamsters, and even a cockatoo. Their apartment complexes, houses, and duplexes were scattered all over James Island. A long way from South of Broad.

She found the last house on the list, pulling into the driveway of a tiny white clapboard behind three other cars. The yard was more dirt than grass, bereft of ornamentation.

The door opened after a couple of knocks, revealing a gangly redhead in his midtwenties, swimming in a pair of oversized athletic shorts and a hockey jersey with the sleeves ripped off.

"I'm Mike," he said. "Are you the pet nanny?"

"Rylee Monroe." She offered her hand.

"Hey, guys!" he called over his shoulder. "She's here."

Two more men thundered up to the door, both around her age. The one with Mike's red hair must have been his brother. The other one had a shaggy fringe of dark hair hiding his eyes. They formed a semicircle around her, saying nothing.

She cleared her throat. "I understand you need a dogwalker?"

A panicked look crossed Mike's face. "A dogwalker? I thought you were a pet nanny or something. You only do dogs?"

She smiled. "No, no. I do most any kind of pets."

He sighed in relief. "Oh, whew. You scared me for a minute." He widened the door. "Well, come on in."

They broke ranks, allowing her to pass through to an open living room, dining room, kitchen area. Dorm room chic, complete with mismatched furniture, pizza boxes, and an impossibly large flat-screen TV sprouting game controllers from all sides.

"This is my brother Randy," Mike said, "and that's Harold."

She nodded at each. "I assume you're all Mets?"

"Me and Randy are. Harold's an Oriole."

The Oriole shrugged apologetically.

"Well, it's nice to meet you all."

Randy led her to the corner, where a huge terrarium gleamed in the light of the sliding doors. Leaping between a token plant and a hollow branch was a fist-sized lime green tree frog.

"This is Shamrock." Randy picked up the frog, then pinched its left foot between his fingers and made a waving motion. "Shamrock, say hello to Rylee. She's going to be your new nanny."

Rylee waved back. "Hey, Shamrock."

They all looked at her expectantly, even the frog.

She held out her hands. Randy transferred the frog into her palm. Its smooth rubbery skin was cool to the touch.

"So how long have you had him?" she asked.

Harold glanced at his watch. "A couple of hours now."

She looked from one to the other. "Logan gave me your address last night."

Mike scratched his chin. "Well, we've been wanting a pet but were afraid to get one since none of us had the time to . . . um, walk it."

Harold rolled his eyes.

They might as well have attached a bicycle pump to her heart. She felt it swelling in her chest. "So you went and bought this frog because Logan told you about me. Is that right?"

Mike shrugged. "The lady at the store said tree frogs are really good for beginners."

Randy perked up. "Yeah. And I've already taught him to come. Watch this." He cupped his palms. "Come, Shamrock!"

The frog gave a slow blink but made no move to jump to him.

He grinned sheepishly. "I guess he needs a little bit more practice."

Harold rolled his eyes again. That seemed to be his role among the threesome.

She placed Shamrock back in the terrarium and gave the guys a few options for how she could take care of the tree frog, all the way up to raising crickets for his dinner.

Randy eyed her skeptically. "So what you're saying is, a beautiful girl like you—pardon me for saying so—will mate and raise thousands of crickets for us?"

"Yes."

The men exchanged a look. "Cool. You got any dogwalker friends you could introduce us to?"

When she finally left James Island, she figured she'd visited most every player on Logan's team.

And none of them needed a pet sitter. They were simply helping out their friend.

Logan.

And Logan was helping her.

Humility, wonder, and gratitude stacked up in her chest. Not only for Logan's gesture, but for that of his friends. Real friends. Who were willing to go the extra mile for him, no questions asked.

She didn't even realize she was crying until she could no longer see the road. Pulling onto the shoulder, she put Daisy in park.

For so long, the only real friend she'd had was Liz. What was it about her that caused her to have shallow friendships—or no friends at all? She'd lived in Charleston all her life, yet she had only Liz. Why?

Was it, perhaps, because she was afraid that when the chips were down, they wouldn't come through for her? That they would abandon her? The way her parents had? The way her clients had?

An eighteen-wheeler roared by, vibrating her windows.

She had to let go. Let go of her fear. She had to knock down the wall she'd spent a lifetime cowering behind.

The thought petrified her. But she kept thinking of those three guys buying a pet, just to help Logan—and subsequently her. The realization that someone would do that for him, for her, filled her with a desperate longing.

I want that, Lord. I want friends like that, too. And I want to be a friend like that to someone else.

She thought of all the opportunities she'd had to make friends, yet she'd shied away.

Well, no more. She was tired of keeping the world at arm's length. Tired of superficial relationships. Tired of being alone.

And if knocking down that wall meant exposing herself to hurt, so be it. Because for the first time she realized hiding behind it was actually more hurtful than knocking it down and risking her heart for what Logan and his friends had.

Okay, God. You're gonna have to help me. Because those are some serious walls and it's gonna take some kinda power to knock them down.

Pulling tissues from her messenger bag, she wiped her face, blew her nose, and put Daisy in drive.

⁓

Logan parked on East Battery, across from the house. He'd worn a light linen jacket for the express purpose of concealing his digital recorder in the breast pocket. Now he turned the device on and slipped it inside.

On the street, he paused to take in the scene. The house now home to the man responsible for the demise of the Monroe family, victims of an exploitation that seemed to know no boundaries.

Karl's silver convertible sat in the drive, the trunk open, a set of matching leather suitcases piled nearby. As he approached the steps to the piazza, Karl emerged with a box. An urn, a plant, and some framed art kept its lid from closing.

He stopped when he saw Logan.

"Are you moving out?"

"What's it look like?" He descended, shouldering his way by, then dropped the box in the backseat.

"I just came from your office," Logan said, watching from a distance. "They told me I could find your dad here."

Karl slung the luggage into the trunk, fitting as many cases as he could, jostling them left and right. Finally, he slammed the lid and hoisted the remaining things into the backseat.

"Are you leaving by choice?" Logan asked. "Or is someone scaring you off?"

Pausing at the open driver's door, Karl turned. "Do I look scared to you?"

"It's just . . . that dog collar the other day. The message inside. It said the same thing as the note left at Rylee's place when that psycho trashed it. I think maybe you know who's responsible. Maybe he's the one blackmailing you. If you want to help Rylee, why don't you tell me what you know?"

Karl slapped the dust off his hands and fixed Logan with a good-riddance glare. "If I want to help Rylee, I don't need your assistance to do it."

He dropped into the driver's seat and yanked the door shut. Logan watched him speed down the short drive and cut the wheel onto East Battery, zooming off like a man on a mission.

Shaking his head, Logan ascended the stairs to the door and knocked.

Grant Sebastian opened up immediately, staring a few moments, glassy-eyed, before recognition dawned. "Oh. I take it he's gone."

"Karl? He just left."

"I see." He took a step backward. "Well, in that case come in."

The first time they'd met, at the police station, he'd been wearing a pinstriped suit. Now, Sebastian's high-waisted slacks and sky blue polo made him look like he'd just come from the golf course.

"So he's gone?" he asked again, as though he couldn't quite believe it.

Logan caught a whiff of alcohol on his breath. "I saw him drive off."

A smile bloomed on the old lawyer's face, a slow but unmistakable grin, reminding Logan of a man who'd matched the winning lottery numbers to his ticket and was just starting to believe his luck.

"Come in. Come in." His voice exultant, he ushered Logan past a stairway and across parquet floors. Whatever his expectations of the old Monroe house had been, Logan was surprised how ordinary it was.

Nice, certainly, but no more opulent than the Davidsons' house or the Petries'. The scale was larger, perhaps, and in contrast to the more lived-in homes of Rylee's clients, this one had a showcase quality, everything arranged with museum-like precision.

Grant waved Logan into his study, a compact, book-lined room with white woodwork and a set of windows looking out onto the bay. One of them was slightly open, admitting a warm breeze, birdsong, and sounds of the street outside.

He went straight to the Scotch bottles on the sideboard, sloshing a generous helping of amber liquid into a pair of glasses. He settled into a wingback chair, offering Logan the facing seat, the one with the view, and handed one of the glasses across.

"To victory," Grant said, raising his tumbler.

Logan clinked glasses but did not drink. He was a little uncertain what they were celebrating. But the lawyer's unexpected mood could work to his advantage. He decided to leave the photocopy of the affidavit in his back pocket for now.

"You don't have any children," Grant said, "so you can't understand."

Logan set his drink on a side table. "Karl's leaving the nest?"

"Being pushed is more like it." Another gulp of Scotch, followed by a laugh. "I never thought I'd see the day. You have no idea how many ultimatums I've given him, how many lines I've drawn in the sand . . . ." He narrowed his eyes. "We're speaking off the record here, you understand."

He nodded.

Grant took another gulp, then settled into his chair. "My wife is out with some friends. She'll be relieved when she gets back. He was supposed to be gone before our return, but it didn't work out that way. Now it's settled, though, and that's all that matters."

"Your wife doesn't care for Karl?" Logan asked.

He tilted his glass, watching the amber liquid as it captured the light. "She says I raised a monster." He finished the drink. "And I'll admit, you don't get to where I am without breaking a few eggs. But I've always tried to offset those necessary evils with a good deed or two."

Anger surged through Logan. Wrenching the affidavit out of his back pocket, he slammed it on the side table. "I'd hardly call this an evil that can be balanced out by a 'good deed or two.' "

Grant picked up the document, fumbling to open his eyeglasses and hook them on his ears. Clearly, the Scotch he'd just consumed was one of many from throughout the day. Perhaps he'd needed some liquid fortification before throwing his son out of the house.

As he flipped the pages, Grant's face collapsed. "Where did you get this?"

"According to Jon Monroe, you defrauded countless widows and orphans during the seventies and eighties. When he confronted you, you refused to make restitution for it. Days after that affidavit was drawn up, Monroe 'disappeared.' Days after he disappeared, his wife took a few too many sleeping pills. What *really* happened to them, Sebastian?"

Grant's face went pale.

Logan squared his shoulders. "You killed them. Both of them. Didn't you?"

His eyes flared. "Get out of my house."

"Monroe threatened to expose you, so you killed him and his wife. Isn't that right?"

Reaching for Logan's untouched glass, Grant took a deep swallow. "You've been watching too many movies, Woods."

"There are plenty more copies where that came from."

Grant's scoff was interrupted by a hiccup. "What? You think to threaten me with *this*? A *legal* document?" His laugh sounded hard and bitter. "Don't kid yourself. This is nothing compared to what I just got rid of."

Logan's breath hitched. "Are you talking about Karl? Did *Karl* kill the Monroes?"

Wobbling to his feet, Grant steadied himself on the wing of the chair. "Karl has problems. Always has. But as far as I know, the Monroes weren't among his victims."

The old man's words slurred, but Logan made them out. The hair on the back of his neck stood. "So Karl has killed in the past, just not the Monroes. Is that what you're saying?"

Sebastian's watery eyes sagged like a bloodhound's, showing red at the bottom. "Jon, he backed me into a corner. I had no choice. But I took care of his girl. Treated her like my own." Grant swayed, and for a moment Logan thought he'd fall. But gripping the chair tightly, he managed to regain his balance.

Logan slowly came to his feet. "Rylee, you mean? You call fleecing her of her estate, her home, and her inheritance *taking care* of her?"

Grant smacked his lips together, then swooped up the glass of alcohol and finished it off. "I protected her from Karl, didn't I? If she'd stayed here, in this house, in this neighborhood, no telling what would have happened. I took that girl clear out to the other side of Charleston. All the way to Folly Beach. I took care of her all right."

The phone on the nearby desk started to ring. Grant lurched for the receiver, knocking it off the base. The person on the other end shouted into the phone. Grant brought it to his ear.

"What do you want?" His eyes flashed with anger. He cut the air with his hand. "Haven't you had enough, Karl?" He gave Logan a look. "Yes, he's here. But he doesn't want to talk to you, and neither do I."

He started to hang up.

"Wait." Logan sprang forward. "Karl, is that you?"

"I paid a visit to a friend of yours just now."

"Rylee?"

"She doesn't care about you. I'm talking about that fat, cigar-smoking piece of garbage who spoon-feeds your stories to you. Only he's not going to be much use to you anymore. He had something of mine. He doesn't anymore."

"What are you talking about?"

"I have a message for my father," he said, "and I don't think he's going to remember much of anything he hears right now. So write this down."

"What's the message?" Logan asked.

"Tell him we're leaving."

"Who's we?"

"Tell him he'll never see either of us again. He doesn't want to have a son, so he won't. That's his choice. But he can't have a daughter, either. That's my choice. You tell him."

"Karl?" Logan gripped the phone. "Karl!"

But the line was dead.

Logan swung around to face Grant. "He said you can't have a daughter, either. What does that mean?"

The old man shrugged.

Logan grabbed him by the shirt front and shook. "What does it mean?"

"He's talking about Rylee," the old man bellowed. "He wants to take her away from me."

Logan didn't wait for more. He left Grant Sebastian trembling against the desk, calling after him in slurred exclamations.

He rushed outside, down the stairs, and across the street. He jammed his keys into the ignition.

Karl was out there somewhere, looking for Rylee. Or maybe he already had her. Logan had to find them.

Only he didn't know where to start.

Chapter Twenty-Eight

The sunlight beating through the windshield made the seats sizzling to the touch, and Daisy's A/C didn't have what it took to cool things down. Rylee's messenger bag lay on the seat beside her. Inside was a new set of keys, a new list of clients, a new start.

Running her fingers over the quilted pink and yellow fabric of her bag, she thought about Logan and the effort he'd gone to on her behalf. As soon as she finished walking Toro, she'd call him. Maybe see if he'd like to watch a DVD at her place tonight.

She checked herself. Make that Liz's place.

The trees along Meeting Street shimmered in the breeze. She parked on the curb, then cut down Prices Alley toward the Davidsons' gate, which was half hidden by a covering of creeping fig.

Despite the heat, chills raced up her arms at the memory of the stalker who'd followed her here and of Robin Hood's break-in. She shifted the bag on her shoulder, the familiar heft of her rollerblades inside.

She'd be able to use them with two of her new pets, and though she'd miss the historic district, the smooth sidewalks on James Island would be a nice break from the jarring she got on the cobblestone walkways south of Broad.

The only sign of the commotion earlier in the week was a tiny ribbon of yellow tape snagged by a boxwood. From the outside, at least. The damage inside the house would take much longer to heal. Her first time back after the break-in had been hard. She plucked the tape off the bush, then made her way to the piazza, slipping her key into the lock.

"Anybody home?"

Barking from deep inside the house, the sound of paws rattling the stairs, nails on the wood, prepared her for Toro. Someone had forgotten to put him in his crate.

He bounded around the corner. She hugged him to her, scrubbing fingers along his short, coarse coat. "Hey there, fella. How's my boy?"

Hearing no other sounds from inside, she grabbed his leash from the hall tree. "Okay. Let's go for a walk."

He gazed up in delight, jumping at her hip, catching his paw on her belt loop.

"Easy, now. Stay down." Laughing, she sat on the steps outside, letting him run free through the side garden while she slipped her shoes off and reached for the rollerblades.

Toro trotted along the beds, pausing to scratch once or twice at the ground. The blooming season had long since withered in the South Carolina heat, but the greenery and verdigris benches still exuded charm and a sense of history.

"Rylee?"

She jumped, losing her grip on the rollerblade laces. In the archway that led to the alley, Karl stood, a crooked smile on his lips.

She pressed a hand to her hammering chest. "You scared me to death!"

"Sorry about that." He raised his open palms in apology.

"So what are you doing here?" she asked.

He walked over, still smiling, and sat down a step below her, leaving a few feet between them. "I should ask you the same thing. Have you ever heard the expression 'returning to the scene of the crime'? If I were you, I'd give this place a wide berth."

"Not a chance." She pointed to Toro, who stood wide-legged in the distance, peering at the new arrival. "I wouldn't miss this guy's workout for the world."

Karl nodded. "You really care about these animals, don't you?"

"I do."

As handsome as he was, as friendly as they'd become while she walked Romeo, she was relieved they'd never gone on that dinner. He wasn't near the man Logan was. Not even close.

She hoped he wasn't here to ask her out again. Standing, she balanced on the cobbled walk.

He cupped her elbow.

She smiled. "I'm good. Thanks."

The breeze was uncomfortably balmy. She grabbed her bag and hooked it over her shoulder. "You ready to go, boy?"

Toro let out a low growl.

"Behave yourself." She made her way across the grass to Toro and gave his head a quick rub. "He's probably on edge because of everything that's happened."

Karl glanced at Toro impassively, the way he might at an inanimate object.

She straightened. "Listen, Toro here is going crazy for a walk, so I better—"

"Rylee," he said, a strange thickness in his voice.

"What's wrong?"

"I'm here . . ." His voice trailed off. "I'm here to rescue you."

She tilted her head. "Rescue me? From who?"

"You know who," he said. "From my father."

311

"Karl, please." She knew things between him and his dad were strained. But she had no desire to get stuck in the middle. "Your dad has done so much for me. It makes me really uncomfortable when you—"

"My father is an evil, manipulative man. Do you know what he did?"

In spite of the sun on her skin, she felt a chill. She crossed her arms, holding on tight. "I'm sorry, Karl, but I'm not going to listen—"

"Rylee." He stepped closer. "He murdered your parents."

She froze. Her eyes wouldn't focus, wouldn't even blink. Then, sucking in her breath, she took a quick step backward, bumping into Toro. Her rollerblades slipped, but she managed to stay upright.

Karl rubbed the back of his neck, smiling to himself. "No, that's not exactly true. *He* didn't kill them. He *hired* someone to do it."

Her chest tightened, making it difficult to breathe. "I'm sorry?"

"I was just a kid. About eighteen." He glanced up into the sky. "Your dad had a document that my dad wanted. So he told Marcel to get it, no matter what it took."

She took quick, rapid breaths, struggling for air. The messenger bag on her shoulder slid to the ground. "Marcel Gibbon?"

Karl nodded. "Back then, he was like a mentor to me. Took me under his wing. To me, he was the next best thing to James Bond. But then, I didn't really know him yet. Just like I didn't really know my dad."

Nausea began to churn in her stomach.

"He took me along, you know. I watched him kill your dad."

Her knees weakened. She groped for the nearby bench, grabbing the back of it for support.

"Marcel let me have your dad's cuff links. 'Something to commemorate the day,' he said." Karl's eyes gentled. His voice grew soft.

"They're fourteen-karat gold. Crested with your dad's alma mater. I wear them around the house sometimes when no one's home."

She was going to pass out. Or throw up. Maybe both. Using the bench as a guide, she hand-walked her way to its front and plopped down.

He sneered. "Or I did. Until that stupid George stole my jewelry casket and tried to make it look like Robin Hood. Then he gave the thing to Marcel, of all people, to fence." He shook his head. "It was your father's, you know. A really cool piece with multiple drawers and doors. I kept my treasures in it. Your dad's cuff links. Your mom's perfume. My law professor's glasses. Everything. Those items would have meant nothing to anyone . . . other than Marcel."

She opened her mouth, breathing in. Blowing out. In. Out.

His lips curled in disgust. "He, of course, immediately recognized the cuff links and the perfume vial of your mom's. And once he did, he realized the significance of everything else." Raking a hand through his thick blond hair, he gave a bark of incredulous laughter. "And he had the audacity to use that stuff against me. *Me.* Can you *believe* that?"

"My mom's perfume?" she rasped, touching her pearl-drop pendant. "You, you killed my mother?"

He sliced a hand through the air. "No. Pay attention. I only *witnessed* your parents' deaths. The others . . . they happened much later."

Her mind started to reengage. She needed to get away. She needed to get help. But her legs were like rubber, and she feared if she stood up she'd pass out before taking more than a few steps.

"It was my *dad* who had your parents killed. Who confiscated the proceeds from your estate sale. Who stole your ancestral home right out from under you. And I'm sick and tired of the way you go all soft around him, like he's some father figure to you or something. It's not right."

Toro had disappeared around the corner. He was somewhere in the yard, but she didn't know where. The faint vibration of her phone came from inside her messenger bag. Too far away to retrieve without being obvious.

Her eyes throbbed in her head. She brushed at them, expecting tears, but the skin, though raw to the touch, remained dry. Her hand was shaking. "If I'd had any idea—"

"And now he thinks he's gotten rid of me. From his house. The law firm. All of it." His smile was full of wicked satisfaction. "He was provoked when he realized everything I'd stolen were items that once belonged to Jon Monroe. But that was nothing compared to his fury when he saw what I did to your apartment."

Her breath caught.

"You should have seen him. He acted like you were his daughter or something. How twisted is that?" He unbuttoned his shirt cuffs, then began rolling the sleeves up to the elbows. "Seems that all this time, it was you he wanted, not me. But don't worry. I'm going to fix that. You're coming with me. And he'll never find us."

Every instinct she had screamed at her to run. Instead, she listened to her brain.

Take it slow. No sudden moves. Big, deep breaths.

She rose from the bench, standing still to make sure her head no longer buzzed or swam. Her legs held firm. Her head was clear.

He slid his hand into his pocket. When he removed it, a folding knife flashed in the light. He snicked the blade open, smiling down at the gleaming edge.

Her voice jumped an octave. "Karl?"

"You're mine."

The words branded on the toilet lid of her bathroom flashed across her mind.

Her phone vibrated again.

He used the knife as a pointer, emphasizing each word with a shake of the wrist. "Give me your hand. It's time to go."

"Karl." She straightened her spine and used the same tone she did with her dogs when she expected them to obey. "Put that away."

Standing between her and the house, he had her bottled up at the corner of the garden. In her rollerblades, she could hardly dart around him. To reach her with the blade, all he'd have to do was lunge.

"I've watched you grow from a child into a woman," he said. "All those years, I'd find myself thinking of you. I'd wonder if wherever you were at that moment, you were thinking of me, too." His gaze raked over her. "Imagine my shock when I discovered my dad had been thinking the same thing."

She reached for her messenger bag.

"Leave it," he said. "I have everything you need. Just come."

She rolled backward around the edge of a garden bench. Toro trotted around the corner, then stopped short. Ears perked. Tail stiff.

Karl glanced at him, weighing the knife.

"Don't you touch him, Karl. I mean it."

He pressed the blade's spine against his lip, like a silencing finger, then gazed almost contemplatively at Toro. The mastiff went into a crouch, baring his teeth.

"If I'd wanted to, I could have done all kinds of things to this guy." He moved the blade back and forth through the air, slicing an imaginary target. "Maybe I still will." He smiled at the prospect.

Barking, Toro charged. Karl's knife hand flashed forward.

Without thinking, she kicked.

Everything happened at once—the dog's yelp, the crunch of her rollerblade wheels sending a shivering impact up her leg, the knife flying through the air.

Crying, Toro limped across the garden and out the gated archway, his leash dragging behind him.

Karl writhed on the grass, the knife just inches from his hand. It had blood on the metal.

They both grabbed for it at once. But he reached it first and lunged from the ground. She swiveled out of the way.

"Come here!" he shouted.

Before he could rise, she scrambled for the wall, jumping, throwing her arms up, reaching for the top. Getting a tenuous grip, she heaved herself up, kicking her leg as high as she could.

Her rollerblade clattered against the brick. She kicked again, hooking the edge, then wrenched herself to the top.

He snapped at her with the knife just as she dropped to the other side of the wall. Landing, she felt a sharp burn on the back of her thigh. Her probing hand came away bloody.

Karl appeared at the top of the wall, gripping the knife like an ice pick.

"Don't you dare run from me," he hissed. "You're *mine.*"

Lifting herself off the ground, she clomped across the neighboring garden, her rollerblades twisting on the grass. Twenty, maybe twenty-five feet away, a paved path beckoned. If she could only reach it, she'd pour on speed.

Every step, the pain in her leg intensified. Like it was splitting. Tearing wide open. She struggled for breath. Her lungs bursting in her chest. Behind her, Karl dropped feet-first from the wall. Landing easy. Rushing forward over the grass.

Chapter Twenty-Nine

Pressing on the accelerator, Logan dialed Rylee's cell. When it went to voice mail again, he tried Harold Hearn—the last appointment she had on James Island.

"Sorry, buddy. She left a while ago. Said she had a dog in the city to walk."

Toro. He tried Rylee's phone again. Still no answer. He sent a text, then dialed Nate, leaving a message. He offered a succinct update and told the detective to get over to the Davidsons' immediately.

He found Daisy parked off Prices Alley, Karl's convertible directly behind it. Logan jumped out and rushed past their cars, brushing his hand against the hoods.

His was slightly warm. Hers was cold.

He ran down the alley, through the open gate into the Davidsons' side yard and spotted her messenger bag in the garden not too far from an antique-looking bench.

"Don't you dare run from me," a voice said.

Frantically, Logan searched for the source.

"You're *mine*."

At the back corner of the garden, Karl Sebastian straddled the top of the wall.

Logan curled his fists and crouched into a fighting stance, ready for Karl to drop down and attack him.

But Karl never even saw him. He swung his leg over the wall, moving away from Logan, not toward him. He caught a flash of metal in Karl's hand. Then Karl dropped to the garden on the other side.

His prey was on the far side of the wall. *Rylee.*

Logan lunged forward, charging across space, sucking up the distance like a jet engine intake.

No thought to the movement. No consciousness even. Just an arrow racing to the target.

Kicking off from the bench, he sailed through the final yard, hooking his arms over the top of the wall. Pulling himself up.

Before he could leap down for the tackle, Karl advanced out of range, jogging forward across the garden. Moving toward Rylee, who lay sprawled on the lawn just short of a paved path. Her rollerblades must have tripped her up. She lifted one hand to ward Karl off. The other clutched her bleeding thigh.

The image of her on the ground locked in Logan's mind with the snap of a mental shutter. His whole body tensed for action.

He hit the ground lightly, bending his knees to take the impact. Sprinting forward. Aiming low. His feet so quiet on the grass Karl never heard. Rylee saw him, though.

"You're really starting to—" Karl must have sensed a change in her. He turned just as Logan exploded into his side.

The collision jarred Logan's teeth. Swept Karl off his feet. They crashed to the ground, Logan grasping along Karl's body for the knife hand.

But Karl recovered quickly. He clawed at Logan's face with his free hand, keeping the blade just out of reach. Looking for an angle to stab.

As they crawled over the ground, muscles straining, Rylee rose in the corner of his eye, staggered backward on her injured leg.

"Get back," Logan yelled. "Get away from us."

He should have kept quiet. Karl sliced wildly, running the knife edge along Logan's forearm. A fissure of blood opened up. A terrible burn went through him. He recoiled, giving Karl a chance to struggle out from under him. To get on his feet. To go after her.

Rylee let out a scream.

Ignore the pain.

All the strength was draining out of him, but he rose to his feet. Not knowing if his arm could still pack a punch, he closed the distance.

This time Karl saw him coming. He bobbed and weaved with the knife, a wicked smile on his lips. Enjoying himself. One false move and Logan knew that blade would be buried deep inside him. *Better that than letting him reach Rylee.*

She teetered on the rollerblades. Logan circled to keep his body between them.

"Run," he said, but it seemed hard enough for her to keep her feet.

Karl edged closer. "She's not going anywhere. And neither are you."

"The cops are coming."

"Really?" Karl cocked his head. "I don't hear any sirens."

He smiled broader, pleased with himself, and that's when Logan struck. He took one step, then launched himself, his strong thighs propelling him.

Karl stepped back, but it was too late. Logan's hand seized his wrist just as their bodies collided, and once again they were on the ground.

Underneath him, Karl twisted, jerking the knife hand free.

The blade flashed. Logan winced, anticipating the stab.

A row of rollerblade wheels crashed down on Karl's forearm, pinning it to the grass. A rivulet of blood ran around Rylee's knee, but she kept the pressure up. Logan glanced up at her, then used all his might to roll Karl over, face down on the lawn.

He snaked his good arm around Karl's throat, then locked in the chokehold with his injured one.

The struggle grew fierce, Karl writhing to get loose. His strength seemed to grow and grow. Logan wasn't fighting just the man now, but the evil inside him. He held on with everything in him, eyes clenched shut. It took an eternity, but finally the power ebbed out of Karl. His muscles grew slack.

"He's going," Rylee said.

Karl let out a final howl of anguish. A sound of despair from a man realizing he's been cheated of his sick reward.

When Logan finally opened his eyes, the beast underneath him lay still. "He's out."

His own body felt heavy as lead. But it wasn't over. There was Rylee's wound to see to. And his own. He pulled his arm free and started to rise.

Rylee exhaled, limping a few paces away before dropping to the grass.

He took the knife from Karl's hand and knelt over her, getting a glimpse of her wound. "Are you all right?"

"He said they murdered my parents." Her eyes were glazed. Her face colorless. "He said it was Grant. He said—"

"Shhhh." He pulled his shirt off, whipping it into a makeshift bandage. She winced as he coaxed her hands away, revealing a deep slice to the back of her leg. Bunching the shirt up more, he pressed it against the wound.

She moaned.

"I'm sorry, baby." He guided her hand to the shirt. "Try and put some pressure on that."

He undid his belt, sliding it through the loops, coiling the strap around her leg to hold the soaked shirt in place, then called 9-1-1.

"An ambulance is on its way."

She gripped his hand. "He's the one. The Robin Hood burglar. The one who tore up my apartment. He told me everything."

They both looked at Karl, now a passive lump curled against the soft grass. His skin flushed from exertion. His body rising and falling as he breathed.

"I was never so glad to see those rollerblades as when you stomped down on his knife hand."

Her hold on him grew weaker. Her lids began to droop.

"Keep your eyes open, Rylee."

She opened them, her pupils huge. "You kind of saved me just now."

He smiled, smoothing her hair down. "I kind of did. You kind of saved me, too."

"He's . . ." She struggled to speak. "Crazy."

"Yeah." He pressed his fingers to her wrist. Her pulse was so faint, he could barely feel it.

"He said Grant had my parents killed." The words were soft, barely audible. Her entire body began to shake. "Gibbon did it. Karl watched the whole thing."

"Shhhh." He stretched out, spooning himself behind her and wrapping her with his arms in an effort to keep her warm.

"He didn't leave us," she said. "It was them. My father loved us."

He laid his cheek next to hers. "Of course he did."

⁓

Logan stood at the rear of the ambulance, its doors spread open. Rylee lay inside it, her rollerblades still on her feet. An EMT wrapped a cuff around her arm and took her blood pressure.

Officers crawled into another ambulance with Karl handcuffed to the stretcher. Nate Campbell closed their doors, then headed toward Logan. "My guys have picked up Grant and George. We haven't found the Cherub's body yet, but we will."

The two friends stood next to each other, neither speaking, while the chaos of the crime scene unfolded around them. Nate kicked at some gravel, shrugging to himself. Logan waited, knowing what was coming.

Nate cleared his throat. "I owe you an apology."

"You owe Rylee an apology. As in, a formal, on-the-air, retraction apology."

The detective's face burned like a teenager caught slipping into the house after curfew. He glanced inside the ambulance beside them, as if he might say something then and there, but the EMT was talking to Rylee.

"I'll take care of it immediately." He stepped closer to Logan. "And I'll do a private one as well. I am sorry, Logan. My only excuse is, I really did think she was guilty."

After a slight hesitation, Logan extended his hand, his knuckles scraped raw.

Nate shook it. "You okay?"

Logan raised his bandaged forearm to show off the second bandage along his side. "Just a few scratches. I'll be fine. She's the one whose whole world just tilted off its axis. So we'll continue this later, okay?"

He climbed into the cab, thanking God her leg would require little more than stitches when he'd feared transfusions were the order of the day. Still, she'd lost a lot of blood.

Patting her good knee, he gave it a squeeze. "It's all over, Rylee. Karl's been taken under custody to the hospital. Grant's being processed right now."

"Gibbon?" she whispered.

"They'll lean on Karl until he tells them where the body is."

Her eyes filled. "He . . . they . . . All this time I thought . . ."

The EMT removed the cuff, made a note on his clipboard, and moved away.

Logan scooted to her side, brushing her bangs back. "I know. It's a lot."

"Nonie won't understand. I can hardly even grasp it all."

He placed her hand against his cheek, then turned to plant a kiss on her palm.

A tear spilled from the corner of her eye. "Toro's gone."

"He's fine," he said. "He's tethered to the piazza."

Her eyes slid closed, pushing more tears to the surface. "Thank God."

He went to work on her rollerblades, loosening the laces.

"He's been hurt," she said.

Logan nodded. "Yeah. But the police went with the ambulance, so you don't need to worry."

"I meant Toro."

Pausing, he looked up. "Toro? No, he's fine. Somebody looked at him already. It was just a nick." He eased the rollerblade off her good foot.

"Poor thing. He's a rescue dog, you know. He's probably scared to death, and he still needs to be walked." She started to push herself up.

"Wait a second." He held his hands up to calm her. "Just wait. There's no way you're taking that dog for a walk. There's no way you're getting out of this ambulance. You're going to the ER, and you're going to let them see to that leg, and you're going to take care of yourself."

"But what about Toro?"

He took a deep breath. "I'll take care of him."

"You?"

Me? "Yes, me."

She sank back against the stretcher. "You'd do that for me?"

"What wouldn't I do?"

She bit her lip. "You better find a shirt first, or you'll shock the neighbors."

He glanced down. He'd totally forgotten he'd used his shirt to stanch her flow of blood. He felt heat creeping up his cheeks.

She smiled. The first one of the day. "It's okay, Logan. You look fine . . . especially to me."

He gave her a hooded look. "So do you, babe. So do you."

He gently removed her other rollerblade.

The EMT returned with an IV bag in hand. "We need to get moving, sir."

Logan nodded. "I'll see you at the hospital once I finish with Toro." Leaning over, he gave her a peck on the lips, then jumped out of the back doors.

She smiled down at him the way the sun does emerging from behind an eclipse. He wanted to grab the edge of the stretcher and give it a pull. To tilt the metal bed until she sledded down into his waiting arms. Never to let go.

Epilogue

If the way man and dog had bonded wasn't so cute, Rylee would almost have been jealous. Though she wasn't sure, in Logan's case, whether bonding was the right word. He awkwardly frolicked with the rescue dog, tossing the Frisbee across the park lawn and running between trees.

The afternoon sun flashed across the distant water. The breeze, balmy as ever, felt good against her skin. She lay down on the blanket, rolling slightly to check the white line on the back of her leg. The wound had healed nicely, but the more she tanned, the lighter the smooth scar seemed to get.

The police had found matches for most of the trophies in Karl's jewel box. They linked the eyeglasses to a Georgetown law professor who disappeared Karl's second year. The dog collar to a golden retriever who'd lived next door to the Sebastians. It had been tortured and left for dead all those many years ago. Karl had been in high school at the time. There were others, folders full of them, but Rylee had stopped Logan from telling her any more. She shuddered. He was more dangerous than she or Logan had ever imagined. According to what they'd learned, Grant had been desperate to expunge Karl from his law firm, his home, his life.

Karl, however, had no intention of giving up his "deserved" lifestyle. So he began to systematically steal the Monroe keepsakes that his father had profited from years earlier.

His message to Grant was clear: *Give me what I want or I'll expose all your secrets.*

Grant's duplicity had left her feeling abandoned all over again. Then memories of her parents would rush to the surface. And the oppressive ache that used to accompany those memories was replaced with a bittersweet peace.

Her parents hadn't left her at all. They'd been taken from her. By Grant and Karl, who awaited trial in jail without eligibility for bail.

Grant's assets had been seized by the courts, including Rylee's ancestral home. But she had no desire to live in a house that had been occupied by her parents' killers.

Shaking herself, she sat up. Off in the distance, Logan was trying to teach the mutt a new trick.

"Just let him play fetch," she called. "That's what he likes."

Reaching for a half-empty water bottle, she drank deeply. Logan had surprised her late one night by appearing at her doorstep with what looked like a miniature German shepherd with who-knew-what mixed in.

He'd seen it racing after a car that was speeding away. Pulling over, he rescued the shivering mutt, which at the time was little more than skin and bones.

The two of them had sat on her kitchen floor while she held its shivering body, cooing and soothing it. His hair was so matted and full of sticker burs that she'd resorted to scissors to remove them all. They bathed him and met at the SPCA the next morning for his shots.

She'd insisted Logan name him. After a great deal of indecision, he finally christened the dog Steve Rogers after his favorite comic book hero, Captain America. And now that he'd signed a three-book contract, he worked out of his home and kept Steve company during the day.

Logan spun the Frisbee to her, but then neither he nor Steve seemed interested in it.

She lifted her sunglasses for a better look. The dog held something while Logan tried in vain to twist it from his grasp.

The mutt growled merrily as they wrestled for the prize.

She lay back down and closed her eyes.

Logan's footsteps approached, and he stretched out beside her. "You finally give up?" she asked.

"If I ignore him, he won't be able to stand it. He'll be over in a minute."

"You hear from Dora today?"

"Yeah. She e-mailed me a jpeg of my cover."

She lurched to a sitting position. "Get out! Why didn't you say anything?"

He smiled. "It's fantastic."

"I can't wait to see it!"

A week after the Robin Hood case had busted open, she'd received a call from Seth Altmeyer. Logan had walked away from a six-figure book deal because he'd refused to include her in the story.

She'd been stunned. Logan had never said a word. Never even asked her if he could include her in the book. When she'd questioned him about it, he'd said no amount of money was worth exploiting her.

After a great deal of coaxing, she finally convinced him to let her read the manuscript. It was fantastic. And had completely stalled out two-thirds of the way through when it became apparent he'd need to include personal details from her life.

But instead of shying away from the idea, she embraced it. What better way to exonerate her parents than by a book that might sell hundreds of thousands of copies?

"Is he back yet?" Logan asked.

"Not even close."

Sitting up, he gave her a quick kiss, then clapped his hands for Steve.

The Confederate Memorial was silhouetted against the sparkling bay. She counted the months that had passed since that first night. Who would have imagined it would all end up like this?

"He's got something in his mouth," Logan said, "but I can't get him over here. See if you can call him."

"Here, boy! Come here, Stevie!"

The dog stopped mid-lope, cocking his head. But he trotted laterally, not moving any nearer to them.

"Looks like he's got a mind of his own today."

"Try again," Logan said. "I don't want him running off too far or I'll have to go after him."

She smiled. "So what? I already know you can run fast."

"Ha, ha. Now would you call him?"

She inserted her fingers in her mouth and gave a whistle. Across the park, Steve's ears perked up. She called his name, and he bounded toward them.

"What's he got in his mouth? I can't tell from this far away." Leaning forward, she squinted and was able to make out a miniature shopping bag, the kind made of heavy stock with a braided rope handle.

"Logan, I think he took that from someone."

There were some people picnicking near the trees where Steve had been. She shaded her eyes, trying to tell whether they were stirring, perhaps missing something.

Steve loped up. Instead of heading for Rylee as usual, he paused at Logan's feet. *Oh, dear.* The top of the bag was wet with saliva and rather chewed up.

"Don't bring that to me," Logan was saying. He waved the dog toward Rylee. "It belongs to her."

"What's he got?" she asked slowly.

Steve edged alongside her leg, dropping his wet package beside her. Logan ruffled his head. "Good boy."

"What is it?"

"Open it up and see."

She pulled the top of the bag apart, reaching inside with her fingertips. She touched a hard, felted surface, round at the edges. Her hand pulled back.

"Open it," he said.

Before she'd drawn the small black jewelry box out of the bag, Logan was already shifting on the blanket, rising, settling himself on one knee.

The box trembled in her fingers. It took two tries to get the lid open.

When she did, a ray of light caught the faceted stone.

"Will you marry me, Rylee?"

She looked up. His warm brown eyes were earnest and filled with hope.

"Yes!" she cried. "Of course. Yes!"

He slipped the ring on her finger, then pulled her to him. Before he could seal his proposal with a kiss, a long, sandpapery tongue swiped between them, catching them both on the lips.

Logan reared back, dragging a hand across his mouth over and over.

Laughing, she wiped her own lips, then threw the Frisbee. Steve charged after it.

She grabbed Logan's shirtfront and pulled him toward her. "You wanna try that again, Woods?"

"I do, but for the record, I'm gonna have a real problem with a wife who gives her kisses out so freely. From now on, all your kisses belong to me. You got that?"

She slipped her arms around his neck. "Yeah. I got it."

Authors' Note

Deeanne sprung the idea of collaborating on Mark, fully expecting him to resist. Instead of putting up a fight, though, he saw the beauty of the plan at once. Even though neither of us had ever collaborated with another author, even though our writing styles and work flow couldn't be more different, we decided to give it a try.

"Let's do it," we agreed.

That was the easy part. Figuring out the story we wanted to tell—and more importantly, *how* to tell it—took more time. Mark wanted to write about Charleston. Deeanne wanted the heroine to be a dogwalker. (In which case, Mark said, the hero will be terrified of dogs!) Little by little, the novel took shape. Then we wrote it. And rewrote it. And rewrote it again.

At first, we figured having two authors work on one story would cut the work in half. Wrong. If anything, it doubled the amount of writing! We both went over every line, every detail, getting everything just right. The result is *Beguiled*, a book neither of us could have written without the other.

Don't try sneaking into Washington Park after midnight, but apart from that, you can walk the streets of Charleston with *Beguiled* in hand, retracing Rylee's routes, experiencing the rendezvous sites for yourself. Even before we put the first words on paper, we knew that Charleston would loom large in the story. If you're inclined, you can sip coffee at City Lights, attend a service at First Scots Presbyterian, or have a meal at Slightly North of Broad. Afterward, stroll down East Battery and try to figure out which house was Grant Sebastian's. To look right for the occasion, you can drop in on Ben Silver, where Logan buys his suit and picks out a dress for Rylee.

And if you're athletic and a little bit crazy, you can attempt to replicate Logan's feat of jumping onto the Confederate Memorial at White Point Gardens. But we don't recommend it.

Confession time: When the story insisted, we tampered with the landscape a bit. Logan finds parking spaces in the historic district a lot easier than you will, and Rylee navigates a few paths on rollerblades that might require exceptional skill in real life. But for the most part the Charleston of *Beguiled* will be recognizable to residents and visitors alike.